A DEAD MAN ON STAFFIN BEACH

A D.I. DUNCAN MCADAM MYSTERY

THE MISTY ISLE
BOOK 5

J M DALGLIESH

First published by Hamilton Press in 2025

ISBN (Trade Paperback) 978-1-80080-024-3
ISBN (Hardback) 978-1-80080-283-4
ISBN (Large Print) 978-1-80080-987-1

Look out for the link at the end of this book or visit my website at **www.jmdalgliesh.com** to sign up to my no-spam VIP Club and receive a FREE novella from my Hidden Norfolk series plus news and previews of forthcoming works.

Never miss a new release.

No spam, ever, guaranteed. You can unsubscribe at any time.

A DEAD MAN ON STAFFIN BEACH

The Isle of Skye

Inner Hebrides, Hebrides

Inner Seas off the West Coast of Scotland

Longitude: 6°13′12W   Latitude: 57°21′43N   Area: 1639 km²

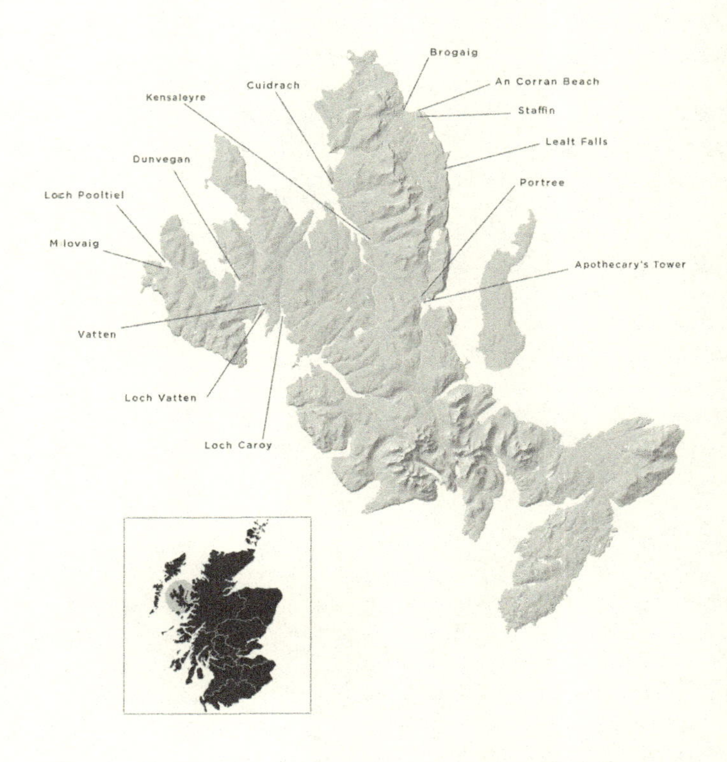

PROLOGUE

THE APPLAUSE CAN STILL BE HEARD as he walks from the stage. It continues on, although muted, as he descends the steps behind the burgundy curtains shielding the backstage activity from the assembled guests. His guide, a charming young lady by the name of Melissa, steers him through the throng.

Several people offer hearty congratulations. A couple even offer him their hands as he passes. Although the attention is positive, and pleasant at a very base level, it still makes him feel a little out of place. That is a feeling he's had to contend with ever since his first novel was published all those years ago. With every passing year, and every passing book, he seems only to garner more adulation whenever he ventures out into the world.

Into the world of publishing at any rate.

In that particular field of enterprise he is something of a large fish now. His name means so much to people. His books, characters and storylines are an ever-present fixture in book shops and on screen, both television and in the cinema. His characters are beloved, and as the creator, so is he.

Having left the auditorium now and passing into the corridors beyond, Melissa leads him back to his dressing room. It isn't quite as grandiose as that, little more than a waiting room with a small two-seater sofa pushed against one wall and a table set beneath a window overlooking the rear alley of the grand building. The sound of London nightlife carries to him through the cracked open window, traffic mainly, along with the occasional shout reflecting how busy it is out there. It's London. It's always busy. Too busy. Too many people. The novelty soon wears off.

"Is there anything else I can do for you, Mr Dunmore?" Melissa asks, smiling sweetly.

"No, no my dear, but thank you. You've been ever so helpful this evening."

"I'll leave you alone then." She glances at the clock on the wall. "The car has been booked for eight o'clock. Someone will come and get you in plenty of time."

He nods, also following her gaze towards the clock. "Okay, thank you."

"You're welcome, Mr Dunmore, and…"

Taking a seat on the sofa, he looks at her expectantly as she hesitates. "What is it, dear?"

"Only… it's been a real honour to be with you, seeing this tonight."

He smiles, feeling his cheeks flushing. He's thankful for the depth of his beard so this young lady wouldn't see his cheeks reddening. There's that imposter syndrome again. It still feels so strange to have people looking up to him for something he'd gladly do even if it didn't pay so handsomely. And it has paid handsomely, for him and for those close to him.

"You're very kind," he says, seeing her eyes lower to the trophy he's cupping in his lap.

"You deserve that, Mr Dunmore."

"As I said, you're very kind."

Melissa picks up on his tone, perhaps sensing that he doesn't necessarily agree with her statement, and she studies him.

"You know," she says, hovering by the door, "we do this event every year."

"I do, yes."

"And every year someone is presented with a lifetime achievement award."

"Aye, very deserving people, in the main."

Melissa smiles, averting her eyes and remaining professional by not commenting on past recipients.

"Well… and I shouldn't really say this, but quite often the recipient isn't particularly well liked. Some authors can be… a bit full of themselves." She says the last, lowering her voice, with a tinge of fear that she's saying too much.

"An egotistical bunch," he says, "some of them, at any rate. Not quite as important as they seem to think they are."

"Yes, that's what a lot of us think too, but tonight… everyone was so pleased that it was you who was coming."

"You're too kind."

That was the third time he'd said that phrase, or something similar. It was his stock phrase, his go-to expression, when praise is heaped upon him. He is undeserving of such things, at least in his mind. He analysed her at this point. She was young, by his count anyway, perhaps in her late twenties or early thirties but, admittedly, the older he got the harder it seems to be to judge the age of others, especially the younger ones. And these days, everyone is younger.

Whenever he ventures out into the public space with what he calls his *author hat* on, people he comes into contact with look at him differently, very differently in comparison with when he is simply a member of Joe Public going about his business. Unrecognised, he's just like any other person, moving more slowly than most and generally getting in the way. In a publishing sphere he is afflicted by what psychologists call the *halo effect*. A shining light that bathes the celebrity in success, success that brings forth both admiration and adulation in almost equal measure. As a writer he is someone. Without that ability for expression, he feels very much like an empty vessel, undeserving of such attention.

"...just there, on the table," Melissa said, bringing his focus back into the room.

"I'm sorry, what did you say?"

"On the table, there. A little gift that arrived for you earlier, but you were already up on the stage. I'll be in the next room if you need anything before they come to collect you to take you to the dinner."

He smiles gratefully and Melissa turns away, leaving him alone in the room. Groaning as he pushes himself off the sofa, he stands and crosses to the table. There is a bouquet of flowers, presented with a red lace ribbon tying the stems together, and alongside it a smart presentation box. Leaning against the vase that the flowers have been placed in is an envelope. It is also red. Setting his award down, he lifts the lid off the box. Inside is a bottle of single malt Talisker.

"Twenty-five years old," he says absently, squinting to read the label on the bottle's exterior due to the size of the print on the label. "Very nice indeed." Picking up the envelope and tearing open the flap on the rear with his thumb, he pulls out a greetings card. On the front is an artist's sketch representing a champagne bottle, the contents exploding upwards in celebration, multiple glasses held aloft by outstretched hands awaiting a refill as fireworks are depicted detonating in the background. Printed in gold, embossed lettering across the top, he reads *Congratulations!*

Opening the card, there is no printed interior message or poem. Instead, a simple message is handwritten inside. Five words that make him involuntarily shiver.

If only they all knew…

CHAPTER ONE

THE SURFACE of the water was relatively calm, and the kayak bobbed around on the water without needing much input to hold position a short distance away from the small group. From here they were simply a mass of arms powering through the water. The storm that had passed over The Rock during the night of Saturday into Sunday had freshened the air. The early morning wild swimmers – the self-styled Wild Ones –were powering through the seawater towards him, approaching the northern tip of Staffin Island. Their route would take them around the island and then they'd loop back along the west side of the island before heading back in to make land on An Corran Beach.

They'd all done this swim multiple times, but it was only common sense to have one person watching over them just in case anyone got into trouble. Today was his turn. They'd gone into the water when it was still dark, although the sky was free of clouds and the sunrise over the mainland in the east was already offering an array of orange and yellow as the dawn broke.

Turning his attention back to his friends in the water, the first of whom was approaching the southern tip of Staffin Island now, he saw his cue to get ahead. Driving his paddle into the water, he set off, passing the swimmers and offering them encouragement as he did so. The tide was against him as he came to the southern tip and he needed to put in more effort to get himself into the lee of the island and offer him some protection from the tidal swell this far out. To think the cattle farmers of old used to swim their livestock out to the island for grazing every year. Now, it was just another grass-laden rock overlooking the dinosaur prints that saw tourists flock here in their tens of thousands every year.

Comfortable in his new position, he rested the paddle across his lap and took a cursory head count. Everyone was present and all were now on the western side of the island and powering towards land. He looked over at the horizon; the Western Isles were still shrouded in darkness but once the sunrise broke over the mountains of Wester Ross in the east that would soon change. Looking back towards the beach something caught his eye. At first he thought it might be a trick of the light. The rock, hard sedimentary shale deposits formed largely during the Jurassic period, is a mix of hard and soft sandstone. Along with limestone it offers different surfaces, colours and textures that reflect light in differing ways. The shadows can trick the mind's eye.

He looked again. He hadn't imagined it. It was there. First checking that his friends were safe and were close enough to land, he turned the kayak, pointed it towards the Skye mainland and began paddling over in the direction of the black sands of An Corran. By the time he arrived at the beach he was breathing heavily and almost fell out of the kayak as he clambered out, splashing through the knee-high shallow water. He came to a stop at the water's edge, still holding the paddle in his hands. He hadn't hauled the kayak out of the water and on a rougher day it would have been immediately dragged out of Staffin Bay and into deeper water. It still might, but right now he didn't care.

"What are you doing, Coll?" a voice called. He didn't answer. Coll's eyes were focused on the rock face barely thirty feet away from him. The road that wound down from Staffin to the parking area off to his left came around the headland in front of him, with a slight drop to the beach below. It was here where Coll was standing.

"Coll?"

He heard the voice this time and looked to his right. Peter was looking at him, hands on his hips, water dripping from his collar-length hair onto his wetsuit, a quizzical expression set on his face. Peter was the strongest of the swimmers, always had been, and was first out of the water. Coll met his eye but couldn't find the words. Instead, he simply raised a hand and pointed. Peter followed the outstretched hand and his lips parted as he saw the same thing. Something unspoken passed between them and they moved off together, Peter falling into step alongside him.

Together, the two of them walked towards the rocks. Others were coming out of the water now and someone called out to them but neither Coll nor Peter acknowledged them. They slowed as they approached what had drawn Coll's eye. What Coll had initially assumed was a dead seal, perhaps one having died or accidentally become entangled in a fishing net, drowning and washing up on the tide. However, upon closer inspection, it turned out to be nothing of the sort.

Hesitant now, Coll looked at Peter, silently hoping he was willing to take the lead but Peter must have been thinking something similar because he hesitated, glancing nervously at his friend. Coll inched forward, but Peter remained where he was. He noticed a discolouration in the sand, it was darker here. The sand was dark anyway, almost black in places, but around the body it was more so. Coll stretched out a hand and as he did so the breeze picked up, blowing across him and lifting the thinning grey hair from the scalp, it fluttered ever so slightly and he hesitated.

"Do you think… you should touch it?" Peter asked from behind him.

Taking a deep breath, Coll reached out and touched the skin of the man's neck. He recoiled from the coldness of the touch. Despite it being the sensation he expected, it shocked him nonetheless. After all, the skin was beyond pale, grey, tinged blue and almost translucent in places where it was at its thinnest. Having never touched a dead person before, Coll reflexively withdrew his hand.

"Is he… is he dead?" Peter asked from behind him. Coll glanced back, seeing his friend had withdrawn further putting a few metres between them now and had been joined by two others from the group.

"I think so," Coll said quietly. Steeling himself, he put his index and forefinger against the man's throat looking for a pulse. He found none. Taking a step away from the body, he composed himself before joining his friends.

"We… we should call someone," Peter said. "Do you have your mobile?"

Coll looked at him and then scanned the other faces who had come to stand with them. The entire group had gathered now, all six of the Wild Ones. Coll knew he should have his phone on him. He was the nominated supervisor today, but he'd left it in the car. They'd never had an issue before, and he'd been casual about it. The car was parked up along the road beside the makeshift sea wall composed of huge granite blocks lining the parking area. The thing was, they'd parked up above the beach and made their way into the sea at this point having met up before dawn. They had to have walked right by this man, Coll carrying his kayak, not half an hour ago and hadn't seen him.

"Who should we call," another man said, but Coll was lost in thought and didn't recognise who it was. "An ambulance?"

"We should probably call a priest," Coll said quietly. "No one else will make a difference now."

CHAPTER TWO

DUNCAN STIFLED A YAWN. He could hear the conversation taking place outside the room in the corridor beyond. The doctor's voice was muffled and only occasionally did he hear that of his sister, Roslyn, as she murmured some measure of agreement or acknowledgement to something that was said. He could step out and insert himself into the conversation if he wanted to but he didn't, not really.

Instead, he gathered up the knitted blanket, made by Roslyn, from where it lay upon the bed and crossed the room to the window. He dropped to his haunches before his mum, gently placing the blanket over her legs and tucking it beneath her arms. She didn't say anything or even seem to know he was there. Her expression was unchanged, simply staring out of the window overlooking the grounds below. Not that she could see much. The rising sun was yet to clear the headland.

The wind was up, not unusual here on the island, and the trees lining the boundary were tilted at an angle that would make Duncan nervous to walk by them. They'd been there for decades though and had survived much worse. The sash window rattled in its frame and Duncan felt a draught brush against him. It was almost as if the storm front had read Duncan's mind and voiced its displeasure at his dismissal of its capabilities.

The hinges of the bedroom door creaked and Duncan turned to see Ros enter. He caught her unguarded expression a fraction of a second before she registered his attention and changed it to depict her more usual forced optimism.

"What did they say?"

Ros looked at Duncan, frowned, and then her eyes darted to their mum, sitting upright in her chair, in her own little world.

"Maybe we should speak later," Ros said.

"Why?"

"Because," she replied, inclining her head towards their mum.

"She's hardly listening," Duncan said, a little more harshly than he intended, and Ros scowled at him. "I mean, you know how it is…"

"Aye, Duncan, but it doesn't mean we should treat her like she's not here at all."

"Yes, of course," Duncan said, embarrassed. "You're right. I'm sorry." He stood up and gently placed an affectionate hand on his mum's forearm, but she didn't flinch at his touch. She hadn't been present, so to speak, during the entire duration of his visit. He approached his sister and Ros lowered her voice.

"They think Mum needs to go for a biopsy."

"Why, what do they think they'll find?"

"They didn't say, not exactly." Duncan sensed she was holding back and he too lowered his voice.

"What is it?"

Roslyn winced momentarily. "They think she might have… you know, cancer."

Duncan was surprised. He glanced towards his mum, although she had her back to him now. "Where are they getting that from? I mean, I know she's no' been too great just recently, but… cancer is a bit of a leap. Do you think I should have a word?"

Ros shrugged. "They're the professionals, Duncan."

"Aye, playing God as usual."

"Oh aye, and I suppose if a member of the public has an opinion on one of your cases I guess you'd give them more weight than your own opinion, right?"

Duncan tilted his head fractionally. She had a point. "Aye well… that's completely different, right enough."

"Is it?"

"Aye. I'm a pro—"

Ros lifted her eyebrows and Duncan hesitated. "You're a what now?" she asked.

"I'm a trained detective."

"And they are trained medical professionals. They don't need you playing Dr Kildare on them."

"Doctor who?"

"Not Dr Who, Dr Kildare. It was a programme on the telly, back in the day." Ros looked at their mum. "Mum used to love the actor who played him."

"Who was that then?"

"Like I'd know, Duncan," she said dismissively. "Honestly."

"You brought him up." Duncan smiled and Ros returned it with one of her own. "So… what are they going to do?"

"Set her up for a scan in the next couple of days, I think."

"Right." Duncan arched his eyebrows and exhaled heavily. He saw a moment of doubt reflected in his sister's expression, the guarded mask of determination that she wore all the time slipping. He reached out and took her hand in his, squeezing it affectionately. "It'll be all right."

"Will it though?" she asked him. He didn't have an answer. Not a good one anyway. "With everything going on, I don't think I could handle any more, Dunc."

"Maybe… it will be for the best—"

She shot him a dark look. "That's an awful thing to say."

"I didn't mean it the way it sounded."

"Yes, you did."

"No… I just meant that maybe it will get to the bottom of what's been causing her discomfort. That's all." Roslyn studied him and he felt the weight of her scrutiny.

"Sometimes I wonder about you, Duncan."

"What's that then?"

"You're a lot more like our father than you care to accept—"

Duncan reflexively coughed in response to her comment. "Well, thanks very much for that one. Now who's speaking out of turn? Talk about punching below the belt."

"I'll kick you below the belt if you ever say something like that again within my presence, Duncan McAdam."

"Duly noted," he said with a trace of a smile. She relented and playfully took a swipe at him which he easily weaved away from. Footfalls and muted conversation signalled the passing of a number of people in the corridor outside. This was unusual. Yes, the facility was busy, after all there was no shortage of patients on the island needing beds but seldom was there much commotion.

Duncan inched towards the door and he found Ros's

curiosity had also been piqued as he found her standing slightly behind him, peering over his shoulder, as he opened the door a little wider so they could see what was happening. There was a throng moving along the corridor, passing their mum's room just as they peeked out. A nurse was pushing someone in a wheelchair along the corridor flanked by several other staff members. They were past the room before Duncan could clock anyone's face but whoever was moving through had family members in tow as well. A lot of family by the look of it.

Once the group had passed, Duncan and his sister stepped out into the corridor to watch. Other people had the same reaction and he saw heads poking out of rooms looking on as well as other interested people standing in the corridor watching the events unfold. The party reached a bedroom at the end of the corridor and Duncan finally caught a glimpse of who was in the wheelchair.

"Ah… that explains it."

"Explains what?" Ros asked. "Who is it?"

"Huxley," Duncan said. "The Right Honourable David Huxley to use his full title."

"I thought he had been made a lord a few years ago?" Roslyn asked.

"Probably," Duncan said. "I can't keep up with the aristocracy and all the baubles they pass out to one another. I'm surprised he's slumming it here with the commoners."

"Honestly, Duncan, I never had you pegged as a republican."

"I'm not!" he protested. "How does the old adage go, everyone is born equal, but some are born more equal than others?"

Roslyn smiled but her reply was stunted by a scream, startling both of them. She almost leapt in fright, and both of them turned to see their mum in the doorway staring beyond them, along the corridor. Before either of them could act, she let out another terrifying scream and Duncan instinctively took another step back, hands aloft. All eyes turned towards them and, as if on cue, his mum screamed again only this time she didn't stop, the pitch elevated to such a level that Duncan couldn't believe she had enough air in her lungs to maintain it for so long.

Roslyn acted before he could and stepped forward, placing a supportive hand on her mother's shoulder only for it to be viciously batted away.

"Mum…"

"Don't touch me, you whore!"

Roslyn recoiled, deeply wounded by the exchange and Duncan moved forward, coming to stand between them. "Mum… let's calm down, aye?" She looked into Duncan's eyes, and there was a brief moment where he thought she recognised him but a veil of shadow descended just as swiftly. Her eyes narrowed and he thought she was looking through him as if he was invisible which, considering her state of mind, was quite possibly the case.

"Don't touch me!" she hissed, but her eyes didn't seem focused. His mum was sporting an impressive thousand-yard stare at this point.

"I won't touch you, Mum," he said calmly, but internally a knot in his chest tightened. "If you don't want me to, I won't. But… do you think we could go back into your room just now?"

A nurse approached and she seemed hesitant to intervene, possibly considering doing so might make matters worse. For her part, Duncan's mum looked to her right over his shoulder, seeing the nurse nearby, and that brought a measure of focus to her expression.

"You won't let him touch me, will you?" she said directly to the nurse.

"I'll no' touch you, Mum,' Duncan repeated calmly, his hands held up wide of his body, offering himself up in as inoffensive a stance as he possibly could. "I promise. Can we just go back inside your room, please?"

"Let me take you inside, Mhari," the nurse said, slowly coming forward. She allowed her to take her arm and seeing as she was clearly unsteady on her feet now, Duncan was pleased. The nurse steered her back into her room, glancing at Ros and Duncan and shooting them a supportive smile before they disappeared from sight.

Duncan exhaled and was pleased to see the onlookers had all returned to their own rooms as well. Many of the residents in this place were suffering from varying levels of dementia among other ailments and there was no judgement from anyone. Many people here were not themselves, or not the people they had once been at any rate. Everyone understood. There was a form of camaraderie in place, but it didn't make any of this any easier.

Roslyn's self-control broke at that very moment, her shoulders sagging as she gasped. Duncan stepped across and she fell into his embrace, putting her head on his shoulder. She wept and he held her close. If anyone passing noticed, they didn't show it and, for once, Duncan didn't care as he made soothing sounds and hugged his sister ever more tightly.

He gave her as much time as she needed and when he felt her pull away from him, he released his grip. He looked into her tear-stained face and she immediately lowered her gaze to avoid his.

"I'm sorry," she mumbled.

"Hey, we'll have none of that," he said quietly. She lifted her eyes to meet his. "We're in this together, you know?"

"It's just so hard sometimes..."

"Aye, and it's no' getting any easier, is it?"

She shook her head. The door creaked open, and the nurse came out to see them. She smiled as Roslyn produced a tissue from somewhere and hurriedly wiped her eyes and face.

"Your mum is settled back into her chair," she said, smiling warmly.

"Thanks very much,' Ros said.

"That's okay. She's calmed down again now."

"Any idea what sparked her off?" Duncan asked. The nurse shrugged. "Only, I've not seen her like that before," he said, looking at Ros. "She's not been like that with you anyway."

"It could be anything… and nothing," the nurse replied. "I'll just go and get your mum a nice cup of tea. It always seems to cheer her up."

Duncan nodded his thanks and she left them. "I don't know how you can tell the difference," he said under his breath and, on this occasion, Roslyn ignored the comment. They walked back into the room together. Duncan's mobile rang just as he pushed the door closed behind them. It was Alistair, his detective sergeant.

"Top of the morning to you, sir," Alistair said brightly. He was never that upbeat, and certainly never first thing in the morning.

"Morning, Alistair. What's up?"

"Why should anything be up?" he replied. "It's a dry, if not bright, morning but maybe that will change later. Perfect for a stroll along the beach, taking in the views…" Duncan could hear the sound of waves breaking in the background. That, and the wind coming down the mouthpiece, Duncan knew Alistair was outside somewhere. This couldn't be good news.

"Where are you?" Duncan asked.

"Staffin Bay," Alistair said. "An Corran Beach if you want me to be precise."

"A great spot."

"Indeed it is," Alistair said, seemingly pausing and shifting the position of his mobile as his words became muffled. He was speaking to someone else. "A perfect spot for some dolphin watching, searching for dinosaur footprints or…"

"Or?"

"If you're looking to dump a body," Alistair said.

"Excuse me?"

"We've got a body, and not just any body… it's what we call in the trade *a real doozy*."

"You have me intrigued, Alistair. I'm on my way," Duncan said, hanging up. He looked at Ros who seemed utterly dejected. Walking over to her, he slipped his mobile into his pocket and embraced his sister. She was watching their mum who was back to her favoured position beside the window, looking out over the grounds much as she had done since they'd arrived to visit her.

"What do we do?" she asked him quietly, leaning on his shoulder. Duncan took a deep breath and exhaled heavily.

"We remember who she was," he said softly. "And in those moments when she comes back to us… we savour them."

"They are happening less and less," Roslyn replied.

"Aye, I know."

"I feel bad for saying it… but how long is this—"

"Then don't," Duncan said, pulling away from her. She looked up at him and he smiled. "You don't need to say it.

We're all thinking the same things, and there's nothing wrong with that. We're only human. It's natural."

"But I feel awful when I wish it was all over."

Duncan pulled her back into his embrace, looking down upon his mum who was humming a nameless tune now. Ros withdrew from him a moment later and he looked at her apologetically.

"You have to go, don't you?"

He nodded. "I do. Alistair has a dead body for me up in Staffin."

"You get all the fun jobs, don't you?" she said with a hint of humour. He wouldn't say it aloud, but he'd rather investigate a deceased body than be here watching his mum wasting away.

"I'm sorry."

"Don't be. I have to get back to the croft soon anyway. Ronnie will be expecting me back. I said I wouldn't be long."

"Give him my best, won't you?" Duncan said, gathering up his coat from where he'd tossed it across the bed.

"I'll do no such thing," Ros said, composing herself. "That'll only set him off, as well you know."

Duncan smiled. There was no love lost between him and his brother-in-law. The animosity was all on Ronnie's side though, as far as Duncan was concerned. It was pretty unfair too in his opinion, but he wasn't going to waste any more energy on trying to improve that situation. Ronnie had made up his mind, and he was a stubborn man. Not like Duncan, who was always open to changing his mind. At least, that's what he told himself.

"You'll give me a phone later, let me know you're okay?" Ros asked him as he leaned over and kissed the top of his mum's head. She didn't react.

"Of course. See you," Duncan said, coming to her now and leaning in to kiss her on the cheek. "It'll all be okay, I promise."

"Save your undeliverable promises for that wee lassie of yours," Ros called after him as he made to leave. He spun on his heel and backed towards the door at the mention of Grace, smiled, and then spun again, leaving the room.

CHAPTER THREE

THE POLICE CORDON was already in place, set up at the bridge over the Stenscholl River. Beyond the river the road wound its way around the headland terminating at Staffin Harbour a little less than a mile down the road. Only one residential property was affected beyond the cordon and Duncan pulled alongside PC Fraser MacDonald who ducked to peer into the car, acknowledging Duncan with a nod.

"Morning, sir," Fraser said, his collar turned up to the wind. It was cold this morning. He appeared to be sinking into his high-vis coat, bracing against the breeze.

The aftermath of the weekend storm had been relatively calm when Duncan left the croft this morning to meet his sister, but the wind was picking up again now as the islanders braced themselves for the arrival of the forecast second front. A hurricane had struck the east coast of the United States a week ago and, such was the way of these things, the storm had made its way north wreaking havoc along the North American coastline before being picked up by the Gulf Stream and rattling across the Atlantic to make landfall over the Hebrides.

The storm had been downgraded, breaking up as it sped east, but it still hammered the Western Isles and Skye, bringing down power lines, and forcing all but the hardiest to hunker down indoors until it passed.

Not that anyone on Skye batted an eyelid to it all. The Misty Isle was the romantic name for their home but Duncan, along with many others, often referred to the island simply as *The Rock.*

"How are you, Fraser?"

"Bearing up, sir. All things considered, I'd rather be at home with my feet up holding a cup of tea."

"How is the wife?"

Fraser frowned, his eye flicking up in a thoughtful pose. "Oh aye, she's all right. She's there right enough. Maybe I'm better off here."

Duncan smiled, turning his attention to the handful of people who were beside the road on this side of the cordon staring towards the turn in the road before you descended to the beach. "We already have the onlookers gathering, I see."

Fraser glanced at them too. "One or two, aye. Staffin folk out for their morning walk. I figure the weather will keep some of the tourists at bay for a bit, but then they'll be here too."

"Got to see those footprints before they head off the island, right?"

"That's about the size of it, sir." Fraser took a step away from the car, gesturing for Duncan to pass by.

"Thanks, Fraser."

Fraser touched his forehead with index and forefinger in a casual salutation and Duncan moved off. He didn't recognise any of the watchers peering along the road, curious to see what the police presence was all about. Word would soon travel though. It always did.

The single-track road continued on and Duncan slowed the car as he approached the bend, looking down and across to Staffin Island as he followed the course of the road. At the foot of the slope was the access to the beach of An Corran, a stretch of blackened sand with the world-famous dinosaur footprints off to the right. Tens of thousands of visitors descended to this stretch of the coast each year to see the footprints for themselves. Passing herds – if that was the appropriate description – of the creatures had left footprints millions of years ago. These then fossilised over time and were still visible in the rock today.

Duncan parked at the end of the run of vehicles; liveried police cars, a forensic van and DS MacEachran's pick-up truck were all present. It was the latter that Duncan pulled alongside. He got out and was immediately struck by a gust of wind, tasting the salt in the air from the spray. The forensic technicians would need to work quickly before the tide came back in. The clock was already ticking. This part of the island may well be shielded somewhat from the Atlantic winds, by its location on the east of the Trotternish peninsula, but the tide would wait for no man.

Moving to stand beside the monolithic granite blocks that acted as a barrier to cars pitching down onto the rocks but also as a breakwater from stormy coastal waves, Duncan peered to his left down towards the beach. He could see the heads of figures moving at the base of the low cliffs, but the scene was still out of sight from his vantage point.

He looked to his right, across the weather-beaten slippery rocks. Tourists would usually be picking their way over them by now, scouring them for signs of the dinosaurs. It would have looked very different here back when the imprints were made in the Jurassic period. Skye was located a lot further south in that period and it would have been a very warm climate. Duncan shuddered, feeling the cold wind permeating the lining of his coat. How much would he give for a bit of that warmth and sunshine just now?

Zipping his coat up, he set off down the sandy path to the beach. Alistair saw him approaching and moved to greet him part way. Duncan took in the scene. The forensic team were beyond Alistair attempting to set up a tent to shield them from the elements whilst they processed the scene. It was proving difficult with the rising intensity of the wind but, while two of them toiled, another was already taking photographs.

"Morning, sir," Alistair said. He eyed Duncan suspiciously as they met.

"What?" Duncan asked.

"You didn't bring coffee with you then?"

"No. Was I supposed to?"

Alistair shrugged. "It might have been a nice gesture, but no bother."

"I'll try and remember for next time," Duncan said.

"No, you won't."

"That's true. I won't," Duncan said, pointing towards the team. He could see Ronnie MacDonald, one of the multiple MacDonalds who made up the uniformed police presence on the island – none of whom were related – standing off to one side with DC Angus Ross, the youngest member of the CID team. "What's the craic then, Alistair?" he asked, narrowing his eyes as he tasted the salt from the sea spray carried on the breeze and striking his face.

Alistair cleared his throat. "One body, a seventy-nine-year-old male, found deceased close to the rocks this morning." He turned his face towards the sea and Staffin Island. "A group of wild swimmers found him just after dawn when they came back in after their water madness."

"It's good for the heart," Duncan said aloud, still looking at the scene a short distance away. "And for the mental health."

"Freezing your arse off on a Monday morning in Staffin Bay?"

"Aye," Duncan said.

"What happened to winding down with a wee dram and a smoke of an evening?"

"You don't smoke," Duncan said as they made their way towards the body.

"Aye, that particular avenue of joy has been closed for a while, it's true."

Duncan acknowledged his detective constable, Angus, and PC Ronnie MacDonald with a nod. The technicians had given up on erecting the tent at this point. There was little to secure the pegs or ties to, the sand offering very little by way of grip for them. From here they couldn't be seen by any bystanders and Fraser was keeping them away at the bridge anyway. If they worked fast, and they would have to work very fast, then the tent wouldn't be needed. Duncan heard an approaching vehicle on the road above and glanced up. It was a blacked-out van with *Private Ambulance* emblazoned on the side in white lettering. The undertakers were here.

"I'm confused," Duncan said, watching the van descend to the parking area. "Is this a crime scene or not?"

"Oh, hedging our bets," Alistair said. "We're not really sure. Which is why I called in the big gun."

"That's me, I take it?" Duncan said and the question was met with a wry smile from his DS.

"Like I said, the swimmers came across him as they came back out of the water."

"They missed him the first time then?"

"Aye, but to be fair to them it was still dark when they went out and here," Alistair said making a sweeping gesture in the air with his right hand, "the rock is dark. Maybe you'd have seen him if he was dressed in pink neon spandex but otherwise fairly easy to miss."

"Fair enough," Duncan said moving to the left of the photographer, keen not to get in his way, as he took another shot and then lowered his camera.

"All yours, sir," he said, and Duncan thanked him.

Duncan stood over the body, immediately surprised. The man was slumped over, lying at the base of the rocks in the foetal position. His hands were raised to his chest, held together almost as if he could have been in prayer, although it would have been an incredibly macabre method of worship if he was. His hands were coloured crimson with dried blood. The blood had run from his wrists, deep cuts visible protruding from the cuffs of his checked shirt, the flow passing over his palms and the backs of his hands, through his fingers, soaking into the sand beneath and around him.

Duncan blew out his cheeks, lifting his focus to the rock face above them. "I don't suppose these injuries were the result of a fall," he said quietly, the words carrying away on the breeze but Alistair still heard him.

"I doubt it very much," Alistair said. "But I can think of worse places to do myself in. Better ones too, mind you."

"Better places?"

"Well… if I gave it some thought," Alistair said, "but it's not my style." Duncan glanced up at him, Alistair was now present to his left, looking over Duncan's shoulder at the body.

"You think it's a suicide then?"

"Yes, and no," Alistair replied. Duncan looked at the body again, studying the cuts to the wrist.

"Professionally done," he said. Duncan had attended the scene of numerous suicides over the years. Most of whom had been jumpers, either from heights, buildings or cliffs, or the preferred option by many who lived in built-up areas, by way of leaping onto the tracks in front of oncoming trains. In Glasgow it certainly felt like the popular method for those so inclined, with one incident a week being fairly commonplace. Those who took their life in this manner though, choosing a bottle of gin or scotch as a bathing companion, would cut their wrists but doing so in a horizontal action. That was pretty ineffective regardless of what Hollywood and television might depict. Following the line of the veins and arteries was far more efficient. That was what he saw in this case here. "He'd have bled out in minutes," Duncan said.

"Aye. He knew what he was doing," Alistair said in agreement. "If it was self-inflicted mind."

Duncan continued his examination, his eyes searching the sand around the body. He didn't see what he was looking for. "What did he use?"

"There's the sixty-four-thousand-dollar question," Alistair said. His brow furrowed momentarily. "Is it sixty-four thousand these days?" he asked, referring to the American TV quiz show. "It doesn't seem like a lot, sixty-four grand, does it?"

"Probably upped it by now along with the rate of inflation," Duncan murmured quietly, deep in thought.

"Aye, and there's plenty of that to go around these days."

"What's that?" Duncan asked, rising from his haunches.

"Inflation. And I don't just mean with regards to what my daughters ask me to give by way of an allowance either."

Duncan sighed, still examining the body. Something wasn't right here. "You might give off the impression you're a cantankerous old sod, Alistair, but you're a real softy where those girls are concerned."

"Oh aye," Alistair said, frowning. "Who's been talking?"

"Where's the knife?" Duncan asked, concluding his search and not finding a blade.

"Didn't find one. I spoke to all of them who discovered him and none of them claims to have seen a weapon or moved anything from the scene."

Duncan looked around, his lips pursed. "The tide carry it out, you think?"

"And leave the body like this?" Alistair shook his head. "Possible but doubtful in my opinion. I will wager the body wasn't fully submerged in seawater. If it had been then it would have been driven against the rocks more and we'd see tissue damage to reflect that, but I don't see any other wounds beyond the slashes to the wrists."

"So, the body must have wound up here as the tide was already going out, you think?" Duncan asked. Alistair nodded. "If the tide was already on the way out then taking the blade with it is possible but—"

"Less likely, aye," Alistair said. "Of course, he might be lying on the blade and simply slumped over on top of it as he expired." He shrugged. "Once the forensic boys and girls have done their thing and we can move the body, we'll see."

Duncan put his hand across his mouth, absently scratching at the stubble he hadn't shaved this morning. There was something else nagging at him too. He hadn't met this man, he was sure of that, and yet he seemed vaguely familiar but Duncan couldn't place him. He took in his appearance. His hair was cut close to his scalp on the back and sides and although heavily balding, there were thin wisps of hair on the scalp that appeared to have a life of their own, aided by the stiffening breeze. He was thin of face, almost gaunt in appearance but how much of that was down to his passing Duncan couldn't be sure. He was dressed in a fairly thin shirt and Duncan could see a white vest beneath it. Curiously, he wasn't wearing any shoes but had thick woollen socks on. Obviously, these were wet through, as was all of his clothing.

The storm had brought with it heavy rain throughout the night, and the idea that anyone, let alone someone of this man's apparent age, would venture out so far from a habitable residence dressed like this, was unfathomable to Duncan.

"Has anyone reported him missing?"

"No, not that I'm aware of," Alistair said.

"What's he doing—" Duncan paused and then looked sideways at Alistair who saw the look and arched a quizzical eyebrow. "Hang on. How do you know he's seventy… what did you say?"

"Seventy-nine, aye."

"How do you know that? Was he carrying ID?"

Alistair scoffed and smiled. "You don't recognise him?"

Duncan frowned. "No, but I'm getting the impression that I should."

"He's only Skye's most famous resident since Bonnie Prince Charlie stopped off here after doing a runner from Culloden."

"You've lost me again," Duncan said, shaking his head and looking at the deceased.

"This is Bruce Dunmore," Alistair said, pointing at the body. "Author of… that book he was famous for writing and the television series that spun off from it. You know the one."

"Which one?"

"The one with what's his name, in it," Alistair said, snapping his fingers. "You know, the one from that thing he was in."

"Oh aye… that one."

"You know the one I mean. Long face… Scotsman but speaks with an English accent for the cameras."

"So good that you can't name him?" Duncan asked.

"Aye… well, if you ask young Angus over there, he records it every week."

"Records it? What on his tape machine?" Duncan asked, restraining a smile.

"Streams it then… is that what they do these days?"

"Aye," Duncan said. "Now you say the name, Dunmore, it rings a bell with me but I thought he left the island years ago."

"Aye, when he hit the big time, he did. Kept the family house on the island though; it's out in Cuidrach."

"He's a wee bit away from home then."

"Especially without his furry boots," Alistair said pointing at the socks on the dead man's feet. "He's got some conversational gig scheduled for the end of this coming week. I saw a poster for it in the town." Alistair arched his eyebrows. "I guess… he's not going to be too chatty."

Duncan's brow furrowed. "Okay, get this lot squared away as quickly as you can. Make sure they comb the beach just in case the knife has been carried some distance from the body. The way this wind is picking up I reckon the incoming tide is going to be high, so they'll have to get a move on with it." He looked across the beach back towards the parking area. "Where are the witnesses? The ones who found the body?"

"They've opened up The Hungry Gull in Staffin for us," Alistair said. "They were all feeling the cold, poor souls. Funny that, seeing as they've just been swimming in the sea. Caitlyn is with them now."

"I'll head up there." Duncan hesitated and Alistair noticed. "What's on your mind?"

Duncan gathered his thoughts. He wasn't sure how to answer that question but he couldn't shift the nagging feeling that all of this, the scene, was somehow way off. It didn't make a lot of sense.

"It's just… all so elaborate. Don't you think?"

Alistair shrugged. "The man wrote espionage thrillers. Cloak and dagger was his sort of thing. You live by the sword, you die by the sword and all of that. Although… on this occasion it's a pen which doesn't really work, come to think of it, but you get my meaning."

"Not really, no."

"I'll give my metaphors a bit more thought," Alistair said, his long coat snapping around his legs on the breeze.

"I'll speak to you in a little while," Duncan said, turning and walking away. This wasn't going to be a simple, cut-and-dried death, he was sure of that. "Why here?" he asked himself aloud as he walked, hunched forward to protect his face from the cold wind.

CHAPTER FOUR

DUNCAN DROVE BACK UP into Staffin to the cafe. It was situated next door to the general store with a small car park off to one side. Now slightly elevated, when Duncan got out of the car he felt the full force of the wind coming across the island. He looked out across Staffin Bay in the direction of the mainland and he couldn't see the coast anymore. It was shrouded in thick cloud and the sky to the west was dark and foreboding. Alistair and the team would have less time to process the scene than he first thought, and he hadn't thought that they had much beforehand.

He stepped aside for a young mother coming out of the mini supermarket, pushing a buggy with a toddler alongside her. He smiled and she thanked him for moving. This early in the morning passing traffic was few and far between. Staffin was quiet. The entrance to the cafe was in the middle of the two buildings and he entered the communal area where toilets were located, taking a right turn along a short corridor to get into the cafe.

He'd been here many times before. It was something of a

well-known haunt for locals and tourists alike, opening up for the season and employing a variety of people from the island and further afield. The cafe closed down when the winter proper kicked in, mothballing the day-to-day business and opening only for special occasions or events.

Pushing open the door to the cafe, several eyes turned to watch him enter and he waved to the owner who was behind the counter, busying herself making food by the looks of it. She smiled and waved back.

"Would you like a cup of coffee, Duncan?"

"In a minute, when you have time, aye. Thanks very much."

"No bother," she said, head down focusing on what she was doing out of Duncan's view.

It wasn't hard for Duncan to work out who the swimmers in the group were. They'd long since got out of their wetsuits and into their dry clothing, but towel-dried hair was obvious. Caitlyn rose from her chair, leaving the group with Robbie, the third constable who carried the name MacDonald, to watch over them. She had a notebook in her hand as she greeted him.

"Hello, sir."

"Caitlyn." Duncan acknowledged her with a nod. "How are you getting on with this lot?" he asked, lowering his voice to ensure they were not overheard.

"Preliminary statements," she said. "Nothing earth shattering coming from any of them, to be honest." Duncan looked past her, scanning the group with a subtle look. There were half a dozen of them. They varied in age but Duncan figured the range was anything from late forties through to sixty-something. Expressions were stern, and there was a conversation going on amongst them although two of the party were on the adjacent table, both nursing hot drinks. They weren't speaking at all, seemingly lost in thought. To be fair, finding a dead body would throw most people if they weren't used to seeing one and others, even if they were.

"Who found the body?"

"The first was Coll McBride," she said, inclining her head towards a tall, slender man who was standing with his arms folded across his chest. He appeared to be listening intently to what one of his friends was saying. "Followed closely by the man who's speaking now, Peter Vandersteen. It was Coll who called 999 when they discovered the body."

Duncan indicated for them to join the party. Caitlyn led the way, introducing the group to Duncan as soon as conversation among the party died.

"This is Detective Inspector McAdam," she said. "He heads up our CID department." There was a general murmur of greeting, but Duncan noticed the two men sitting slightly away from the others at the next table didn't make a sound although one of them did glance up at him when he was introduced. Duncan nodded towards him having caught his eye but the man lowered his gaze before he made the gesture.

"Thank you all," Duncan said, "for agreeing to remain here to speak to us. I'm sure it's been something of a shock for all of you, and not what you'd have been expecting when you got out of your beds this morning." A few heads bobbed in agreement. There was an understandably sombre air surrounding them. "DC Stewart will continue taking all of your statements, so if you can bear with us a little longer I'd be grateful. However, a couple of questions from me—" a cup of steaming coffee was passed to him and Duncan accepted it gratefully. "I understand that you were all out in the bay for a morning swim, is that right?"

"Aye, it is," Coll McBride said, nodding sagely. "It's not an organised thing, so to speak, but we have a text message group and if someone drops in a time to meet for a swim then people will come along if they can."

"How many of you are there?" Duncan asked.

Coll rocked his head from side to side, exchanging a quick look with a couple of others. "No more than eight or nine but usually a minimum of a half dozen, much like this morning."

"How often?"

"Once a week, maybe more if the weather holds."

"Always swimming from the bay here?" Duncan asked, purely making conversation to put everyone at ease.

"More or less, aye," Coll said. "Sometimes we'll brace out but we all live here on the Trotternish and so it's an easy spot to get to whatever the time of day."

"Did any of you notice anything out of the ordinary this morning?"

"Other than the dead body?" the man Caitlyn pointed out as Peter said quietly.

"I was thinking more about when you arrived," Duncan said, clarifying his question. Peter held up an apologetic hand for having misunderstood. "Anyone strange hanging around, an unidentified vehicle. Something like that?"

"There was that van," a man said. Duncan looked at him, silently inquiring after his name with a look and a simple hand gesture. "I'm David," he said. "David MacQuarie. My wife and I run the post office up in the village there."

"Right. You remember seeing a van? What sort of van?"

"A white one."

"Okay, a white Transit type or a camper?"

"Oh right, sorry," he said, shifting in his seat. He seemed to be a well of anxious energy, but that could simply be the shock of the morning's events kicking in. "Er… it was a camper type, pretty new, I reckon. It had curtains… or blinds covering the windows. I don't know the make though."

"Did anyone else see this?"

Several people shook their heads, but one or two nodded. Neither of them could offer Duncan any more detail on it though, other than it was parked up along the sea wall.

"Was it still there when you came out of the water?" Duncan asked. The group exchanged looks but no one could say one way or the other. Distracted by the discovery of Bruce Dunmore's body, it was quite possible that the van left while they were on the beach and not necessarily while they were still in the water and none of them noticed. It wasn't unusual for a camper to park there overnight.

Although not an official campsite, and therefore no facilities were present, in Scotland a person had the right to camp anywhere they chose to, provided they were not on someone's private land. You could find holidaymakers pitching tents or campers almost anywhere on the island. On the whole, people cleared up after themselves and no harm was done. This spot would be quite appealing although they'd likely want to be up and away early on to find food or washing facilities. The camper was interesting but not necessarily out of the ordinary; not in Duncan's mind, at least.

"Did you see anybody in the area or pass other cars on the way in?"

There was only one access road down to An Corran Beach and it was narrow in places. Anyone else loitering or passing through would be highly visible, even in the darkness of the predawn light. Again, everyone exchanged looks but the general consensus was that nothing untoward or unusual had been seen. He wasn't confident of drawing anything useful out of the group, at least not straight away. On occasion, people can be overwhelmed by events, misremembering or inadvertently omitting a detail only to recall later something that turns out to be quite significant.

"I'm sorry," Peter said to Duncan, joining him as he stepped away from the party, leaving Caitlyn and Robbie to continue recording what they did remember along with their names and addresses. "We're not very useful, are we, Detective Inspector?"

Duncan smiled. "Don't worry about it. I'd rather you were entirely honest than try to come up with something just because I asked."

"Do people do that?"

"Yes," he said. "Not through a desire to feed their ego by being part of something momentous, although that happens as well, but often it's because they really have the urge to help and feel guilty when they can't."

Peter nodded. "I get that, yes."

"I can't quite place your accent," Duncan said, curious, although people were drawn to live in the wilds of Skye from all over. "Dutch, is it?"

Peter smiled. "Close. Brabant."

"Belgium," Duncan said. "Fairly close."

"Not too far at all," Peter said. "Although, I've lived here on Skye for almost as much time as I lived in my home country."

"What brought you over here?"

"What's not to love?" Peter countered. "The life, the landscape… and my wife, of course."

Duncan smiled. "Got you."

"Are you married, Detective Inspector?"

"No, not yet," he said, suddenly having the urge to shift the conversation on as Grace came to mind.

"You should try it. It's good for the soul."

"I'll certainly give it some thought."

"Well, don't leave it too long."

"Tell me, did you know the deceased?" Duncan asked, keen to change the subject.

He shrugged. "I can't say that I did, no." He looked across to his friends. "Most of the guys did but I must admit that I'm not much of a thriller reader and I don't even own a television set, so his name and body of work are lost on someone like me."

"Right," Duncan said, also casting a glance over the assembled friends.

"Why do you ask?"

Duncan didn't want to answer that particular question. He had his reasons for asking it, but none that he wanted to share. Not yet anyway. He decided to duck the question with his reply.

"Like you, Mr Dunmore's body of work has passed me by. I was just looking to get a steer on how well known he is among the islanders. I seem to be in the minority, so far."

"Then I am standing alongside you, Detective Inspector."

CHAPTER FIVE

Bruce Dunmore's family home was located in Cuidrach on the western side of the Trotternish. Once the body had been safely removed from where it was found on the beach, and transferred to the mortuary to await Dr Dunbar's post-mortem, Alistair joined Duncan and together they drove around the headland and down to the residence.

The house was south of Uig, and a short distance from the main A87 which led to the ferry terminal serving the Western Isles. Duncan knew the access road into Cuidrach headed west almost to the cliff's edge before turning south and looping back to rejoin the main road having passed the ruins of Caisteal Ùisdein, colloquially referred to as Hugh's Castle. Not that they drove that far south, taking a branch road north along the coast on a single-track road which terminated at the Dunmore house, located in the shadow of a copse of long-established mature trees.

Two cars were parked outside the traditional, white-painted house which had an enviable view over the mouth of Loch Snizort Beag to the south and as far west as the Outer

Hebrides on the horizon. The isles of Lewis and Harris were vague outlines today but on a clear day the details of the land mass would easily be visible with the naked eye.

Turning his focus onto the house, Duncan could see it was likely at one time to have been a simple two-roomed, single-storey property but had been added to on several occasions over the years. This had led to a greatly increased footprint and part of the more recent construction – still probably fifty years previous – had added a second storey into the roof area. The property was neatly maintained, the boundary fences and landscaping of curated vegetation was well manicured. The house was quintessentially Hebridean, just what one might imagine a house somewhere in this location would look like.

"Is he married?" Duncan asked Alistair as their boots crunched on the stone chips lining the turning area in front of the house.

"I've no idea. There's no next of kin I could see on file for him."

"We'll tread carefully then," Duncan said, shooting his DS a quick look as he rang the doorbell.

"I always do, don't I?"

Duncan snorted and was about to reply but the door opened almost immediately. A woman in her fifties, Duncan guessed, stood before them. She cast a swift eye over both men, apparently curious as to who they were when she didn't recognise them.

"Yes, can I help you?"

She was dressed in casual wear, a light woollen jumper above jogging bottoms and trainers. Her hair was tied up, likely in order to keep it clear of her face rather than in a fashion context. She also sported a floral print apron over her clothing, and she was clutching a set of yellow rubber gloves in her hands.

"DI McAdam and DS MacEachran," Duncan said, opening his wallet to show her his warrant card. She was taken aback.

"Oh heavens. Whatever has happened?"

"May I ask who you are?" Duncan said politely.

"I'm Flora," she said looking between the two men. "I'm Mr Dunmore's housekeeper. Has something happened?"

Duncan glanced at Alistair. "May we come inside for a moment?" Duncan asked.

"Yes, of course,' she said, stepping back and opening the door wider, holding it in place to stop it from closing on them as they entered.

Inside, the house was very much as one might expect having seen the exterior. Everything was in good order from the paintwork to the windows. Much of the interior clearly hadn't been updated for decades but it was all of a high quality, although the house didn't seem to have a very lived-in feel to it. It wasn't quite like entering one of the many holiday homes or rentals that Skye had to offer, having more personal effects, pictures, books and trinkets on show that collect over the years. However, it was also devoid of the clutter of everyday life that accumulates over time. Perhaps employing a housekeeper mitigated such things.

Duncan would love to have a housekeeper, but on a police salary that was never going to happen.

Flora led them through into a sitting room which had an oversized glass wall, not visible from the approach road to the property, which overlooked the water offering a panoramic view of the Waternish headland, the Ascrib Islands and the Western Isles beyond. It was quite simply breathtaking, even on a day such as this one. The housekeeper's demeanour had shifted in the short time since she'd opened the door to them, where she'd been curious as to who they were, to now, where she stood in the centre of the room, her features shrouded in shadow with the visible daylight behind her coming through the window. She was wringing her hands anxiously.

"Has something happened to Mr Dunmore?"

"Why do you ask?" Alistair said before Duncan could speak. She looked at him nervously.

"He wasn't here when I arrived this morning," she said, glancing between them. "His car is outside and, at first, I thought he might have gone for one of his early morning walks." Her eyes darted between them again. "He… he does that from time to time. And that has me worried."

"Why would that worry you?" Duncan asked.

"In this weather, what we had over the weekend… and he likes to walk close to the cliffs on his route." She frowned deeply, her eyebrows knitting. "And he has seemed rather frail of late."

Duncan sensed there was something else behind her concern, but he parked the thought for the moment. "Miss—"

"Mrs," she corrected him, "but please call me Flora. Everyone does."

"Flora, does Mr Dunmore live here alone or does he have any family—"

"No, no," she said quickly, "Mr Dunmore isn't married. He's widowed, and the couple had no children."

"Siblings?" Duncan asked. "We have nothing on file for his family."

"He is an only child," Flora said, concern edging onto her tone now as well. "What is going on?"

"I'm afraid I have some bad news for you," Duncan said.

"A body was discovered this morning, and we believe it to be that of Bruce Dunmore."

"Oh heavens," Flora said, raising a hand to her mouth. "Poor Mr Dunmore. Did he… fall?"

"Investigations are ongoing at this time," Duncan said, wincing momentarily at having to use such formal speech. Flora didn't seem to notice and suddenly looked unsteady on her feet. Alistair moved first, placing a supportive hand on her arm. It was just in time as her weight became too much for her shaky posture and Alistair helped her to sit down on the sofa.

"I'm so sorry," Flora said, embarrassed. Alistair passed her a glass of water he'd got for her from the kitchen. She accepted it, sipping from the glass before placing it down on the coffee table. "I don't know what came over me."

"It's the shock," Duncan explained. "It can happen at any time."

"Of course, yes," she said. Duncan sat down opposite her.

"Flora, if you're feeling up to it, could I ask you a few questions?"

"Yes, certainly," she said, absently toying with the hem of her jumper. "Anything I can do to help, of course."

"When did you last see Bruce?"

She thought hard, her forehead creased. "I saw him yesterday… he was still here when I left for home."

"And what time was that?" Duncan asked.

"It would have been a little after six o'clock," she said, her eyelids fluttering as she looked heavenward. "I'd made him his supper and left it in the oven to keep warm while he finished up."

"Finished up?" Alistair asked.

"Oh right, yes. He was in his study, working. He doesn't

like to leave thoughts unfinished." She smiled warmly at Duncan. "That's what he's always said, don't leave things unfinished."

"And he was referring to what?" Duncan asked.

She shrugged. "His writing I suppose," she said. "A fresh chapter or something, I don't really know."

"But you spoke to him before you left?"

"Yes, but only through the door." She inclined her head, adopting a stern expression. "Mr Dunmore doesn't really care for people in his study, ever."

"And how was he, in himself I mean?" Duncan asked.

"Well… I think it's been a trying time."

"Trying? How so?"

"Well, this last weekend was the anniversary of his wife's passing."

"Aye, so he used to be married," Alistair said. "To a woman, I mean." He shrugged at Duncan's fleeting glance. "You never know these days."

"Yes, Annie passed a few years ago now, three…" she looked thoughtful again, "no, four years ago now. Cancer. It all came about very suddenly." She turned her eye to the mantelpiece where family photos were on display. Duncan got up and crossed to them, casting an eye over the images.

"Is this her, Annie?"

"Yes, that's her and Bruce. I think that was taken at their home in Glasgow a couple of years before she passed. Looking back, you can see she wasn't quite herself."

"You knew her well?"

"Oh no, not Annie."

"You've been the housekeeper here for how long?" Duncan asked.

"Years," she said proudly. "At least for the last decade…

no, more than that." She blew out her cheeks. "Doesn't time fly. I think it's closer to fifteen years."

"But you didn't know Annie very well?"

"They hardly spent any time on the island," Flora explained. "My mother… going back a few years now, was the housekeeper for Mr Dunmore Senior—"

"Here?" Alistair asked.

She shook her head. "No, no. Originally, the Dunmores owned a manse over near Kilmuir, Dunvegan way. Mr Dunmore – junior – sold the property after his mother passed away but they also owned this place. Why he kept it on, I'll never know but… they kept me on too, to look after it while they were away."

"How often did they visit?"

She pursed her lips, but it didn't take a great deal of time for her to answer. "Hardly ever. I would receive a telephone call from Mr Dunmore every few months and if I needed anything I could always contact him, but other than that… I never really saw him."

"Why do you think he stayed away?" Duncan asked.

She shrugged. "I don't know. Perhaps his wife, Annie, didn't care for the island. It's not to everyone's tastes, after all."

"True," Duncan said. "However, he's returned here to live now?"

"Yes, he contacted me some time ago and let me know he was intending to move back, and could I make sure the house would be ready for him." She smiled, sitting forward, evidently proud of her work. "Not that I had to do much. I've always treated the house as if Mr Dunmore would return at any moment."

"Why the change of heart?" Duncan asked. "About him

returning to the island, I mean."

"I don't know. I didn't ask and if he wanted me to know then he would have told me, wouldn't he?"

"I suppose so. He never gave away any indication to you?"

"No. But… people always leave the island in search of something greater and then, sooner or later, they come back, don't they?"

Duncan caught Alistair looking at him from the corner of his eye. "What was he working on, do you know?"

"Another book, I think. Not that he said."

"You never saw what he was working on?" Alistair asked. "Having a sneaky peek over his shoulder?"

"Certainly not!" Flora replied, indignant. "I would never do such a thing."

"No, of course not," Alistair said. "Silly of me to suggest it."

"Mr Dunmore is very precious about his privacy. I would *never* betray that."

"Quite right," Alistair said. "I would never suggest otherwise. I just thought, when you were cleaning his study… you might see something on his desk, is all that I meant."

"I never enter his study," Flora said.

"Never?" Duncan asked.

She shook her head. "It was forbidden. I think—" she stopped suddenly, glancing around as if someone might overhear her. Satisfied that they were indeed alone, she still lowered her voice. "I think he was a little superstitious, you know."

"About what?"

"He had rituals he adhered to."

"Rituals?" Alistair asked, somehow managing to keep the

disdain from his tone, which Duncan was impressed by. "Like… religious ones or… something else?"

"It may have been a religion to him," Flora said. "He could be a bit funny about things."

"For example?" Duncan asked.

Flora shook her head. "I should probably not say any more. It wouldn't be fair."

Duncan decided not to press the matter this time. If he felt it necessary in the future then he might revisit the conversation.

"And how would you say Bruce has been this past week, bearing in mind it was the anniversary of his wife's passing?"

"I would say… he's been preoccupied of late and," she cocked her head, "sad."

"Very sad?" Alistair asked.

"Withdrawn," Flora said thoughtfully. "That would be more apt."

"Is that usual?"

"How would I know? I've worked for the family on and off for years but this is the first anniversary since his wife's passing where he's been here for me to see him."

"You had concerns about his welfare when you arrived at work this morning," Duncan said. "What did you think might have happened to him?"

"Only that he may have… fallen…"

"Fallen?" Alistair replied. "Or jumped?"

"No, certainly not!" Flora said, but by the manner of her reaction, Duncan figured that was exactly what she had feared. "Although…"

"Although?" Duncan repeated.

"He was very down over the weekend."

"About Annie?"

"I don't know. He didn't really confide in me in that way," she said, despondent.

"Who did he confide in, do you know?"

Flora arched her eyebrows. "You know… I wouldn't have said that he had many friends on the island. When he first came back I never knew him to have visitors. No one came to the house that I saw for several months… but recently…"

"He's had visitors?" Duncan asked.

"Y-Yes… from time to time."

"Do you know who?"

"No, not really. You see, no one would visit during the day whilst I was here, but I would see signs that he'd had visitors of an evening. Like I said from time to time, and not what I would ever say was regular."

"You never saw anyone actually visiting?"

Flora hesitated, and Duncan saw the eyelid of her left eye involuntarily flicker as she did so. It could have been a muscle twinge but, then again, it could equally have been a telltale micro expression.

"No… not really."

"Sorry if this sounds pedantic, Flora, but that's not a very clear answer."

"Well… aside from Mr Dunmore's agent, who I've met once or twice recently – this week in fact – there was only one other person I ever saw come around," she said, hesitantly.

"The agent," Duncan said, "who is that?"

"I was never formally introduced but he's staying at the Portree Hotel, in the centre."

Duncan nodded. "And the other person you mentioned?"

"I was running behind that day, my chores had taken longer than I'd anticipated and I had to rush to get away.

After I left, I realised I'd left my mobile here at the house and so I had to drive back to pick it up. Mr Dunmore was in his study, where he had been for much of the day, and I let myself into the house with my own keys as usual, and… I heard raised voices. They were coming from the study and moments later, that's when he came out and almost bumped into me. I wasn't listening in or anything, but my mobile was on the sideboard there," she said, gesturing to the unit in the hall beyond.

"Who was it visiting with Mr Dunmore?"

Flora looked between them, breaking eye contact with Duncan and lowering her gaze. "It was Campbell," she said, biting her lip, her eyes dancing between Duncan and Alistair. "Campbell McLaren."

Alistair inhaled steeply and Duncan was surprised by the pair's reaction. He sent Alistair an inquisitive look, but Alistair was focused on Flora.

"Were they friends?" Alistair asked.

Flora shook her head. "I've no idea. I've never heard mention of him, and I'd not seen him at the house before."

"You said their voices were raised—"

"Maybe, yes," she said. "That's what I thought but I guess they could have just been speaking loudly. I don't really know."

"What *might* they have been saying to one another?" Duncan asked.

"I don't know," she said, Duncan inclined his head and Flora persisted. "I don't know, honestly. I was just so surprised to see someone at the house that it caught me off guard."

Duncan looked at Alistair again and the look he returned suggested they'd talk about it later. Duncan accepted that with a curt nod.

"Flora, would you mind if we had a look in Mr Dunmore's study?"

"I don't think he would appreciate that—"

"I don't think he'll object," Alistair said, raising a solitary eyebrow.

"I… suppose not," Flora agreed. She looked to Alistair's left, into the hall linking the newer construction to the older. "It's along the way there, last door on the left."

Duncan and Alistair left her in the sitting room. She appeared drained by their conversation, and Duncan found himself wondering why. They came to the door to the study and Duncan tried the handle only to find the door locked. He looked around for a key but there wasn't one in view. He tried the handle again but it was steadfastly secure.

"Did you think you could unlock it with the power of your mind or something?" Alistair asked drily.

Duncan ignored the sarcastic remark. He analysed the door. It was solid oak, and wasn't likely to give without some immense pressure. "We'd better hope he had his keys in his pocket I guess," Duncan said.

"If he did for himself then we don't need to bother, do we?" Alistair countered. Duncan tested the door again, once more for good measure before giving in.

"No, I suppose we don't."

He turned and they both saw Flora standing at the entrance to the sitting room, arms folded, watching them intently.

"You never did say what happened to Mr Dunmore."

"When we know," Duncan said softly, "I promise we will tell you."

Flora escorted them back to the front door and once they were outside, the front door safely closed and they were walking back to the car, Duncan glanced at Alistair.

"Tell me about Campbell McLaren."

"A proper bastard," Alistair replied flatly, hauling open the driver's door and climbing up into the cab of his pick-up. He looked over at Duncan as he also got in on his side. Alistair turned the key in the ignition and glanced sideways at Duncan. "So I'm told anyway."

CHAPTER SIX

THE LUNCHTIME TRADE in the hotel restaurant appeared to be dissipating when Duncan and Alistair entered the hotel lobby. The Portree Hotel dominated Somerled Square, barely a stone's throw from the police station. It was an imposing old stone building and had been trading in the island's capital for almost one hundred and fifty years. The reception desk wasn't occupied and they had to wait in the lobby, Duncan casting an eye over the grandeur of the setting. Alistair nudged him, indicating a clutch of promotional flyers on a small table just inside the lobby entrance. Bruce Dunmore's name was emblazoned upon it.

"It would appear that this was where our man was going to be for his meet and greet later this week," Alistair said. Duncan picked up one of the leaflets and examined it.

"He wasn't charging for the event," he said, surprised. The event was due to take place on the coming Saturday. "I'll bet it would have been packed out too."

A young lady approached the reception desk, greeting

them both with a warm smile. Duncan identified himself and subtly displayed his warrant card.

"We're here to see someone we believe is one of your guests," Duncan said.

"What is the name?" she asked politely, turning to the monitor on the desk. Duncan looked at Alistair who was scrolling through an internet page displayed on his mobile.

"It says here that Dunmore is represented by Connor Booth at Harlequin—"

"Mr Booth is just through that archway in the bar, sir," the receptionist said. "I spoke to him not five minutes ago. He's on the left-hand side, sitting at a table overlooking the square." Duncan thanked her and he led the way through into the hotel bar. The restaurant may have been fairly busy at the end of lunchtime service but the bar was quiet with barely a handful of patrons sitting down. Duncan saw a man as described, pointing him out to Alistair and the two of them made their way over to where he was sitting.

Booth saw them approach, putting his mobile phone down on the table before him as they reached the table.

"Mr Booth?" Duncan asked and the man nodded.

"Indeed," he said, smiling. "How can I help you, gentlemen?"

"DI McAdam and DS MacEachran," Duncan said. "Could we speak to you about your client, Bruce Dunmore?"

"Of course," he said, gesturing with an open hand for them to join him. Duncan pulled out the chair opposite while Alistair slid onto the bench seat before the window. "How may I help?"

"I'm very sorry to inform you that Mr Dunmore's body was found this morning." Booth was visibly shocked and before he could ask, Duncan confirmed the news. "I'm afraid he was pronounced dead at the scene shortly after he was found."

"My God!" Booth said, open-mouthed. "W-Whatever happened?"

"We are trying to ascertain the circumstances of that just now," Duncan said. He sat forward, resting his elbows on the table. "Can you tell me when you last had contact with Bruce?"

Booth was momentarily silent, expressionless and then seemed to pull himself back into focus, exhaling heavily. "I… yesterday. I saw Bruce yesterday. We met for lunch, a late lunch…"

"And what time did you part company?" Duncan asked. "Do you remember?"

Booth's forehead furrowed. "A little after three, I think." He nodded to himself. "Yes, I recall the clock sounding at the top of the hour."

"And how was he?"

"Bruce?" Booth asked, Duncan nodded. "He was… in good spirits, all things considered."

"All what things considered?" Duncan asked.

"Well… you're aware of the passing of his wife?"

"Yes, it was the anniversary of her passing at the weekend."

"Right, yes," Booth said. "It's always a tricky time for Bruce to negotiate. She was very much a piece of his world… more so than his writing, if the truth be told." He sat forward, fixing an intense gaze over Duncan. "You're certain… I mean, positive that it is Bruce who was found?"

"There hasn't been a formal identification yet, no," Duncan said but he was keen to ensure false hope wasn't offered as soon as he saw hope exhibited in Booth's expression. "But your client is very well known, and enough people have identified him for us to be absolutely certain."

"Damn," Booth muttered, sighing. "That's a crying shame. So soon after he returned to his birthplace as well."

"Yes, that's interesting to me," Duncan said, sparking a curious look from the agent. "Why did he return to Skye? From what we understand from his housekeeper, Bruce never seemed to spend much time on the island in recent years."

"No, that's true," Booth said, thoughtfully. "Come to think about it, Bruce was one of the few people I know who always referred to the island in a rather disdainful way when it came up in conversation. I must admit to being perplexed by his announcement that he was going home."

"So why would he move back? You're only adding to the background that he wouldn't care to do so," Duncan said. "It seems a bit out of character. Not that I knew the man at all."

Booth was silent for a moment and then shook his head. "That's a good question. I'm afraid I can't answer it though, at least not with any confidence. He'd had a health scare recently, and generally had been feeling unwell, scaling back his public commitments this past six months or so. That might have something to do with it."

"He never discussed the move with you?"

"No, not at all. I think he was already back in the family home before I received word of the move. But… although we have known each other for many years, it was broadly a business relationship. Bruce was never one for idle chit-chat. A very… closed off man, I would say." He splayed his hands wide. "Not that we didn't get on, it's just that Bruce is a lot like most of the authors I know and represent."

"In what way?" Alistair, who had been silent until now, asked.

"Well, authors have very creative minds, active imaginations and have a lovely way of entertaining their readers – well, the good ones do anyway –but, how can I put this delicately… they spend an awful lot of their lives alone, and it is by choice."

"They don't enjoy the company of others?" Duncan asked.

"Generally speaking… no. That's not to say they aren't sociable types. They are often quite delightful people but they find solace in their own company. After all, I can't imagine many people who could sit in a busy office and concoct stories along the lines of Bruce's. Far too much distraction."

Duncan processed that information. It made sense. "Did he have friends, close friends, I mean? People he would go to if he was in need of support, for instance."

"I dare say there would be," Booth said. "Bruce was a very amenable man. People loved to be in his company."

"Care to throw some names into the mix for us?' Alistair said.

"I'm afraid I can't help you there…" his eyes narrowed as he looked at Alistair. "DS…"

"MacEachran."

"Right, yes. Sorry. I'm not one with the ear to keep details in mind." He chuckled. "Thankfully, I am simply the negotiator on Bruce's behalf. Or, at least, I was. Terrible news, dreadful."

"Again, apologies for bringing the bad news," Duncan said. "What was this event that was scheduled for the weekend?"

"The one just gone or this weekend?"

"He had an event over the last weekend?" Duncan asked. "We weren't aware of that. When was it?"

"Saturday," Booth said. "Bruce always preferred weekend

events. He liked to treat his working week much as one might if they went to the office every day."

"If I had the choice," Alistair said, "I'd make sure I never had to treat the working week by being in the office every day."

Booth smiled. "Each to their own, Detective Sergeant. Bruce had his habits, his routines, and he was fastidious in following them."

"For example?" Duncan asked.

"He walked every morning, whether he was here on Skye, at his home in the West End of Glasgow or attending a function in London. It was his thing. Everyone knew that. He documented it in numerous articles. That… and always smoking a cigar once he finished the final draft of a new book. It was… his celebration. His only vice, too, I should add."

"He didn't care for a wee dram of an evening then?" Alistair asked.

"No, not these days. Bruce was strictly teetotal."

"Was that a new thing?" Duncan asked, reading between the lines.

"Fairly new, yes." Booth's gaze lifted to the ceiling as he thought of something. "Possibly six months or so, maybe more."

"Did he drink too much?"

"That's subjective," Booth said, ducking the question.

"How was he, in himself?"

"Well, I think," Booth said. "When I came up at the end of last week and we met for dinner he seemed very bright. I even commented on it."

"He was happy?" Duncan asked.

"I couldn't say for sure, but he was energetic, composed

and he looked like he was sleeping better. I think the move had been good for him, I have to say."

Duncan sat back. "What you just said there, about him sleeping better—"

Booth held his hands aloft. "I'll repeat, Detective Inspector, that we did not share personal thoughts and feelings, other than regarding his work, but… I will say that he seemed much more settled here. It was noticeable from the last time I met with him."

"It's the island," Alistair said. "It does that to you. If you let it."

"I'll take your word for it, DS MacEachran. I, for one, cannot wait to get back to the mainland." His eyes shifted to the bar where a young man was clearing away glasses and prepping the bar for the evening no doubt. "It's difficult to get a decent cup of coffee around here."

"How long were you planning to stay for?" Duncan asked.

"Until after this coming Saturday's event." He seemed glum. "I suppose I won't have to stay that long after all."

"Do you usually spend over a week with one of your authors?" Duncan asked. Booth shook his head.

"No, certainly not. Highly unusual."

"Then why on this occasion?"

"Bruce had finished the first draft of his latest manuscript, and we were planning on running through it this week—"

"And you often do that in person?" Duncan asked, failing to mask his surprise.

"No, not at all. Usually, he would send it through to me via email and I'd spend a week or so going over it before submitting it for the first round of edits."

"Then why the change?"

"Good question," Booth said. "It's one I would also like the answer to as well..." he looked at Duncan inquisitively, "but I think we will both have to speculate, won't we?"

"He never told you?"

"No," Booth said, disappointed. "I was due to see him again on Tuesday – that's tomorrow, isn't it? – and he promised to go through it all with me then."

"What did the two of you discuss over dinner when you arrived?"

"The marketing plans for the new book, as outlined by his publisher. Believe me, they are just as keen to learn what this new book was all about!"

"They agreed to publish something without knowing what it was?" Duncan asked. That didn't strike him as good business sense.

"When you have someone as successful as Bruce Dunmore on your books, trust me, you give him free rein to do as he pleases. His last book sat at the number one spot for seven weeks. This book already has television and film producers stumbling over one another to obtain the rights to it. Have you any idea how much of a feeding frenzy there is for the next Dunmore thriller?"

"A big one," Duncan said, "so it would seem."

Booth stretched his arms out theatrically to each side. "Huge!"

"Shame he'll never finish it then, I suppose," Alistair said. Booth lowered his arms, a dejected look momentarily crossing his face.

"Yes, that's true," he said.

"A posthumous publication perhaps?" Alistair asked. Duncan could see a little gleam in Alistair's eye. He didn't care for this man, but you wouldn't know it unless you knew Alistair.

"I suppose that's possible," Booth said, and then he cleared his throat when he saw them both staring at him. "A little early to think of anything like that though."

"You would think so," Alistair said flatly.

"Where was this other event?" Duncan asked. "The one this past weekend. Saturday, you said?"

"Yes, it was a much smaller event though, a book signing at a local shop here in Portree," he said, raising a hand in the air and hesitating as he tried to get his bearings and point in the general direction of the shop. "It's on the run along Bank Street, just over the road before the harbour."

"I know it," Duncan said. "How did it go?"

"It all went off without a hitch, by all accounts. A popular man is – was – Bruce." He frowned again, deeper than before. "Tragic. Absolutely tragic." His eyes shifted to Duncan. "Tell me, what do you think happened? Was it a heart attack or something?"

"We're looking into it," Duncan said. "Did Bruce have any reason to be up in Staffin?"

"Staffin?" Booth repeated. "I'm sorry, I don't know where that is."

"Up the way," Alistair said. "On the east coast of the Trotternish."

"The what?"

"You haven't spent much time on Skye, have you, Mr Booth?" Alistair said. Booth grimaced.

"Not my sort of place," he said lowering his voice as he checked they wouldn't be overheard. "It's all a bit… too much like island folk, if you know what I mean?"

"Well, it is an island, Mr Booth," Alistair said without a flicker of humour or sarcasm. Booth cleared his throat.

"I meant no offence," Booth said.

"None taken," Duncan said. "I assure you. What are your plans for the coming days?"

"I… will probably be around for a little while. A few days at least."

"Tie up loose ends?" Alistair asked.

"Yes, along those lines, I should think." Booth looked at Duncan. "Is there anything else that I can assist you with, Detective Inspector?"

"There is one thing," Duncan said.

"Name it, please."

"Bruce had no living relative that we know of—"

"That's correct. He was an only child and ever since Annie passed away, I believe he has lived alone."

"Therefore we are struggling to find someone who can provide an official identification."

"Oh…" Booth said, his face dropping. "I see… well, couldn't the housekeeper—"

"I was thinking that you would be a better option," Duncan said, seeing as you've known him for such an extended period of time."

"Well… I—"

Alistair chimed in. "It would be the gentlemanly thing to do," he then looked at Duncan. "Wouldn't you say so, sir?"

"I would," Duncan said.

"Well, in that case…" Booth frowned, and seemingly unable to come up with a good reason not to do it, he nodded curtly. "Anything I can do to help."

"Thank you," Duncan said. "I'll contact the hotel reception when we have a time and I'll send a car for you."

"Is that really… really necessary?"

"We wouldn't want you to get lost," Duncan said, standing up.

"Right," Booth agreed, staring straight ahead now.

Duncan thanked him and Alistair fell into step alongside him as they made their way out of the hotel to make the short walk across Somerled Square and into the police station.

"You didn't like him very much, did you, Al?" Duncan asked.

"No. A spiv," Alistair said, checking for no buses arriving into the station before stepping out to cross the road. A number of passengers were gathered on the platform awaiting their connection. "I've never liked people like that, kind words, silver tongue… a tenner says he's only sticking around to see if he can find a copy of Bruce Dunmore's latest book kicking around somewhere."

Duncan chuckled. "That's cold, you cynical old sod."

"Mark my words," Alistair countered, "a man like that would sell his own mother if he thought he could make a few quid."

"You sound pretty sure of that."

"Hah! You're no different," Alistair retorted as they entered the station lobby.

"What do you mean?" Duncan asked, punching the code into the security door to allow them access whilst acknowledging the clerk on the public-facing desk.

"You didn't like him any more than I did."

"Again," Duncan said, holding the door open for his colleague, "what do you mean? I said nothing of the sort."

"You," Alistair said with a wicked grin, "making him do the identification of the body. That isn't necessary—"

"That was done with purpose," Duncan countered. They were walking up the stairs to the CID office now. "Do you find it hard to believe that the man's agent, who's been with him for years, and is scheduled to be up here with him for over a week, has no idea of what he was working on, who his friends are and, most importantly, he went around the houses by way of asking how Dunmore died. It was like he was avoiding the question but dying to ask it."

Alistair stopped halfway up the stairs, leaning on the handrail. "You wanted to see how he'd react to seeing Bruce dead, didn't you?"

Duncan inclined his head. "Or how he'd react to me asking him to, aye. I don't think he strikes me as a stone-cold psychopath… and if he is involved then it might turn his stomach to see what he's done."

"You think he's involved?" Alistair asked as Duncan resumed his climb.

"I have no idea at the moment," Duncan said, rounding on him. "But what I do know is, as you so studiously pointed out, that I didn't like that man one bit. You know when you come across someone and your skin starts to… crawl—"

"Aye, had that once or twice."

"Well, it's instinct and I've learned to trust that feeling."

"Of course, if he doesn't react at all then he might still be involved," Alistair said. Duncan tilted his head. "He might just happen *to be* a stone-cold psychopath."

Duncan checked his watch. It was almost three o'clock now. "Damn," he said quietly.

"What is it?"

"I told Grace I'd pick her up from work. Her car's in the garage."

"You go, I'll hold the fort here," Alistair said.

"Okay," Duncan said, descending the stairs. "I'll not be long." He stopped, looking up at Alistair. "And when I get back you can fill me in on Campbell McLaren."

"Campbell?" a voice from below said and Duncan turned

to see the custody sergeant passing the foot of the stairs. Duncan nodded a greeting and the officer stopped, hands on his hips. "Are you talking about old Inspector McLaren?"

Duncan looked back up at Alistair who smiled. "The very same."

"Inspector?" Duncan asked the custody sergeant. "You knew him?"

"Of him, aye. A right bastard."

Duncan shook his head. "Does anyone actually know this man to dislike him or is it simply a popular opinion to hate him?"

The custody sergeant shrugged, turning the corners of his mouth down and setting off, rounding the corner and disappearing from sight.

"I told you," Alistair said. "The man's reputation is formidable."

"Aye, you did. How come I've never heard of him."

Alistair shrugged. "You should pay more attention."

"I'll no' be long, Alistair," he said, shaking his head as his DS grinned at him.

CHAPTER SEVEN

GRACE WAS WAITING OUTSIDE on the pavement, underneath the overhang of the bar's entrance when Duncan pulled up. She hurried over and got into the passenger seat keen to get out of the now steadily falling rain.

"Sorry I'm a bit late," Duncan said.

"You wouldn't need to be sorry if you were on time," she said, leaning over and kissing him.

"I'm still sorry."

"No bother, Duncan. It's okay."

"Any word on your car?" he asked as he checked his mirrors to pull away.

"A rocker cover gasket has failed," she said, fastening her seatbelt. "Whatever the hell that is?"

"That'll explain why the engine is covered in oil. When will you get it back?"

"They have to order it in, so a couple of days. In the meantime, you'll just have to drive me around like my chauffeur."

"Terrific," Duncan said.

"My ever so slightly grumpy chauffeur, I might add," she said, looking sideways at him. "What's up?"

"Is something up?" he said. She fixed him with a stern look, a knowing look and he relented, shaking his head and smiling. She knew him too well. "I've caught a case," he said, negotiating the tight turn onto Bank Street. A lorry was dropping off goods to the mini Co-op and half the road was blocked. A mobile home was trying to negotiate the bend at the top of the hill and the usual high-quality level of parking outside the hotel there was helping to back up the traffic. Duncan sighed. "Not going anywhere for a bit, by the look of it."

"So… what's really on your mind?" Grace asked, accompanied by a searching look.

"A dead body was—"

"No, what's got to you? You're always on some case or another and most of them have you wading through awful people doing awful things, so that's nothing new. What's up?"

Duncan gathered himself. Grace was right. He hadn't really thought much about it, work having got in the way and done a pretty good job of distracting him. "I dropped in with Ros to see Mum this morning."

"Oh yeah, how'd it go?" He looked at her and she winced. "That bad, huh?"

He nodded. "She's getting worse." He sighed. "Today… is the worst she's been in a while. She screamed at Roslyn… and me to be fair, but I could see it really cut through with Ros." He inclined his head, glancing up the hill to see that the mobile home was still yet to find a way through. Their best bet was to see the lorry depart first. "I'll not repeat what she said, but it was awful. To hear and to see how it hurt her."

"Ros?"

"Aye."

"There's more though, right?"

Duncan nodded. "They think Mum... that she might have cancer."

"Aww Dunc... I'm sorry, that's awful."

"Well... it is what it is." Someone displayed their displeasure by sounding their horn. "Impatient sods," Duncan said and his patience evaporated too. He blasted his own horn, not at anyone in particular but more just to vent his frustration. Still, no one moved.

"What's the prognosis?" Grace asked.

"We're not there yet," he replied, looking to his right. "They want to schedule a biopsy and we'll take it from there I suppose."

"Okay. Let's hope for the best—"

Duncan accelerated suddenly, swinging the car over onto the other side of the road and pulling into the kerb.

"A little advance notice of that would have been nice," Grace said, arching her eyebrows at Duncan.

"Sorry," he said, switching off the engine. He nodded towards the book shop he was parked in front of. "Do you mind if I just pop in here?"

Grace peered past him, eyeing up the bookshop which also sold artist supplies, maps and island-related material. "I know we aren't moving, but are you in dire need of something to read?" she asked with a smile.

"I won't be a minute," he said, clambering out before ducking his head back into the car and meeting her curious look. "I promise."

"I'll be right here," Grace said. "Not doing very much." He walked up to the bookshop, pushing open the door. There were a couple of customers browsing the book shelves, and he made for the person behind the till.

"Good afternoon," he said, smiling. He was warmly greeted.

"Can I help you?"

"I was wondering if you could, yes," he said, showing her his identification. The customers who were in the shop headed for the door, thanking the lady he was speaking to for her help. She waved them off.

"Police?" she asked. "How can I help?"

"You hosted a book signing at the weekend—"

"For Bruce," she said, smiling. "Yes, he is such a lovely man."

"It went well then?"

"There was a healthy turnout yes, but I think more people will be planning to go to the one he has booked for this weekend."

"The one at the Portree Hotel," Duncan said and she nodded. He didn't think it wise to tell her that that wouldn't be going ahead.

"He was very good with the audience. He really took the time to answer people's questions," she explained. "Although..."

"Although?"

"He seemed a little distracted, I thought, as it went on. Maybe that was just him. – I'd never met him before – or maybe he was tired. He looked rather frail."

Duncan thought that was in stark contrast to how Connor Booth had described him, but maybe it was all relative and by her own admission, she'd never met Bruce before.

"Aside from looking frail, how was he?" Duncan asked.

"Like I said, it went well. I could see he was getting tired towards the end but a man of his age, that's not surprising, is it?"

"No, I suppose not."

"Why do you ask?"

"Just routine," Duncan said drawing a smile from her. "What?" he asked innocently.

"I've read enough detective books to know that no policeman ever asks a question because it's routine."

Duncan smiled, glancing out through the window to see Grace looking at him. She raised her arm and pointed – in an exaggerated way – at the watch on her wrist. He waved to her.

"Tell me, was there anyone who… perhaps wasn't such a fan of Bruce who attended the event?"

"No. Not at all," she said. "What a curious question."

"Just routine," Duncan said, with a hint of a smile.

"There was one though… but he wasn't actually at the signing. I saw him speaking to Bruce outside, after we'd wrapped up. I was just locking up and I saw them talking."

"Why did it get your attention?"

"It looked… a little heated."

"They were arguing?"

She shrugged. "I don't know about that, and Bruce had his back to me. The man he was talking to didn't seem particularly pleased though. I did wonder whether I should go out, seeing as he was much younger than Bruce and he did look quite aggressive."

"But you didn't?"

"No need. Just as I was watching they went their separate ways." She smiled. "Perhaps I misinterpreted what was happening."

"Perhaps." Duncan was thoughtful. "I don't suppose you know who he was speaking to, do you?"

"Oh yes, it was Iain," she said. Duncan pursed his lips. "Iain Lambert. He owns Skye Lights."

"The window company?" Duncan asked. She nodded. "I've seen their little vans around the island."

"That's the one. It was definitely Iain. I've known him for years."

"I don't suppose you heard anything of whatever it was they were talking about?"

"No, sorry. The door was closed."

A car horn sounded and Duncan glanced out to see Grace leaning over. She tapped the horn once more for good measure. "I should go," Duncan said.

"She is keen, isn't she?"

"I'm supposed to be driving her home."

"Better not keep her waiting."

"No," Duncan said. "Oh, this altercation – or whatever it was – was it seen by any of the other attendees?"

"Probably. It was right at the end and Bruce left along with everyone else."

"I don't suppose you have a list of names for those who were here?"

"It wasn't that organised," she said, but there were only seven or eight people here. I could jot their names down for you, if you like. I know them all and I'm sure they wouldn't mind."

"Thank you, that'd be helpful."

"No problem at all."

When Duncan got back into the car, a list of names secreted in his pocket, he found the windows were all steamed up and the temperature inside the cabin had dropped. It felt chilly now.

"Sorry," Duncan said. "It was to do with—"

"The case, aye. Home," Grace said, pointing at the clear road now the traffic had all passed through. She tore open the packaging of a pasty and when the smell reached Duncan's nose his stomach growled. He hadn't eaten at all today, having skipped breakfast because he needed to meet Roslyn early. He hadn't given it much thought until now.

"Where did you get that from?" he asked.

"I went into the Co-op while you were gassing in there."

"Did you get me one?"

"No, I didn't," she said, smiling and taking a bite. "If you're good I'll let you have the end of this one."

"Define good."

"Getting me home before I wee myself would be a start. The toilets are backed up at work and, unlike the lesser half of the species, we lasses need a functioning toilet." Again, she pointed forwards. "Drive like your life depended on it, Duncan McAdam. But not too fast, because I need a wee and I don't want the seatbelt pulling too much."

"Got it," he said, spotting a gap in the traffic and pulling out. Once they were moving, Duncan called Alistair via the Bluetooth connection in his car.

"Yes, boss?" Alistair said, answering quickly.

"Iain Lambert," Duncan said. "Everything you can find on him along with any possible connection he might have to Bruce Dunmore."

"On it," Alistair said, hanging up.

"I know Iain." Grace said. "He's a nice guy, comes into the bar from time to time. What's he been up to?"

"We'll soon see," Duncan said, focusing on his driving.

CHAPTER EIGHT

HAVING DROPPED Grace back at the croft, where they were pretty much living together these days, her place being used less and less at this point, Duncan returned to the station. Duncan gave Alistair a heads-up when he reached the outskirts of Portree and his DS was waiting for him as he pulled up outside the station. He got into the passenger seat and Duncan didn't even have to engage the handbrake.

"What did you find out about Iain Lambert?" Duncan asked. Alistair, hands in his pockets and knees raised awkwardly, sat almost hunched in his seat. He was a tall man and found the dimensions of Duncan's car a little cramped. That was one reason he preferred to drive when they were out in the field.

"There isn't a lot on him," Alistair said, "from a policing point of view at any rate. He's not been in trouble with us before. A few speeding fines and some points on his driving licence over the years, but probably about average bearing in mind his age." Leaning his head back against the rest, he looked sideways at Duncan. "What's our interest, if you don't mind me asking?"

"He was seen having words with Bruce this past Saturday afternoon. The exchange looked a bit heated, according to the eyewitness who saw them together."

"Any idea what it was about?"

"No, nothing was overheard," Duncan said. He glanced at Alistair. "I thought we would go and ask."

"No harm in asking," Alistair said, settling into his seat more. "You sit low in this car, don't you?"

"That's because it's a car and not a monster truck, Alistair."

"Aye, right enough. Each to their own I guess." Duncan could tell from his tone that he didn't mean that at all.

"How did the team get on at Staffin?"

"Didn't find a blade anywhere on the beach," Alistair said. "The body has been transferred to the morgue and your man Connor Booth is going in to identify him officially just now. Then Craig Dunbar can get on with the post-mortem." His brow furrowed. "Curiously, when I was having a good look at the body, we found shards of glass in his hair."

"Glass?" Duncan repeated and Alistair nodded.

"Aye, not much but it was thick. I mean, thicker than a wine glass but not as thick as a windowpane, if you know what I mean. A shard is probably not right either. It was more like a fragment, a chunk for want of a better word. Barely a couple of millimetres across," he said holding his thumb and forefinger aloft, almost touching.

"Anything else leap out at you?"

"No. Other than that, it was a pretty run of the mill suicide." He sniffed. "Aside from the location," he said, wrinkling his nose. "Don't get me wrong, I'm all for creating a beautiful environment as the backdrop for a momentous, life-changing – indeed life-ending – event but I've never known anyone to be all that bothered about atmospherics and aesthetics when it comes to doing harm to themself, if you know what I mean?"

"I do," Duncan said. "That's been bothering me as well. I know it's a beautiful location, but that's something you don't tend to think about when your head's not right."

"Aye," Alistair said, "but these creative sorts are a bit emotional, aren't they? So… who knows what he was thinking."

They turned off the main road and onto the industrial estate on the western edge of Portree moments later, barely a five minute drive from the town centre, Duncan slowing the car so they could see which of the units was occupied by Iain Lambert's business. It was on the far side of the estate, and they drove through it passing the many small and medium enterprises that serviced the island's needs. There was so much more business operating on the island beyond tourism and hospitality and most people never saw it.

There were half a dozen parking spaces in front of the unit, three of which were occupied. Two were works' vans with the stencilled logo and contact details of Lambert's business emblazoned on the side and the other was a blue Range Rover, several decades old. None of the vehicles looked particularly new and the paintwork was fading on the vans, some of the lettering had peeled away from the surface and been cut off at some point.

"I can see he's busy," Alistair said, with no attempt to hide his sarcasm. The doors into the unit were open but there was no showroom to speak of. Once inside there was a simple carpeted lobby with another set of doors leading into an open space. There were some mock-ups scattered around the room, the glass panes noticeably absent, displaying what was available to order. A fake wall was put up here and there with window frames, minus their glass, in place along with a set of contemporary folding, sliding doors which seemed all the rage at the moment. Duncan thought it odd to consider installing such doors on a property in Skye. Somewhere warmer with far less wind and rainfall certainly, but how much use you'd have for the functionality on the Misty Isle was questionable.

All around the space there seemed to be bits and pieces of packaging or strips of plastic and aluminium, all seemingly without a proper home and cast to the side, remaining wherever they landed. Duncan had been into closing-down sales when big stores on the mainland had seen their parent company go into administration, the staff selling off everything inside in the final days of trading. It was organised chaos, and this place had a similar look and feel to it.

"Hello!" Duncan called seeing no one around.

"I'll be right with you," a voice came from somewhere in the rear. The unit had been partitioned at some point and Duncan peered through an opening, looking into the rear of the building. This was a storeroom, and he saw rows and rows of old window frames, clearly old because they had blackened mould and detritus in the frames as well as on the glass in many cases. They must store old windows they replace, having them shipped off once they reach a certain threshold. Either that or he was hoarding them in some twisted fetish for second-hand uPVC glazing.

Duncan joined Alistair, casually looking around the unit, but they didn't have to wait long. A red-faced man came out of the rear, wiping his hands on a cloth which he threw aside, smiling as he came to meet them. He was wearing jeans and a coloured jumper which matched the rosy glow of his cheeks.

"Good afternoon," he said, jovially, looking between them. "Sorry about that, I was just... dealing with an order."

"No problem at all," Duncan said, producing his warrant card. "DI McAdam and DS MacEachran."

"Police?" he said, the smile dissipating. "W-What can I do for you?"

"We're looking for Iain Lambert."

He held his hands up. "That's me, guilty as charged!" he said, forcing a smile which was fleeting. "What... er... can I do for you?"

"You are acquainted with Bruce Dunmore?" Duncan asked but in such a way as to make it sound more like a statement.

"Bruce?" Lambert asked, failing to mask what Duncan thought was genuine surprise. "Yes, I know Bruce. I have done for a long time."

"Are you friends?" Duncan asked.

"I wouldn't go that far," Lambert said. "I've known him for a long time. He was friends with my father back in the day. Well," he said frowning, "they worked together for a time."

"You get on with him?"

"Yes, of course. What's all this about?"

"You were seen with Bruce this past Saturday, in Portree."

"Oh... yes, I did bump into him as it happens," Lambert said, concentrating now. "We were on Bank Street, I think. Yes, I'm sure it was. He'd just come from some book signing or reading he'd given." He shook his head. "Something like that anyway. So?"

"I'm told you exchanged words and that it was a little heated, as if you might be arguing," Duncan said.

Lambert hesitated, then exhaled heavily, his eyes flitting between Duncan and Alistair. "No, I wouldn't say so. Not heated exactly. We were just talking."

"Okay," Duncan said, adopting a conciliatory tone. "What were you not arguing about?"

Lambert scoffed. "Look, I did some work out at his place and… er…" he shook his head, "he hasn't paid me yet, and I was asking him about it. That's all." He laughed nervously. "It's hardly worth bothering the police about."

"Some work, you say?" Alistair asked and Lambert nodded. "What kind of work?"

Lambert reacted by holding his hands out wide. "I fitted some windows obviously. What else might it be?"

"Is it a lot of money he owes you then?" Duncan asked.

"Not a lot, no," Lambert said, defensively. "I'm entitled to ask for it though, aren't I?"

"A coincidence, you two bumping into one another just after he leaves his event, isn't it?"

"Well…" Lambert frowned. "I suppose so."

"How did Bruce react?"

"He… er…" Lambert's demeanour changed, becoming impatient. "Look, I'm sorry to ask this, but what has it got to do with you?"

"Bruce Dunmore was found dead this morning, Mr Lambert," Duncan said. Lambert gasped. "And we need to establish his movements over the weekend and see what was going on in his life. That's why we're here."

"I… I don't know what to say," Lambert said, his shoulders sagging as he took in the news. "Dead you say? How?"

"He was found out at Staffin, on the beach first thing this morning."

Lambert was open-mouthed, a vacant look in his eyes. "Dead."

"I'm afraid so," Duncan told him. "When did you do the work on his property?"

"Um…" Lambert was seemingly lost in thought, and Duncan wasn't sure he'd heard the question.

"Mr Lambert, when did you do your work for him?"

"It was… it was a few weeks ago now. At the beginning of last month."

"And how did you find him?"

"Fine," Lambert said. "Much the same as always, you know? Bruce wasn't a man for change, not really. He was always a very steady sort of a man, if you know what I mean?"

"Have you had any other contact with him recently, prior to speaking to him on Saturday or even afterwards?"

"No, no, I can't say I have." He held Duncan's gaze. "I've no reason to."

"Other than to obtain payment, you mean?" Alistair said.

"Yes, that's… that's it, yes."

"Okay, Mr Lambert," Duncan said.

"I'm sorry I couldn't have been more help to you."

"You've been very helpful," Duncan said.

"I have?" Lambert replied. "Great."

"Your father, what's his name?"

"Douglas," Lambert said. "Dougie really. Only my old grandmother ever called him Douglas."

"And you said they were friends—"

"More like colleagues, but they knew each other."

"Are they still in touch at all?" Duncan asked.

"No, my father passed away."

"I'm sorry," Duncan said.

Lambert shrugged. "Thank you but it was a long time ago now." Duncan took out one of his contact cards and passed it to him. Lambert accepted it, staring at the front.

"Just in case anything comes to mind that you think might be useful to us."

"Of course," Lambert said. "I'll be sure to call you."

Duncan thanked him and he left the room, Alistair a step behind him. Back at the car, Duncan glanced towards the unit and saw Iain Lambert at the window watching them. Under Duncan's gaze he turned and disappeared from view.

"If you believe him," Alistair said, "then this was a waste of time."

"Aye," Duncan replied, unlocking the car. "If you believe him."

"So..." Alistair said drawing a deep breath. "You think he's lying as well then?"

Duncan cocked his head. "Did you see any new windows out at the Dunmore house in Cuidrach?"

"No, I can't say that I did. And for one, Bruce Dunmore has hardly spent any time on the island in years, so how does this guy know if he's not one to embrace change." Duncan leaned against the car, laying his forearms against the roof and glanced back towards Iain Lambert's business unit. "Another thing, since when does a business chase people in the street for payment?"

"Aye, and this place doesn't exactly look like a going concern," Alistair said. "For a fibber, Iain Lambert isn't very good at it, is he?"

"I'd happily sit down and play a few hands of poker with him, that's true," Duncan said with a wry smile.

CHAPTER NINE

ONCE THEY WERE BACK in Portree, Duncan was sitting at his desk nursing a hot cup of coffee watching his team through the window in the CID operations room. They were quietly going about their tasks populating the information boards with detail, piecing together Bruce Dunmore's last few days. Once that was clear, they would continue working backwards to build the timeline of events leading up to and including his death. Until they had something definitive to conclude this was a suicide, Duncan had every intention of keeping an open mind.

Duncan's mobile rang and he answered without looking at the caller ID.

"Duncan," a familiar voice said. "Craig Dunbar."

"Hello, Craig," he greeted the pathologist warmly. "I didn't expect to hear from you so soon."

"And if you are expecting my report then you will be disappointed, because I haven't got there yet. A chap by the name of Booth has just been in with—"

"Yes, I arranged it. Is everything confirmed?"

"We are certain this is Bruce Dunmore, aye. I must admit, he's older than I thought, but that's down to looking at the photo printed inside his books. It must have been taken some years ago."

"None of us look better with age, Craig."

"Never a truer word spoken," Dunbar said. "Although, much like a fine wine, I'm improving with age. At least, this is what I tell my good lady at home."

"How does that work out for you?"

"Hmm… not well."

Duncan smiled. "What can I do for you, Craig?"

"I just thought you would like to know," he said, apparently shifting some paperwork near to him as the sound carried, "that your man here, Bruce, had an interesting final few hours."

"Go on," Duncan said, his curiosity piqued.

"I understand that there is a question mark surrounding the death, suspicious or otherwise. Now, I can't definitively state that he didn't take his own life – not yet at least – but I can tell you he was restrained at some point."

"Restrained?" Duncan asked, standing up and trying to catch Alistair's attention in the other room. His DS noticed and came through, closing the door behind him. "How was he restrained?"

"Bound at the wrists," Dr Dunbar said. "Looking at the pattern of the indentations to the soft tissue at the wrists, a thin binding material with a straight edge. That rules out rope or any form of cord. Likely plastic, thinner than five millimetres—"

"Cable ties?" Duncan asked.

"That would be my guess, yes," Dunbar said. "It looks to

me as if his hands were not bound in prayer, but crossed like an eagle in flight, if you can picture such an image."

"That would make them easier to bind."

"He struggled against them though. The edges have dug into the soft tissue, even cut it in places but with the amount of blood at the scene, drying on the hands and so forth, I'm not surprised they were missed."

"Contrary to popular belief, they aren't very efficient for binding someone. They're easily breakable."

"I quite agree. People often confuse these zip ties, cable ties, with the zip cuffs that are used by the military for snatch-and-grab operations but those are much thicker and primarily used because speed is of the essence. However, a man of his years might struggle to break them. It is fairly easy when using speed and a little force but he might not have been capable."

"They were gone by the time his body was found. Can we conclude if they were removed prior to death?"

"That's a tough one. I'll consider it during and once I've performed the post-mortem. The damage to the skin of his wrists was recent prior to death. One can surmise that from the degradation of the tissue along with the body's regeneration time and formation of any bruising. There is no sign of either in my initial inspection but, as I say, I haven't got going yet. I just thought you would like to know as soon as possible."

"You were right, Craig," Duncan said. "Thanks very much."

"I'll have my report for you as soon as I'm done. I should be through this evening and I can let you know my initial thoughts then and follow up with the details tomorrow."

Duncan hung up and put the mobile down on his desk, exhaling heavily.

"I suppose you're going to drop something interesting on me," Alistair said.

"Bruce Dunmore was tied up before he died." Duncan wrinkled his nose. "Now that doesn't mean he couldn't have taken his own life, but—"

"It certainly adds a layer of complexity to it all," Alistair said. Duncan was about to speak but Angus Ross knocked on the door and he beckoned the young detective constable inside. "What is it, Angus?"

"I thought it'd be a good idea to keep my ears open for any unusual reports floating about," Angus said, inclining his head, "just in case like you know?"

"And?"

"A hiker has called in an abandoned vehicle. It's up on the high point, between Flodigarry and the Balmaqueen turn-off. You know, up the way, behind that old disused toilet block by the side of the main road."

"There's a track that runs up there from the road, isn't there?" Duncan said. Alistair nodded.

"Aye, there's an old ruin on the cliff edge overlooking the water too, I think."

Angus continued. "The hiker said one of the windows has been smashed in, and so it's not likely to be another walker leaving their car to come back to. He was concerned. He thinks he might have seen signs of blood as well. It's no' far from Staffin. It could be a coincidence…"

Duncan exchanged a glance with Alistair, who shrugged. "Did the caller give us the registration number?"

"Aye," Angus said, referring to the pocketbook in his hand. "I checked with the DVLA and the car is registered to a local woman, Flora McQueen—"

"Really?" Alistair asked, almost laughing.

Angus was puzzled. "Aye. You know her?"

"We've met," Alistair said, looking at Duncan. "Shall we go for a drive?"

DUNCAN COULD FEEL the wind buffeting the pick-up when Alistair stopped the vehicle. Although they were at a high point, with a sweeping panoramic view from north to south of the coastline, the area where the car had been abandoned wasn't visible from the road side. The ruins were in a shallow depression just over the crest of the rise and the car wouldn't have been discovered but for the passing walker. That in itself was a stroke of luck. There were several charted walking routes from nearby but almost all of them led up onto the Trotternish Ridge which formed the backdrop to their location when looking inland.

The car was a small hatchback. It wasn't particularly old but neither would it be classed as new. They hadn't reported the find to the owner, Flora, Bruce Dunmore's housekeeper. That was something Duncan wanted to do in person. Duncan stopped as he approached the car, dropping to his haunches to inspect the ground at his feet. They were up on the cliffs here, it was rugged, rocky and the only vegetation besides the wild grass was a patch of heather clumped nearby. Even so, the land mass was showing signs of slipping towards the sea with several step changes in levels if you were willing to tread close to the edge and look down. The volume of rainfall had left this area sodden underfoot and Duncan was looking at tyre impressions.

"Something like yours?" Duncan asked Alistair, inclining his head towards the pick-up.

"Aye, similar size," Alistair agreed. "Could be a commercial vehicle. One of the estate off-roaders maybe."

"Agreed," Duncan said. "What would it be doing all the way out here?"

"What would anyone be doing all the way out here?" Alistair countered.

Duncan glanced towards the car, assessing it from his current vantage point. The wheels of the car were turned outwards and, glancing down at the soil around the base of the rubber, he saw they'd gouged a path out of the surface rather than ridden across it. It was almost as if the driver had been turning the car around and been too aggressive with the combination of acceleration and the turning of the steering wheel. There were no footprints in the mud however. The ground was sodden and the weight of vehicles could churn it up but they were so high up that the water would run off, and so grass and heather flourished here despite the harsh environment. Lower down, the ground would be incredibly boggy.

Rising from his haunches, Duncan resumed his walk to the car. The information provided by the hiker tallied with what he saw here. The driver's side window was smashed in with only the perimeter inches holding together whereas much of the glass had fallen into the interior. The glass had shattered but held, as it was designed to do to minimise injury to those inside the vehicle in an accident, however it had then been knocked through. The fact that much of the glass was inside the cabin was indicative of someone on the exterior trying to get in rather than someone inside trying to escape.

Duncan did find a spattering of broken glass on the ground at his feet outside the car but then, peering inside, he assessed the trajectory of where the bulk of the glass had landed. He could see fragments on the passenger seat and, angling his head to improve his view, there was more in the passenger footwell too. Whoever struck the glass did so with quite some force. The driver would have been showered in glass and probably carried some of the pieces with them when they got out.

Duncan pulled on a set of forensic gloves, keen not to damage any trace evidence and watching his footing, he carefully opened the driver's door. Alistair was on the other side of the car peering through the passenger window. He also carefully opened his door so that he could see the same as Duncan and they exchanged a knowing look. They were reaching similar conclusions as to what had happened here, and it didn't look like it was a positive outcome. The overcast skies reduced the ambient natural light and Duncan used the torch function on his phone to illuminate the interior. The light reflected off the broken pieces of glass and Duncan found some had a dull shade to them. Examining further, he found what he thought was dried blood.

The car key was still in the ignition and leaning in closer, he noted the position denoted the ignition and engine should be on. However, the engine wasn't running and no icons were lit up on the dashboard.

"The ignition is on, but it looks like the battery is dead."

"Trying to start the car to get away and stalled it, perhaps?" Alistair suggested.

"Perhaps," Duncan repeated, "or he may have kept the car running while he was waiting for the heating and the wipers, and didn't see the threat coming. How long does it take for a battery to fully deplete?"

Alistair thought about it. "Depends on the state of it, along with how many systems were running off it too. This isn't a luxury car, so I don't see heated seats and the like, but it's a few years old so the battery will have cycled a lot of times. If the lights were left on… a few hours will certainly do for it, I should imagine."

Duncan couldn't go inside and he was reluctant to do much more until the vehicle was properly examined. However, he could see a mobile phone was in a small cubby of the central console and in the door bin he found a wallet. Tentatively lifting it out from its resting place, between thumb and forefinger, he gently opened it. There was a significant amount of cash inside to be carrying in a mobile phone case, probably close to one hundred pounds in various denominations along with several credit cards.

Holding it aloft, he turned the interior of the leather wallet so that Alistair could also see a small plastic window below the slots for the credit cards. Tucked inside this sleeve was a driving licence. Bruce Dunmore's face stared out at them.

"Now we know the real reason Flora was so anxious," Alistair said.

"Aye," Duncan agreed, "and it wasn't because he'd gone off for a walk either."

"We told her he was dead, and she didn't mention that he'd borrowed or taken her car. Assuming she knew of course."

"I suspect it's the former. You'd know if your car went missing, wouldn't you?" Duncan asked.

"No one drives my truck but me."

"I think we can rule out robbery as a motive, seeing as they left his cash, cards and mobile behind."

Duncan withdrew from the vehicle, shivering as he felt the first drops of fresh rain beginning to fall. Glancing at the seat he could see the fabric was darker on the driver's seat than on the others. The car had been here some time, the interior exposed to the elements by the broken window. He looked around. The peaks of the mountains in the distance behind them were hidden by cloud cover and the surrounding landscape was rugged and open with nothing to act as a windbreak. They were exposed up here. It was a desolate beauty. There was simply nothing here; no houses, no people. No one to see comings and goings. Perhaps that was the point of Dunmore being up here. Presuming it was Dunmore who'd driven the car anyway. Duncan thought of the glass Alistair spotted in the dead man's hair. He was confident that Bruce Dunmore was driving this car.

For a fleeting moment he wondered if Flora might have driven him up here but then dismissed it. Her surprise seemed genuine enough when she learned of her employer's passing, but she definitely knew more than she'd let on. He was keen to speak to her again.

"What was he doing all the way out here?" Alistair asked, coming around the car to stand alongside Duncan, his coat snapping against his legs as they were buffeted by the wind; its strength increasing.

"It's only speculation just now," Duncan said, raising his voice to be heard above the howl of the wind, "but I'd put money on it that Bruce was meeting someone out here. Let's face it, he wouldn't have driven up here over the weekend to get a closer look at the storm."

"The same person who went on to kill him?"

"Or drove him to suicide, aye," Duncan said.

"That'd take some doing to motivate him to do that."

Duncan cocked his head. "You think so?"

"Don't you?"

Duncan pursed his lips, then sighed. "I think everyone has a limit. To reach that limit, all you need to do is know what buttons to press."

"You still thinking it's a suicide?"

"I'm not ready to rule anything out," Duncan said, the earlier conversation with Craig Dunbar coming to mind. He turned to face Alistair just as they both heard the approach of a car picking its way up the track from the main road below. A liveried police car came into view, the steadily falling rain illuminated in the headlights, Ronnie MacDonald was at the wheel. Duncan nodded towards the newcomer. "Ronnie can secure the car until we can get a forensic team out here. You and I need to revisit Flora McQueen and see what she has to say for herself. Maybe she'll be a little more forthcoming this time around."

"Do you ever wonder why everyone we meet can't seem to tell us the truth?" Alistair asked with a rueful smile, hunching his shoulders as the rain was driving at them in waves now.

"I try not to take it personally, Alistair."

Alistair inclined his head. "You tell me the truth, don't you?"

"Of course," Duncan said, moving to greet Ronnie who was now out of his car and hastily pulling on his all-weather high-vis coat. Duncan called to Alistair over his shoulder as he walked. "Except for when I tell you everyone likes you, obviously."

"It goes without saying," Alistair replied.

CHAPTER TEN

Flora McQueen lived in Bernisdale, a small township on the western side of Loch Snizort Beag. If Bruce Dunmore's housekeeper had been expecting them then she hid it very well, her mouth falling open when she found them on her doorstep.

"Hello, Flora," Duncan said.

"Mr McAdam… I…"

"We've come about your car, Flora," Alistair said. She made to speak, her lips moving but no sound came from within as her eyes flitted between them.

"Who is it, love?"

Duncan looked past Flora into the house. It was a small property, of recent construction and very much in keeping with the style that the planning authorities in the Highlands and Islands seem to prefer.

"It's… the police, Freddie." She glanced over her shoulder and looking back at Duncan she seemed anxious. "Freddie is my husband," she said quietly.

"Police?" A man came to the door, casting a wary eye over Duncan and Alistair. His expression was stern and he put a supportive arm around Flora's waist. Duncan took out his warrant card, showing it to him, and he gave it a cursory inspection. "Is this about Dunmore?" Whereas Flora always referred to Bruce Dunmore in a very deferential manner, perhaps because he was her employer, Freddie didn't appear to have the same reverence. The way he said the man's name was a little off, bearing in mind his body was barely cold.

"No, this is another matter," Duncan said. Freddie nodded, his expression softening, if only slightly.

"Are you going to invite them in, love?" Freddie said, smiling at Flora.

"That's okay, Mr McQueen," Duncan said, stopping Alistair in his tracks, who was about to enter the property. "We just wanted a quick word with your wife. We won't be stopping long."

"Suit yourself,' he said with a shrug. Looking sternly at his wife, he turned away. "Don't be long, will you. We're due over at the pods in an hour."

"No, no," she said. "I won't."

Freddie walked away and Flora kept half an eye on him, not speaking until he was safely out of earshot. Even then, she still kept her voice low.

"Thank you," she said. "I… appreciated that. Freddie…" she hesitated.

"Would you be willing to step outside for a moment?" Duncan asked. She nodded, gathered her coat from a rack beside the entrance, slipped on her wellington boots and came outside, pulling the door to behind her. It wasn't raining at the moment but judging from the dark mass on the horizon that wouldn't be the case for long.

Flora led them away from the house, down a slight incline and they soon came upon a five-bar gate which opened into a fenced paddock. A couple of ponies were grazing at the far end of it. Duncan held the gate open and the three went through, Alistair taking the weight of the gate from Duncan and closing it to ensure the horses stayed secure. "Freddie doesn't really care for Mr Dunmore," Flora said. "He never has done."

"I had that impression. Why is that?" Duncan asked. She shrugged. "Was he happy you were working for him?"

"No, I can't say he was but my mother worked for the Dunmores and they were happy to employ me as well. It's not like we can pick and choose out here. You take whatever work is available… and… Mr Dunmore paid well." She sniffed. "I mean, very well, considering he was never here."

"You said he came back infrequently."

"That's right. On average I'd say once a year, if that some years. Like I told you before, he would call from time to time and if I had an issue with the house then we would speak, but not all that much."

"How come Bruce was driving your car, Flora?" Duncan asked. She didn't respond immediately, but she did stop walking. From where they were standing they had a stunning view across the head of Loch Snizort Beag. A small boat was moored just off the far side of the loch, bobbing on the gentle swell that accompanied the wind. The forecast suggested it was about to get a lot rougher but this far inland, sandwiched between the Trotternish and the Waternish peninsulas, they would be fairly well sheltered from the worst of it.

"He asked me if he could borrow it." She looked at Duncan, inclining her head. "I said yes."

"He had his own car. Was something wrong with it?"

"No, not as far as I know."

"Why ask to borrow yours?"

She shook her head. "He didn't say." She looked glum. "And I didn't ask."

Duncan found that hard to believe. "Where was he going?"

"He said… he had to meet someone, and he didn't want to attract attention."

Duncan had seen Bruce Dunmore's car parked outside his house in Cuidrach. It was a Mercedes and certainly stood out as not common on the island; but it wasn't a bright red Ferrari.

"When was it he asked to borrow it?"

"He called me late on Saturday to ask. I took it round for him on Sunday morning, after service."

"You went to church?"

"Of course. Freddie and I always go, every week," she said. "Unless we're ill."

"Who was he meeting?"

"I don't know. It wasn't my place to ask."

"Did it strike you as odd?"

"Yes, a little." She smiled ruefully. "But Mr Dunmore is – was – eccentric, to say the least." She turned to face Duncan now, glancing at Alistair who was standing a couple of steps behind Duncan. "And he has always been very good to my family. After my father passed away, he looked out for my mother, offering her work when she needed it and being ever so understanding when she was struggling."

"Struggling?"

"Yes," Flora said, frowning. "I was very small and my father left us with nothing. We had no other family on the island, my mother and father were both only children to elderly parents and that removed the support network around us. Not to say that people didn't help out, because a few people did, but it's not the same as family." She sighed. "And my father wasn't very well liked."

"Can I ask why not?"

"He was a very God-fearing man, and a strict disciplinarian," Flora said. "He had that instilled in him from a very young age by his own father and I think he just carried it on. It didn't make him someone that others warmed to. It might also have something to do with his age when he became a parent," she said, pursing her lips. "He was mature by the time he had me, much like his father was when they had him, and he was quite set in his ways by then. We all are once we hit our late thirties, aren't we?"

"You said he left, your father—"

"He passed away. It was quite sudden."

"I'm sorry."

"Don't be," Flora said gently. "I don't really remember him. I was only three, nearly four, at the time. I have some old photographs that my mother kept, but only that along with a handful of stories to remember him by." She took a deep breath. "And most of those are quite negative, reflecting him in a bad light more often than not. As I said, he wasn't well liked and very few people mourned his passing."

"Bruce Dunmore?"

She shrugged. "I don't know, but he certainly took pity on my mother. His kindness earns a lot of loyalty from me, DI McAdam." She offered him a contrite look. "Which is why I didn't tell you about him taking my car at the weekend. I thought that whatever he was doing… it was none of my business and if he needed my help, then I sure as hell wasn't going to refuse."

Duncan thought on it for a moment, allowing conversation to drop as he contemplated what she'd said. "Flora, what do you think Bruce was doing at the weekend?"

She laughed involuntarily, but it was a dry sound and

without humour. "I have no idea what he was doing. Not this past weekend anyway."

"What else then?" Duncan asked. "I can appreciate your desire to be loyal but… the man is dead, and it looks like someone else had a hand in it."

"I don't know—"

"Come on, Flora—"

"I really don't," she said, "but I will say one thing, and that's that I'm pretty sure he wasn't writing a new thriller."

"You said he didn't confide in you."

"No. He didn't. Never on a personal level but… there was one evening… it was late evening. I was finishing up and I found the door to his study was open. He was in there, so I wasn't snooping or anything like that, and I just wanted to say goodnight but I found him slumped over his desk with a half-empty bottle of scotch beside him."

"He was asleep?"

"Yes, he'd passed out or gone to sleep," she said. "I can't be sure. Anyway, I went in because I wanted to check he was all right. His breathing was shallow but nothing to be concerned about. I considered waking him, but…" she shook her head. "Anyway, I didn't want to disturb him. If he was drinking heavily, and felt the need to, then it wasn't for me to judge or get involved."

"But you saw something else, am I right?" Duncan asked. She nodded. "What was it?" Her expression clouded, darkening. "Flora? What did you see?"

"Photographs," she said quietly, nervously looking around to ensure they wouldn't be overheard. They were alone without another soul in sight. Even the horses were giving them a wide berth, although keeping an eye on them – the paddock's intruders.

"Photographs of what?"

She frowned. "People… children, teenagers mostly."

"Family?"

"No, no," she said, shaking her head firmly. "These were old pictures, many of them discoloured. They would have been taken back in the seventies or eighties, I would guess. Some were black and white, but others were colour shots. All of them were showing their age. And there was the building. The school building."

"What, here on Skye?"

"Yes, but no one was in uniform or anything like that." Her eyes darted to Duncan, looking fearful. "They were nothing weird or anything. I mean they were normal shots, boys playing on the field, larking about together. That sort of thing. It was nothing… weird. They were laid out across his desk and he had been making notes."

"What had he written?"

She forcefully shook her head. "I didn't look. It's not—"

"Your place," Duncan said. She nodded.

"It wasn't my place. I already felt as if I was intruding somewhere I shouldn't have been."

"When was this?"

"Ooo…" her eyebrows knitted in concentration, "a month, six weeks ago, maybe. I'm not sure but it was recent."

Duncan shot a sideways glance at Alistair whose expression was unreadable. He remained stoic. Duncan looked back at Flora who was staring out across the water now, her arms folded tightly across her body, evidently feeling the cold now they'd stopped walking.

"Did you ever mention this to Bruce?" Duncan asked.

"Oh no, not at all. I wouldn't want him to know I'd been

into his study and… certainly not that I'd seen him… in that state."

"And you think this all had something to do with the book he was writing?"

"I think so," she said. "It makes sense. I'm not a writer but it looked like he'd gathered a lot of things together, like it was the result of research or something. I suppose he could have been writing one of his thrillers, but he always writes Cold War-themed books and these photos just seemed so out of character for that."

"You read his books?"

"As soon as they come out," she said proudly. "I have every book he's ever written at home. Freddie moans about it. He says we'll need to build a bookcase just for Mr Dunmore's books alone at this rate." She was despondent then. "I guess there will be no need for that now."

"You said you don't have access to his study," Duncan said. "Is that true?"

She bit her lip gently, tilting her head to one side. "Not officially. I mean, I never went in there… only that one time, but I do know where he keeps a spare key."

"I think we need to access his study," Duncan said to Alistair.

"I think that should be our next step, aye."

"I can show you where the key is," Flora said to Duncan. "It's well hidden and you'll not find it without me."

"I thought your husband said you're expected elsewhere," Duncan said.

"Hah," she said, dismissing the comment with a flick of her hand. "It won't hurt him to do a little extra graft without me."

"You work together?"

"Yes, we do changeovers for rental properties all over the

north and west of the island. It's good work, although the end of the week can be a bit hectic because that's when people like to come and go. Although," she said, smiling, "these days people often book two-to-three-day mini breaks and that keeps us busy throughout the week rather than all at the back end. There are only so many properties you can reach on a Thursday or a Friday, but short breaks spread the load."

"I appreciate your help," Duncan said.

"I'm sorry I didn't tell you sooner," Flora said. "It's just… it was a shock, and I didn't know what I should do for the best. I feel… indebted makes it sound so transactional between me and Mr Dunmore but it really isn't like that."

"If you're happy to come with us over to Cuidrach, we can make sure you get back afterwards."

"Anything I can do to help, Mr McAdam."

Duncan genuinely appreciated her help, but the thought occurred that when he voiced the idea that Bruce Dunmore had been murdered, Flora never asked who by. She didn't comment at all. He added her lack of a reaction to the growing number of oddities swirling around this case. He was also intrigued to open up the study and see just what Bruce Dunmore was keeping so secret from everyone around him.

"What do you reckon?" Alistair asked.

"Are there any lights on programmable timers in the house?" Duncan asked Flora. "Security lights or similar?"

"No. Why would we need that? This is Skye."

Duncan nodded.

"We should take a look," he said, turning to Alistair. He looked back at Flora, reading her anxious expression. "May I take your keys?"

"Yes, of course," she said, fumbling inside a little canvas bag. She produced a ring of keys, handing them to him. "The front door is the one with the green sticker."

Duncan examined the keys. There were four of them. "Green sticker," he repeated, locating the key with a small green circle stuck to it.

"The white one is the back door from the kitchen. Red is the French doors off the dining room and the other is for the external store."

"Thank you," Duncan said, smiling to try to reassure her. "We'll just go ahead. If you can stay here, in the car, and once we've had a quick check then we'll come and get you. Okay?"

She nodded, but he could see she was on edge. Duncan hoped that this wasn't an extension of her withholding pertinent information from him.

"I'm sure you just left a light on, don't worry," he said.

Duncan heard Alistair take a deep breath before opening his door, having to use some force to do so as the wind drove straight at him across the water. Duncan also got out and, hunkering down inside his coat, he joined Alistair and together they hurried to the cover of the overhang above the front door, which could be found on the southern gable end of the house.

Duncan slid the key into the lock and gently turned it. The

action was almost effortless, and the door cracked open with barely a sound. Not that they would hear it from the outside, but Duncan was keen not to alert anyone inside to their presence. Of course, if someone was inside then they could have seen the approach of the pick-up along the coast road, but the course of the driveway brought them up to the side of the house where the main access door was located. The windows of the property were predominantly facing to the east and the west, the grassland to what was the rear or out across the water towards the Western Isles at the front. Unless they were unlucky and someone inside happened to be looking directly towards the approach road, then their arrival may have passed unnoticed.

Duncan glanced at Alistair, and he silently nodded to indicate he was ready. Easing the door open, Duncan listened carefully. There were no sounds coming from inside and he didn't see any sign of movement. Pushing the door wide, he entered, handing the responsibility of gently closing the door behind them to Alistair. He closed the door and they both stood in the lobby, listening. Still, they heard nothing. Walking slowly forward, Duncan gestured with his forefinger to the right and Alistair peeled away from him and into the kitchen.

The light that Duncan could see was coming from the sitting room he'd been in on their previous visit, and he reached the doorway, paying attention to the shadows emanating from within the room. If anything broke them, crossing through the light casting the shadow, then he would know someone else was present. Holding his breath, he waited. Nothing. Alistair appeared to his right, having looped around the hallway and come out of the second door to the kitchen, taking up a position slightly behind Duncan on the other side of the narrow corridor.

Duncan chanced a quick glance into the room. There was nothing there. He relaxed a little, drawing breath and then entered the room. Everything was in place. Flora must have simply left the lights on after all. On the other side of the sitting room was another doorway leading into the corridor that linked the old house to the newer section where Bruce Dunmore's study was located. Alistair swiftly crossed the room to check the link corridor while Duncan, confident that they'd been overly cautious, considered calling Flora inside to find the key to the study.

"All clear?"

Alistair's voice carried. "More or less!" he called back. "I don't think we'll need Flora's help, though."

Duncan was intrigued, following Alistair's route, he entered the corridor and found his DS standing outside the study door. The door had been securely locked when they were last here, and the lock was still in place, only now the door was ajar, the latch-plate no longer in the door frame. Instead, where it should be there was a gaping hole where it had been forcibly separated from the frame. The wood was split, warped and twisted at an odd angle, the timber splintered. A cursory inspection revealed black marks and indentations around the housing where the locking bolt met the frame and these marks were mirrored on the door's edge. This hadn't been executed with precision. Duncan guessed a wrecking bar had been used or something similar, almost gouging the lock out of the housing.

"Who needs a key?" Alistair said drily.

Duncan sighed heavily. Alistair eased the door open and slowly entered the study. Expecting the study to be ransacked, Duncan was surprised to find everything in relatively good order. The study was large, perhaps originally a downstairs bedroom or snug, and easily big enough. A set of French doors opened out onto the front of the property, making the most of the view, and Duncan found these were still locked and no key was present.

A partner's desk took up much of one end of the room. It was crafted from what looked like polished walnut, with a green leather inlay covering almost a third of the surface. He noted cables protruding from a cut-out on one corner, but they were not connected to a laptop or similar. However, there was a keyboard, mouse and a monitor. He went over to the desk, watching his footing just in case there were footprints or anything on the floor that might be damaged. He need not have worried because the study appeared well presented. If not for the damaged door, then nothing would seem out of place.

Duncan didn't find a tower unit for a computer and figured Dunmore must have worked off a laptop, but it was missing.

"Did they find a laptop in Flora's car?" Duncan asked.

"Not that I'm aware of," Alistair said, "but I've only had a few texts from the team. You think he would have taken it with him to see whoever it was he was meeting up there?"

"I wouldn't," Duncan said absently. "But that's just me."

A drawer pedestal was under the desk and Duncan found all but one of the drawers was locked. The top drawer had suffered the same fate as the door to the study and had been forced, the contents seemingly riffled through but not emptied out. Presumably, the person responsible knew what they were looking for. Whether or not they found it was another question. A more standard burglary, carried out by someone on an opportunistic hunt for valuables would never concern themselves with taking such care. These drawers would have been wrenched out, their contents emptied onto the floor. Speed was everything, in and out in five minutes or less because every second spent in the property was another second where they risked discovery and capture.

Alistair pointed beyond Duncan and he turned, seeing a cabinet door behind him was ajar. There were three cabinets at floor level with open shelving above where Dunmore had various photographs, books and other items displayed. Duncan extended his sleeve over his hands so as not to contaminate any potential trace evidence and slowly pushed the door open. Inside, he found a safe. It was almost two feet tall and a little over a foot wide. There was no combination lock but two keyholes, both of which had a key in them. The door to the safe was ajar and Duncan dropped to his haunches and took a deep breath before he opened it further.

By this time Alistair had joined Duncan, taking up a position behind him to his right. The safe was made of cast iron, welded at the joints and Duncan would wager it had a decent amount of fire-resistance to it. Moreover, it would take a significant amount of time to breach the casing by way of an oxy-acetylene torch. Other than that, dynamite could be effective provided you didn't care about the integrity of whatever was inside. The safe's interior was split almost fifty-fifty between the base level with a single shelf above, both lined with dark green velvet. It was empty. Duncan sighed heavily, pinching the bridge of his nose between thumb and forefinger.

"What would I give to know what Bruce Dunmore kept in here?" Alistair said quietly.

"Whatever it was," Duncan said, "it looks like someone was so keen to get a hold of it that it may have cost Dunmore his life." Duncan rose from his haunches, casting a critical eye around the study once more. Other than the forced door and the drawer under the desk, nothing appeared out of place. It was all very odd.

Duncan found Alistair inspecting a shelving unit in one corner. There were picture frames, books and several trophies that must have been awarded to the author over the years. Seeing nothing to pique his own interest, Duncan came alongside him, his eye drawn to the photographs. The better-quality images were more recent, the colours were far more vibrant and the detail was clearer. There were others though, grainy shots that Duncan guessed were in some cases decades old. There were black and white photos as well, and Duncan recognised parts of the island in some. His attention was drawn to one image in particular, and he stared at it.

"Duncan?"

He looked away from the photograph, glancing sideways at Alistair who was giving him a strange look. He appeared to be awaiting a response. "Sorry… I was miles away there for a second. What did you say?"

"I said you look like you've seen a ghost."

Duncan didn't reply, instead he turned back to look at the photograph again. It was old, grainy and taken in the late sixties or early seventies, Duncan was sure of that. A younger Bruce Dunmore, identifiable by his slender facial features, pronounced nose and recessed chin, standing in front of a building that Duncan didn't recognise. The building looked like it would be in keeping with those found on Skye, dark stone blocks with a honed-slate roof. An engraving was visible on a plaque mounted on the wall to Dunmore's left and, squinting due to the size of the lettering, Duncan read it as St Benedict's Boys' Home. Dunmore was standing behind one teenager, his hands resting on the smiling boy's shoulders, with others to either side along with other men who Duncan guessed were staff members. Some of the staff didn't look altogether much older than the children they were looking after. He didn't recall such a home on the island, though, but this picture was taken years before he was born.

"St Benedict's," Duncan said quietly.

"What was that?" Alistair asked.

Duncan shrugged. "I've never heard of it."

"Then why are you staring at it?" Alistair asked. Duncan still had his mobile phone in his hand and he raised it, zooming in and taking his own photograph of this particular image but ignoring the others.

"Have forensics come out here as soon as possible," Duncan said absently, his mind elsewhere.

"Of course," Alistair said, reaching into his pocket for his own mobile. "Are you okay?"

"Aye, fine," Duncan said, turning away and slowly walking out of the study. "I'll just have a quick word with Flora."

"Fair enough," Alistair said as Duncan walked away from him, but he felt his eyes on his back as he left the study. "Anytime you feel like sharing, you just let me know," Alistair said under his breath.

CHAPTER TWELVE

When Flora saw Duncan emerge from the house, she got out of the car. She looked nervous, wringing her hands before her as he approached. She didn't seem bothered by the falling rain although it had eased since they'd left her in the car.

"Is everything okay?" she asked. "Only, you've been gone some time."

"It turns out we won't need you to unlock the study after all," Duncan said, but he didn't offer a reason as to why. "When did you leave here, yesterday?"

She thought for a moment. "Shortly after you left," she said. "Early afternoon. Why?"

Duncan glanced back at the house. "Who else has access?"

"The gardener," she said. "Phillip. He does a lot of the gardens around this part of the island. Nothing major, just keeps on top of the lawn."

"Does he have keys as well?"

"Only to the outside store."

"Not the main house?"

"No," Flora said, shaking her head. "He has no need. I'm

the only one who has a key." Duncan pondered that. The main house was secure when they arrived. Whoever broke into the study didn't have to do the same to get into the main house.

"Did you lock up when you left?" Duncan asked her and she nodded. "Are you sure? Yesterday was a bit of a shock for you. Maybe you forgot?"

"No, I would never. I made extra sure when I left yesterday that the house was all locked up. The last thing Mr Dunmore needs is for me to let him down now." Her forehead creased and she looked disconsolate. "I suppose, it doesn't really matter now, does it?"

"Who would have access to your set of keys other than you?"

"No one. I mean, I guess my husband but… as I said before, he doesn't really come out here unless it's to pick me up or drop me off, but I use my own car most of the time."

"Yesterday?"

"He picked me up," she said, nodding then lowering her head. "I… don't have my car at the moment."

"Did he come inside?"

"No, he waited in the car, and I'd called him to let him know I was ready."

"He was alone?"

"Yes, why do you ask?"

"Just routine, Flora, don't worry." She appeared to accept his explanation. "Did Mr Dunmore ever mention St Benedict's to you?"

"The boys' home?"

"Yes. Was it here on the island?"

"It was," she said. "A long time ago. That's where my father knew Mr Dunmore from. They both worked there."

"I've never heard of it," Duncan said.

"Oh… it closed a long time ago," Flora said, thinking hard. "I think it was closed in the eighties, maybe earlier. I'm not sure."

"And your father worked with Bruce?"

"Yes… well, he volunteered," she said. "My father, I mean."

"And Bruce?"

"He worked there," she said. "If my memory serves, he was one of the managers or supervisors looking after the boys."

"What sort of home was it?"

"I'm afraid I don't know," Flora said. "It's not something my father ever talked to me about but my mother mentioned it. It is why Mr Dunmore did so much to help her after my father passed away. He was a very kind and community-spirited man, Mr Dunmore."

"Okay, thank you," Duncan said. "If you want to wait back in the car then I'll arrange for someone to run you home as soon as possible or you can call your husband and have him collect you."

"You… don't need to get into Mr Dunmore's study?"

"We have it in hand," Duncan said. Flora was confused but she did as Duncan said and got back into the car. Alistair came to meet Duncan at the front door.

"Forensics will be here within the hour. I've arranged for some uniform to come and keep an eye on the place until they can get here. We can drop Flora back at hers… then back to the station?"

"Aye, there's something I have to do first."

"Anything I can help with?" Alistair asked.

"No, just an… errand I forgot to run."

"Oh, did yer, aye."

Duncan nodded, ignoring Alistair's watchful expression and, taking out his mobile phone, he wandered away from him selecting Roslyn's number.

"Hello, Duncan," she said. "I wasn't expecting to hear from you so soon."

"You said to call."

"Aye, that's true but since when do you ever do what I ask you to?"

He laughed. "Right enough. Are you still with Mum—"

"No, I'm back at the croft. Why?"

"How was she when you left?"

Roslyn's voice became distant. "She was calm but not much different to when you left, to be fair. Why?"

"I was just wondering. I'm going to call in on her, have a chat."

"Okay. Is everything all right?"

"Aye. Why do you ask?"

"It's just… you sound distracted, that's all."

Duncan rubbed the side of his face. He felt a headache coming on. He was pacing around the side of the house and when he looked back, he could see Alistair was watching him. He heard a car approaching along the access track and saw a police car come into view. "I have to go," he said.

"Duncan, are you sure everything is okay?"

"Yeah, yeah, don't worry," he said, hanging up.

ALISTAIR FOUND a parking space in front of the police station in Somerled Square. Duncan got out, closed the door and looked across at Alistair as he got out of the other side.

"I'll be back in an hour or so." Alistair nodded but didn't

say anything. After they'd dropped Flora back at her home, conversation had been limited on the drive back to Portree. Duncan was lost in thought, and he suspected Alistair realised something was on his mind but didn't press him on what it was.

Alistair disappeared into the station lobby and Duncan drew his coat about him, grateful for the break in the rain, and made his way across the square for the short walk to his mum's residential care home. Although he'd been more involved in his mum's life since he returned to the island, helping to take some of the weight off his sister's shoulders, he was suddenly struck by how little he knew about his family's past.

The last few months had seen a significant decline in their mum's health. Her dementia was getting worse, her outbursts becoming more frequent and her lucid moments sparse. To learn of her more recent health complications being a suspected cancer only made Duncan more fearful that the time he had with his mum was growing ever more precious. The opportunity to complete the gaps in his knowledge of where he came from, not the place, for he knew that but he was conscious that the man he became was a result of his life experience. To understand himself, he needed to understand the people who raised him.

This was even more pertinent today, more so than he ever realised previously.

Duncan had to increase his pace because it started raining again before he reached the residential home on the outskirts of Portree. He was grateful to be inside, shaking off his coat in the lobby, and he caught the eye of someone sitting in one of the chairs beside the front door. She was flicking through screens on her mobile when her gaze drifted up to Duncan.

She smiled and he recognised her. Katie Matheson. He returned her smile and she hurriedly got up and came across to greet him.

"DI McAdam," she said. "Lovely to see you again."

"Hello, Katie. How are you keeping?"

"Very well," she said, glancing past him towards the reception desk. No one was present. "I don't suppose you're here to see Lord Huxley, are you?"

"No," Duncan said. "Why would I be?"

"Oh, I just wondered seeing as you're here. I put two and two together—"

"And came up with seven," Duncan said, drawing a smile from the young journalist. "Is that why you're here?"

"It's a story," she said, shrugging.

"Slow news week?"

"And… yes, it's a slow news week," she said, "and someone else got assigned the big story of the year. How's that investigation going by the way?"

"Which one?" Duncan asked innocently. She smiled. They both knew she was referring to Bruce Dunmore's death. The whole island would be talking about it by now. Word travels like wildfire on Skye irrespective of any official announcement.

"Don't worry, I'm not on that story anyway," she said accompanied by a sigh. "More's the pity. That's not why I'm here."

"Is an old man being admitted to a care facility particularly newsworthy?"

"It is," she said, "when he used to be a prominent shadow cabinet minister and the right-hand man to a future prime minister."

"I guess so," Duncan said, finding it difficult to believe that anyone would be interested in reading an article about a man who'd dropped out of public office a decade ago. He had been elevated to the House of Lords in recent years but, as Duncan understood it, it was an honours appointment for previous service rather than because he was an active participant in the political sphere these days.

"Although, I must admit I never thought this was the sort of thing I'd be running around after when I first got into journalism."

"What did you expect to investigate on Skye?" Duncan asked, mildly amused.

"I don't know," she said. "I thought it would be a stepping stone to bigger things, you know? I got into this to be an investigative journalist, to get to the truth of things and not… documenting bake-off fetes and which celebrity has visited the island." She wrinkled her nose. "Naive, aren't I?"

Duncan smiled. "No, not necessarily. And it's a good thing to seek the truth." He shrugged. "It's what I do for a living every day."

"Ah… they'll probably shelve whatever I write until the excitement around Bruce Dunmore's death subsides anyway." Duncan arched his eyebrows at her matter-of-fact tone. She exhibited the appropriate expression of contrition when she caught his eye. "I didn't mean that the way it sounded. Sorry. What brings you here then?"

"I'm just visiting a family member," Duncan said, checking his watch. "Speaking of whom, please excuse me?"

"It was good to see you," she said and Duncan wondered if she actually meant it. He'd come across a number of journalists over the years and many were shallow individuals simply looking for a story. They were more often than not tabloid journalists and, to be fair to them, it was their job to seek out stories and the more salacious the better when it came to the red-top newspapers. On the island, Katie seemed to be in it more for the passion of journalism rather than to make a name for herself. Perhaps that was the difference between regional news and the nationals.

Duncan found the nurses' station unoccupied when he entered the wing of the home where his mum stayed. There appeared to be a number of people at the far end of the corridor coming and going from the room that he'd seen Lord Huxley wheeled into when he was last here. Arriving at his mum's room, he gently knocked and entered. She was sitting in front of the window again, and she didn't look over towards him when he entered.

"Hello, Mum," he said cheerfully. She maintained her gaze out of the window, looking over the gardens. He went to her, kissing her forehead before pulling another chair alongside hers and sitting down with her. He took her right hand and held it between his own palms. "Mum?" he asked, squeezing her hand gently. Her eyes drifted over to his and he thought there was a flash of recognition. "It's Duncan."

A trace of a smile crossed her lips, and he smiled at her. "You're a handsome young man," she said. The smile faded, replaced with a look of concern. "You're tired."

"Constantly, these days," he said, his smile broadening. He hadn't interacted with her like this for days if not a week or so.

"You need to sleep more."

"I'll try, Mum. Honest, I will," he said, lifting his hand away from hers and reaching for his mobile phone. He unlocked the screen by looking at it and, having already opened the photograph he took, he turned it towards her. "Mum, I found an old picture of Dad." Her eyes narrowed as she studied the picture. She smiled but it was fleeting and dissipated as quickly as it arrived. "Have you seen this?"

"Duncan… he was handsome too," she said quietly, staring at the image. "Not as handsome as you are, though."

Duncan had to stay focused, aware that she could slip away from him at any moment. "Did he ever speak to you about his time at St Benedict's?" She turned her gaze away from the image, staring back out of the window. "Mum, St Benedict's. Do you remember anything about it."

His mum began to hum a nameless tune, but Duncan persisted, feeling mounting frustration which he heard in his own tone, getting up from his chair and bringing the screen back before her, almost forcing her to look at it.

"Mum, did Dad ever mention the boys' home?" She didn't respond, and it was like she was able to stare straight through the image as if it was invisible to her. "Mum?"

"She's gone, Duncan."

He turned to see Roslyn standing at the door, arms folded across her chest, a stern look on her face.

"I was just—"

"Just *what* were you doing, Duncan?" she asked. "Besides pressuring your own mother." Duncan rose, drawing a deep breath as he looked down on his mum, still humming her tune and looking out of the window. Roslyn came further into the room.

"What are you doing back here today anyway?" he asked.

"After you called… I wanted to know what you were up to. I didn't know you were planning to give her a hard time."

"I was hardly giving her a hard time."

"Really? Because that's what it looked like to me—"

"You don't understand," Duncan said, shaking his head.

"No, I don't. What's with all the questions about Dad all of a sudden?"

Duncan winced. He didn't know what to make of it all, and

how could he articulate his thoughts to Ros when he didn't understand them himself.

"St Benedict's," Duncan said, passing his mobile to her. She looked at the screen. "St Benedict's Boys' Home," he said. Roslyn took a deep breath.

"Aye, Dad was there for a while."

"Why was—"

"An evil place," their mum said suddenly. Both of them looked at her, but she was still staring out of the window. "A place for lost souls," she all but whispered. Duncan crossed the room, retaking the seat beside her. If she noticed, then his mum didn't show it.

"St Benedict's?" he asked her. "The boys' home was evil, is that what you're saying?"

"Such pain," she said, her eyes glazing over.

"What pain, Mum? What happened there?"

Roslyn came over and she lowered herself, placing a supportive hand on one of her mum's. "Mum? Is it about Dad?"

"Mum?" Duncan asked, squeezing her forearm. "Mum, what is it about the home that was painful? Did something happen there… to Dad?" She began to hum again. Duncan felt a flash of irritation. "Mum!"

"Duncan!" Ros snapped, reprimanding him. "Can you just leave it?"

"I need to know, Ros—"

"Why? Why do you need to know now, after all these years," she said, chiding him and checking over their mum who looked agitated by Duncan's tone. He shook his head. "Honestly, Duncan. I don't know what gets into you at times, I really don't."

Duncan stood up and paced the room. Roslyn fussed

around their mother, placing a blanket across her lap and ensuring it covered her legs.

"I'm sorry," Duncan said. Ros stood up, stepped away from their mum, who had quickly settled, and crossed to him, handing his mobile phone back. He glanced at the photo he'd taken. "Did she ever mention it to you?"

"About Dad staying at St Benedict's?" He nodded and she shook her head. "No, not really. I knew he had a spell away from the croft at one time when he was in his teens, I think it was." She looked at the photo. "That's probably it, wouldn't you say? He looks… what, thirteen there?"

Duncan was studying the photo. "Aye, probably. Why would he be at a boys' home though?"

Roslyn shrugged. "It was hard times working the land. Raising a family then would have been tougher than it is now. Granddad… he was a tough old sod, wasn't he?"

"An abusive old sod, you mean," Duncan said. Roslyn didn't object to his description. "Like father like son, eh?"

"You'd better hope not," Ros said. "Besides, it may not be as bad as you think."

"How do you mean?"

"Well, the school children who lived further afield on the island used to stay at the school boarding house, didn't they? There were no buses back then ferrying people around the island. I remember there being talk of the boys' home and it wasn't just for orphans or troubled kids, but for those whose parents struggled. Dad… could have just been there to make life on the croft easier if things were a bit rough. He was only away for eighteen months or so as I recall. When he came back to the croft he finished school and took over the croft. He would have been fifteen then."

"Aye, when Grandad died. Maybe you're right," Duncan

said. "I remember there was a boys' home attached to the boarding house when we were at school. Archie stayed there for a time. That was a similar situation in his family."

"Well, there you go," she said. "Maybe this… what did you say it was called?"

"St Benedict's."

"Aye, that was probably the forerunner to that one. How is Archie anyway?"

Duncan felt a guilty pang in his stomach. He hadn't checked in on his friend for a while. "Oh, he's fine, you know."

Roslyn rolled her eyes. "So, you haven't been to see your old pal recently then?"

"I've been a bit snowed under of late—"

"Loved up with young Grace, I should imagine."

Duncan felt his cheeks reddening. "Aye, she's grand so she is, you know how it is."

Roslyn smiled. "Try not to mess this one up, Duncan. She's good for you. Will you give Archie a phone? And make sure you give him my best too, while you're at it."

"I will." Duncan glanced at the clock. "I need to get back."

"Oh before you go, what's all this about Bruce Dunmore being found dead up Staffin way. Is that true?"

"Aye, it is."

"That's a shame. I loved his books."

"You've read them?"

"Hasn't everyone?"

"Aye, of course," Duncan said, arching his eyebrows fleetingly. Roslyn smiled, knowing he hadn't read them at all. He gave her a quick hug and headed for the door. Pausing as he opened it, he looked back at her. "What do you think Mum meant about it being an evil place and a place of pain?"

Roslyn was thoughtful. "I don't know. Dad struggled at

school, didn't he? You remember that he was brought up only speaking Gaelic in the house and the school insisted on speaking nothing but English when he was there. Grandad used to thrash him when he spoke English, and the school did the same if he dared to speak Gaelic… it's no wonder he was a mess by the time he hit his teens!"

Duncan smiled ruefully. "Aye, must have been tough for him."

Roslyn inclined her head in his direction, sarcastically replying, "You sound almost sympathetic."

Duncan wrinkled his nose, holding his thumb and forefinger in the air in front of his face, pinching them together to the point where they nearly touched, as he backed out of the room.

CHAPTER THIRTEEN

"DUNCAN, ALISTAIR!" Dr Dunbar said as the two detectives entered his office. "You're keen. I only spoke with you, Alistair, half an hour ago."

"We're not paid by the hour, Craig," Alistair said with a smile. "You know that."

Duncan returned to the station just as Alistair was getting off a phone call. Craig Dunbar had completed his post-mortem, and they immediately set off to see him at the morgue. Alistair hadn't asked where Duncan had been or what was troubling him but Duncan felt his detective sergeant's watchful eye upon him several times during the short drive across Portree.

"I have to hand it to you two gentlemen," Dr Dunbar said. "You are really justifying the expenditure on my position these days."

"We're happy to be of service," Alistair said. "Although we can hardly take all of the credit. After all, we don't supply the bodies directly, being simply the middlemen, so to speak."

"Indeed but historically, all of this work had to be done at

Raigmore up in Inverness. They were talking about centralising services again…" Dunbar sighed theatrically, "and as much as I love Inverness – which I do –I'd much rather stay hereabouts."

"We'll see if we can keep the supply going for you then," Alistair said drily. Dunbar didn't notice or went along with the artificial sentiment. "Thank you kindly, DS MacEachran."

"What can you tell us about Bruce Dunmore's demise?" Duncan asked.

Dr Dunbar cleared his throat, picking up the folder from atop the pile in a tray on his desk. He opened it, putting on his reading glasses.

"An interesting set of results, I must say," Dunbar said, reading over his summary. "He was in his eightieth year and, aside from being deceased, was in good health."

"Good health?" Duncan repeated. Dunbar nodded, still scanning his notes.

"Aye, he was. For his age, obviously. I would say he was ageing fairly well. His primary organs, heart, lungs, liver, – the ones we always suspect will be in terrible shape in a man of this generation –were all in better condition than I would normally find in a man approaching his eightieth birthday."

"We understood him to have been ill in the past year," Duncan said.

"Really?" Dunbar asked, his brow furrowing.

"So we were told, aye."

"I dare say I hope I'm in as fine fettle as he was when I'm his age," Dunbar said, peering over the rims of his glasses at Duncan. "Preferably with my heart still beating, it goes without saying." He pursed his lips, checking in case he missed something. Shaking his head, he sat back. "No, he was a healthy individual. I'm afraid you have received some erroneous information there, Duncan."

"Can you confirm the cause of death?"

"Aye, that's simple enough. Blood loss, as a result of the nasty cuts to his wrists. He would have bled out within minutes after suffering those."

"Can we rule out suicide?"

"I can't, no," Dunbar said. "However, my personal opinion is such that I doubt it."

"The binding of his wrists?" Duncan asked. The pathologist nodded.

"Plastic zip ties, as I said to you over the telephone, Duncan." Dr Dunbar produced an image from within the file, passing it across to him. Duncan studied it. The indentations along with the abrasion of the soft tissue were clear to see. "The plastic ties were eight millimetres in width, two thick, and tied tightly enough to cut the skin in several places and to cause those abrasions in the tissue. He may have tried to work himself free and that caused the edges, although smooth, to cut into the skin. My best guess, though is that wasn't what happened."

"What did happen?"

"I think he was transported to An Corran, and it was during this period that he was jostled and bounced around and it was that, along with a bit of a struggle, perhaps, that caused the injuries. I found some microscopic fibres, manmade, lodged in his hair. I've sent them away to the lab in Glasgow to determine exactly what they are but I suspect carpet fibres from a car's footwell or a boot lining."

"We could match those fibres to a vehicle," Alistair said.

"If you can find a suspect vehicle then that should prove easy enough, yes," Dunbar said.

"Was he killed on the beach?" Duncan asked, frowning.

"There was certainly sand in the wounds of his wrists," Dunbar confirmed. "However, that could have been after his body was placed there, carried across the open wounds by the seawater. I took the liberty of checking the tidal flows for that night and the following morning. I would put him in position no earlier than four in the morning. Otherwise, I would expect to see more signs of nature's finest Scottish tidal system leaving her mark upon him. Not least, I would have seen his body hauled out to sea on the receding water. We likely would never have found him."

"You said *placed*," Duncan queried.

"I believe he was, yes."

"Placed and not dumped?" Duncan clarified.

"There is no indication that he was dropped from the road above," Dunbar said, mimicking a falling body with a raised hand, driving it down onto his desk with a slap. "Even landing on wet sand I would expect to see some damage as a result of such a fall. After all, he had either been dead for a short time or was still alive – albeit barely –when he found himself on the beach." Dr Dunbar shook his head. "No, no, he was carried or dragged – I doubt walked judging by the blood loss – to where he was discovered around dawn on Monday morning."

Duncan pursed his lips, thinking hard. He was still considering the same question he'd asked himself on the morning of visiting the scene, *why there* on the beach at Staffin?

"You're wondering why, aren't you?" Dunbar asked.

"Am I that readable?" Duncan replied. "There are countless other places where you could choose to dispose of a body. Many of them where a body might not be discovered for days or weeks—"

"Or years," Alistair said. "If ever."

"Let's say, just for the sake of the conversation," Duncan said, "that Bruce Dunmore was murdered in Staffin and that's why they left his body there, because it was convenient to do so… why on the beach? There's one road in and out. Driving along it, even in the early hours, you're running a grave risk of being seen by someone. People are up and about at all hours and if you're the only vehicle moving then there's a chance, however small, that you'll be seen."

"Aye," Alistair said, frowning. "Why take the risk when there are far easier, and remote, places to do it?"

"That's what I'm struggling with too," Duncan said.

"Maybe your killer has an eye for the dramatic?" Dr Dunbar said. "It's a beautiful spot, a tourist location. Maybe they are looking to make a name for themselves. He is a big name. That's some scalp they've taken here." He coughed nervously. "Forgive the theatrical analogy. I'm just… er… getting into the mind of the flamboyant murderer."

"It is beautiful," Alistair said, "and one of thousands in these parts."

"Which brings us back to either Craig's suggestion – forgive me – but I really hope you're way off the mark here, or there's something about An Corran that marks it as a significant disposal site," Duncan said.

"I think it best if I don't step out of my lane, Duncan," Dr Dunbar said, picking up his report again. "However, I can tell you that the toxicology report came back showing a heavy dose of non benzodiazepine in his blood stream."

Duncan's eyebrows knitted. "What is that used for?"

"Treatment of acute sleeping disorders, insomnia and the like."

"Available over the counter or by prescription?" Duncan asked.

"They are controlled substances," Dr Dunbar said. "It would need to have been prescribed as they are incredibly addictive and often used only as a last resort if other medications or treatments don't work, and even then only for short periods of time in as small a dose as possible. The withdrawal effects can be rather nasty."

"Presumably they can knock a person out?" Duncan asked.

"That's the point, aye," Dunbar said. "There are only two currently licensed for issue in the UK."

"Was Bruce Dunmore under the treatment of his doctor?"

"Not that I can see on his medical file, no," Dr Dunbar said. "And in any event, the levels I discovered in his blood would be far in excess of what would be prescribed by a general practitioner." He frowned. "A competent one anyway."

Duncan pondered what this might mean. Either he was forced to take the drug, or ingested it unwittingly, or he may well have taken it deliberately but for what reason Duncan couldn't fathom. "Do they offer any side effects that might make someone take too many on purpose?"

"Only if you want to knock yourself out for a longer period," Dr Dunbar said. "There are no hallucinogenic side effects and they aren't *happy pills* for want of a better description. The side effects are significant, but we're talking about memory loss, sleep walking, potential for violent outbursts that are not premeditated—"

"Could he have harmed himself during such an outburst?" Alistair asked. Dr Dunbar cocked his head.

"I suppose that's not beyond the realms of possibility." He arched his eyebrows. "I wouldn't rule it out, but he wouldn't have bound his own wrists with zip ties as a result of a sleeping pill overload."

"Did you find anything else of note?" Duncan asked. Craig Dunbar studied his notes again.

"The glass in his hair – I believe you suspect that was from the window of a car he was sitting in – is that correct?"

"I think so, aye," Duncan said.

"It certainly matches that, but we'll need to wait for an official confirmation from the lab," Dunbar said. "He had some bruising and abrasions on his knees, elbows and on his upper body, consistent with being in a cramped space, wedged against hard surfaces…"

"From being wedged into the boot of the car maybe?" Duncan suggested.

"That would figure, yes," Dr Dunbar said. "There's no evidence of a beating or anything like that though. I found no trace evidence underneath his fingernails – they were cut very short – and there were no defensive wounds to hands, forearms or legs if he'd curled up in a ball to protect himself," Dunbar said, raising his hands and arms up around his head as a boxer might when under attack. He sat back in his chair and smacked his lips. "The short answer is, that this is the least violent murder I have ever come across."

Duncan found that last comment rather sobering. It spoke to a planned killing. When it came to murder, Duncan always hoped that it was not premeditated. As awful as a murder was, if it happened as a result of drugs or alcohol, losing one's temper or similar, that was far better than someone coldly planning to murder another human being.

"You've given us a lot to think about, Craig," Duncan said. "Thank you."

Neither Duncan or Alistair spoke until they'd left the morgue and were outside, bracing against the driving wind.

Duncan had to raise his voice to be heard as they walked to the car.

"I want you to have Angus look into An Corran," he said. "Have him sift through any reference to the beach we may have on file. Any mention of crimes, missing people, accident or injury… hell, even folklore stories if any come to mind." Alistair nodded. "There's a reason they left him there, and it might give us a steer as to who did this and why."

"What about the break-in at his study?"

"Let's hope whoever did that made a mistake and left us some fingerprints. Have a uniformed presence go door to door in Cuidrach, see if anything out of place has been noted these last couple of days."

"This is all a bit weird, isn't it?" Alistair said to him, and Duncan agreed. "Can I ask you something, sir?"

That question piqued Duncan's interest. Although he outranked him, Alistair hardly ever referred to Duncan with the reverence required by his rank. "Sure."

"What was it that spooked you about that photograph?"

Duncan took a breath. He could explain but he couldn't see it as relevant to the case.

"The picture of Dunmore outside that boys' home…"

"Aye, what about it?"

"It's…" Duncan looked away, staring at some far-off point in the distance. He shrugged. "Forget it. It's probably nothing."

Alistair offered him a searching look. "Really? Because it looked like something."

Duncan forced a smile. "You think too much."

"Fair enough," Alistair said. They'd reached the car now and Alistair unlocked it. They both got in and Alistair asked casually, as he connected his seatbelt, "Do you think we should look into that angle of his life, or the boys' home more generally? It was this time period where he had his roots on the island. If this is tied to his being on Skye, then it stands to reason that a motive could be rooted in his past."

Duncan blew out his cheeks. "It was a long time ago. He's been away from the island for years."

Alistair inclined his head with a half-smile. "Maybe some scores take that long before they have the opportunity to settle them."

Duncan sighed. "Aye. I suppose it wouldn't hurt to keep an open mind. We should look into it."

Alistair agreed with a curt nod and started the car. "I'll say one thing about those drugs in his system."

"Aye, what's that?" Duncan asked.

"They wouldn't half make him more malleable, don't you think?"

Duncan nodded solemnly.

CHAPTER FOURTEEN

DARKNESS HAD FALLEN over the Isle of Skye by the time Duncan pulled up outside the house. The worst of this storm front appeared to have passed through now and the rain had ceased falling. The thick cloud had been replaced by clear skies although the wind was still fierce and took Duncan's breath away as it struck him face on when he got out of the car. Looking across the loch he saw the twinkling lights of the houses in Treaslane, plumes of smoke rising from their chimneys as the occupants settled in for the evening.

A dog barked excitedly from behind him and Duncan turned in time to see the approach of Archie's dog. It bounded up to him, Duncan stooping to pet it.

"Hello, gorgeous!" Duncan said, making a fuss of the creature who leaned into him, resting his head against Duncan's leg.

"That animal would be a rubbish guard dog," Archie said, stepping out from a shed at the rear of the croft house. Duncan smiled, still ruffling the fur around the creature's neck.

"You wouldn't be without him."

"No, that's true," Archie said, coming closer and moving into the light emanating from his house. He had an armful of sticks. "You coming inside? I need to get the stove going. I'm hungry."

Duncan followed his friend into the house, the dog trotting along beside him, and he closed the door once they were inside. With a grunt, Archie knelt and dropped the bundle in his arms on the floor beside the stove. It was an old cast-iron, double oven stove in Archie's kitchen. Most people these days had switched to electric or used bottled gas, but Archie remained steadfastly old school with the way he lived. Several of the internal walls of the house weren't even plastered; bare stonework visible.

Archie was adding the sticks to the stove, and he had larger logs ready to put in once the fire took hold.

"Have you thought about upgrading," Duncan said, "and going a bit more modern?" Archie looked up at him, peering through his shock of ginger hair hanging down across his eyes, the whiskers of his beard moving as he pursed his lips. "Nothing too excessive. Maybe just catch up to the last century."

"Modernity," Archie muttered. "People crave it, see it as the answer to all their ills when all it does is add more needless rubbish to your life. It makes it harder, not easier."

"Aye, on your knees getting a fire going so you can heat yourself some mince and tatties is great fun."

Archie pushed the door to, almost closing it but creating a through draught to pull oxygen into the fire. He peered through the crack of the door, keeping a watchful eye on the growing flames. "So… what do I owe for the visit?" Archie cast a wary eye up at Duncan.

"Do I need a reason to visit my best friend on the island?"

Archie snorted a laugh. "No, of course you don't." His gaze narrowed. "Someone hasn't been on the phone to you, have they? Having a moan."

"Who would do that?" Duncan asked. "Do you have a guilty conscience about something." Archie grinned, looking back at the flames, opening the door and adding a larger log to the growing fire. He closed the door and brushed his hands before standing up.

"No, I've been keeping my head down of late."

Now it was Duncan who scoffed. "So you haven't been hanging around your favourite haunts along the banks of the Varrrigal or Skeabost rivers of late, trying to catch your supper?"

"No, I have not," Archie said indignantly. "Not recently anyway." He moved to the sink and filled a kettle with water, pausing as he switched off the water and glancing nervously at Duncan. "Has someone been talking?"

"Not that I've heard," Duncan said.

"Good." Archie cleared his throat, putting the kettle down and switching it on. "Not that there's anything to know anyway," he said through the side of his mouth.

"How have you been keeping?" Duncan asked, looking around. The kitchen was a mess and looking through into the living room, Duncan saw a similar scene in there, lit up by the flickering light from an open fire. It was quite normal for Archie to live like this though. He was a hardy sort and, living alone as he did, he didn't care much for the niceties that most people, including Duncan, hankered for.

"I've been well," Archie said, taking two mugs out of a cupboard and holding them aloft. "Thank you for asking. Tea?"

Duncan nodded. "Please. How is the croft?"

"Ticking along nicely," Archie said, reaching to a nearby shelf for a box of teabags. He put the bags in the mug and turned to Duncan, folding his arms across his chest, his piercing blue eyes staring at him. "But you didn't come out here to discuss crofting practices, did you?"

"No, but it has been a while and—"

"You've been busy with wee Gracie, haven't you?"

"I have," Duncan said. "And things have just been busy. Sorry."

Archie sighed. The kettle clicked off and he lifted it, pouring the water into the mugs and shaking his head. "You could always have picked up the phone."

"Well, that would be quite a feat," Duncan said, with a wry smile, "because you don't have a phone." Archie ceased the pour, pursed his lips and then glanced sideways at Duncan.

"Fair point. I'll give you that," he said, continuing to make the tea. Once the tea was brewing, Archie smiled at him. "Okay, so you're forgiven."

"Very benevolent of you," Duncan said.

"I try, Dunc, I really do." Archie pointed to the fridge behind Duncan who fetched the milk, passing it to his friend. "So… what's so important that it brings you out here?"

"Do you recall a boys' home on the island from back in the day, St Benedict's—"

"Hah! Brutal Benedict's… aye," he said. "I do. My brother was there for a while."

"Was he? I didn't know that."

"Aye," Archie said, his forehead furrowing in thought. "Would have been 76… or 77, I'm not sure."

Archie's half-brother, Frankie - sharing the same mother - had been several years older than his sibling and he left Skye to join the army when he turned sixteen. Duncan never really knew him, only meeting him once or twice when he was a young boy and wouldn't be able to pick him out of a line-up. In any event, he'd been killed serving in the Middle East in the early nineties.

"It closed in the late seventies, didn't it?" Duncan asked.

"Um…" Archie thought hard. "82… I think, but I could be off. I can't remember if it was after the Falklands ended or after Charles married Di." He shook his head. "Around then anyway. Why do you ask?"

"I remembered you had a stint away from home—"

"Aye, but that was at the school boarding house, you know. That was different, completely unconnected."

"Ah, I see. Shame, I was hoping to pick your brains."

"I've got a decent enough memory and Frankie talked about it a bit. Although, what he had to say was pretty much rumours from back in the day rather than his own experience. I think the staffing line-ups had changed by the time he was there."

"You said it was called Brutal—"

"Brutal Benedict's, aye," Archie said. "It was run by some of those types who associated with the fanatical wee frees of the time, but ones who couldn't get work in the actual churches, you know, the proper mental ones?"

"Too devout even for the Free Churches of Scotland?" Duncan said. "That… must have taken some doing."

"Aye, well if you believe the stories anyway."

"What stories?"

"Corporal punishment was a thing back then," Archie said. "If you didn't follow the rules or maintain the standards then you could expect a hell of a thrashing." He rocked his head from side to side. "And bear in mind that the boys staying there were often the troubled souls, the ones whose parents had either washed their hands of them or couldn't cope with them… not easy kids, mind."

Duncan nodded. "Did Frankie experience any of this?"

"No, not that I'm aware of," Archie said. "If he did, he didn't say anything to me anyway. He talked about surviving it though, so it still couldn't have been a lot of fun but he also said he met his best pals while he stayed there." He shrugged. "It can't have been all bad, I suppose."

"What about the staff, any names get mentioned at all?"

Archie pressed his tongue into his cheek, eyeing Duncan warily. "What are you up to?"

"Up to?"

"Aye, what's all this about, asking questions about a children's home that closed forty-odd years ago?"

"Just looking into the background of a case I'm working, that's all."

Archie rolled his tongue along his bottom lip, his eyes fixed on Duncan. "The only case you could be spending time on is the body they found on An Corran, Monday morning."

Duncan cocked his head. "That's a possibility, aye."

Archie laughed. "Bruce Dunmore… was he connected to St Benedict's then?"

"It would appear so," Duncan said, but he was quick to add, "not that it has anything to do with his death as far as I know."

"Oh aye," Archie said, his face splitting a broad grin beneath the mass of red beard. "Pull the other leg, it's got bells on it."

"No, I'm serious," Duncan argued. "I'm just looking at all the angles—"

Archie held up a hand. "Don't worry, I'll no' say anything to anyone."

"Thanks, Archie. I'd hate to start an unfounded rumour."

"Ah forget it. No one would believe me anyway. I'm just the mad old crofter from Kensaleyre after all."

"That's harsh," Duncan said. "You're not old."

Archie chuckled, passing Duncan a freshly made mug of tea. It was uncomfortably hot to the touch and Duncan set it down on the dining table beside him. "How come Frankie ended up there anyway?"

"Ah, his old man found it all a bit too much once he'd parted ways with Frankie's step mum, you know? From what Frankie told me, she was quite a combustible character herself and she didn't like having a lad around who wasn't hers. His dad didn't take it too well when she packed up and left with someone else; the failure of a second marriage and all. He used to like a drink and would knock Frankie around a bit, taking his frustrations out on him..." Archie hesitated, wrinkling his nose and looking apologetically at Duncan. "You know what that's like."

"Aye," Duncan said, remembering his own childhood with a flash of similar images passing through his mind. He could relate to Frankie's experience.

"Anyway, Frankie was quite pleased to be away from that; but out of the frying pan and into the fire, so the saying goes."

"But you think it was different then, when he was staying there?"

Archie shrugged. "I think so, aye. I mean, still not great from what Frankie used to say but better than running the gauntlet at home."

"Was Bruce Dunmore's name ever mentioned?" Duncan asked.

"No, I can't say it was. Not that I can remember any names from that time. I'm not sure Frankie ever mentioned any names specifically. I was only a wee lad at the time and if he did, I don't remember." He fixed Duncan with a stern gaze. "Where's all this going? Do you think Dunmore was working at St Benedict's when all this nasty stuff went on or something?"

Duncan arched his eyebrows. "That's what I'm wondering but, to be honest, it's only speculation. We're just trying to figure out a reason why someone might want to kill him."

"So... old Bruce was murdered over at Staffin?"

"Keep that to yourself, Archie," Duncan said, lowering his voice conspiratorially. "That's not common knowledge yet."

Archie exhaled deeply. "Well, well, well... look what happens when life imitates art."

The irony was not lost on Duncan either.

CHAPTER FIFTEEN

DUNCAN FOUND the team were busy at work when he returned to the CID operations room in Portree. Alistair beckoned him over and Duncan joined him just as he patted Angus on the back, leaving the young detective constable to get on with his task.

"How did you get on?" he asked.

"Archie has a half-brother who spent time at St Benedict's, but other than some old storytelling about the staff being pretty old school with their discipline, he didn't really have much to say."

"Maybe his brother could help?" Alistair said.

"Afraid not," Duncan said, shaking his head. "He died years ago whilst serving abroad in the army."

"Shame."

"Aye," Duncan said, surveying the room. "Where are we at here?"

"Angus is picking through the history of the beach up at Staffin. He hasn't found anything of note yet, although he is having to filter out hundreds of references to dinosaur footprints."

Duncan smiled. "This will be a new reference for An Corran, and I'm sure it won't be popular with the tourism office."

"I don't know," Alistair said. "Have you seen the queues for the ghost walking tours of Edinburgh? Dark and macabre sells right enough."

"That doesn't make me feel good about human nature."

"I've got something else though," Alistair said, crossing to his desk. Duncan followed. "I ran a search in the national police computer for any references to the boys' home, but it drew a blank. Now, St Benedict's closed down years ago, as you know, and so any references to the place in our files was likely only to feature in the hard copy archives. It was too long ago to make the transfer to digital."

"Stands to reason, aye," Duncan said.

"So I went down there and just had a look through the old index cards."

"I presume you're going somewhere with this?" Duncan said, stifling a yawn. They'd covered a lot of ground today and he realised he was flagging, having missed both breakfast and lunch.

"There was a reference to St Benedict's in the index cards."

"Okay, you've got my attention," Duncan said. "Was there an incident?"

"I'd love to know," Alistair said, turning away and picking up a faded green folder from his desk. He handed it to Duncan who, failing to mask his confusion, accepted it and opened it in his hand. He glanced up at Alistair and then down at the folder in his hands. It was empty.

"What's this?"

"That is the folder for crime reference number IS/2354/11," Alistair said. "Are you impressed that I memorised it?"

"Very," Duncan said, lifting his eyes from the empty folder and up at Alistair. "I'll be even more impressed if you tell me why I'm looking at an empty folder."

"I'm guessing our colleagues of the day could not only memorise the crime reference number, but also the contents of the case file, because they didn't feel the need to write anything down."

"Aye, that is pretty clear," Duncan said, holding the folder higher to dramatise the point. "Where are the contents?"

Alistair inclined his head. "The folder is just as I found it in the archive."

Duncan heaved a sigh. "Do you know anything about it?"

"Only the name of the detective who created the file," Alistair said. "He was a detective constable at the time, Campbell McLaren."

"There's that name again," Duncan said. He gently bit his bottom lip. "Perhaps it's time we paid him a visit."

"A word of advice," Alistair said. Duncan nodded. "Tread carefully."

"I always do," Duncan countered. "Besides, you said you didn't know him."

"I don't but everyone who knows anything about him says he's pretty formidable."

"I've never known you to be afraid of anyone, Alistair."

"Only my wife," he said, quietly. "Only my wife."

CAMPBELL MCLAREN LIVED IN VATTEN, a small hamlet a few miles south east of Dunvegan, on the shore of a loch bearing the same name. The drive out from Portree took just shy of three quarters of an hour and when Duncan pulled up at the house, he cast an eye over it from the road, before driving through the gates and parking close to the front door.

The retired policeman was living in a converted barn. The property had only one neighbour, a croft house only a short walk away which was probably where the original owner of the barn had lived. The property had access directly onto the waters of Loch Vatten, and although Duncan couldn't see them now due to the darkness, he was certain there was a stunning view across towards MacLeod's Tables, the famous mountains that dominate the skyline of the Duirinish peninsula.

Duncan got out of his car and approached the door. A security light came on as he reached the porch and he noticed a camera mounted on the wall off to one side above him.

"Once a policeman, always a policeman," Duncan whispered to himself. He rang the doorbell, hearing an excited bark come from inside which got louder as the dog came to investigate. He didn't have to wait long before he heard a key turn in the lock and the door swung open. He was met by a heavy-set individual. His hair, once dark, was now a salt and pepper grey with a widow's peak. He was almost as tall as Duncan and appeared to stand with a slight hunch. This wasn't surprising as Duncan knew he was in his mid-eighties.

"Can I help you, young man?" he asked.

"DI Duncan McAdam," Duncan said, producing his warrant card. "Campbell McLaren?" he asked.

"The very same," McLaren said, barely looking at Duncan's identification. He did, however, study Duncan's face for a moment before stepping back and gesturing for Duncan to come inside. "Don't stand on ceremony, laddie. We're letting the heat out."

Duncan followed him inside, closing the door behind him. He bent low and held his hand out for a little West Highland terrier who was still making a fuss about Duncan's arrival, but the dog held back just out of Duncan's reach. The barking had ceased, unusual for a westie, and likely because his owner seemed happy enough with the guest. He cautiously came closer, sniffing around Duncan's legs.

"Hello, wee man," Duncan said holding out the back of his hand to the dog. It sniffed his hand, then allowed Duncan to pet him for a brief moment before he turned tail and ran off into the house.

"You'll have to ignore Jocko there," McLaren said. "He's a grumpy wee thing, but his heart is in the right place." He winced. "Much of the time, anyway. Come through." Campbell McLaren led them along a short hallway and into a sitting room, moving with a sprightly gait that belied his age. If Duncan didn't know better, he could easily imagine the retired policeman would pass for a man some two decades his junior. A stove was alight in one corner, the room feeling oppressively warm for Duncan's tastes, but his eye was drawn to a picture window alongside a large sliding door which opened out onto a stunning view. The clouds had parted and moonlight flooded Loch Vatten, glinting off the surface of the water which ebbed with the strong breeze. Duncan could see a boat at anchor just off the shoreline and a dark expanse of land was visible on the horizon. The mountains.

"A cracking spot you have here," Duncan said.

"Aye, it's not too bad at all," McLaren said, grimacing as he moved to Duncan's right and eased himself down into a chair. Duncan noticed, glancing at his left leg. "Arthritis," he said, rubbing at his knee joint. "Knees and ankles. Too many years spent running up and down the hills of this island." He sighed. "No one tells you that when you're a young man, that your joints wear out pretty quickly once you hit a certain age."

"And what age is that?" Duncan asked. "Just so I know what to expect."

McLaren laughed. "It's different for everyone, lad." The pain seemed to ease and he stretched his leg out, wiggling his foot. Satisfied he put his foot down and gestured for Duncan to take a seat. Duncan looked behind him and sat down on the corner of a sofa. There were several tartan blankets thrown over the leather and Jocko leapt up onto the other side away from Duncan and curled up. "Did you say McAdam?"

"Aye, Duncan McAdam."

"Big Dunc's wee lad, are you?"

Duncan nodded. "Aye. He was my father."

McLaren nodded solemnly, his lips pursed. "I'm surprised big Dunc's lad wound up in the service."

Duncan smiled, flicking his eyebrows momentarily. "None more so than me."

McLaren smiled as well. "It was a shame about your father."

"You knew him?"

"Didn't everyone?" McLaren replied. "Something of a tear-away your father." He held up his hand. "No more so than any of the other lads on the island." Duncan didn't feel like discussing the good and bad of his father, pretty sure the conversation would be largely focused on one more than the other. "So, DI McAdam… what brings you to my door at this time of the evening? It must be something important."

"Aye, sorry about the timing," Duncan said. "But it is what it is."

"Nae bother, lad," McLaren said. "It's nice for Jocko and

me to have a visitor. Things get a bit dull around here when the weather drives everyone indoors."

"Is it just you here then?" Duncan asked, spying several photographs around the room depicting Campbell with a woman, and others that looked like family snaps. There was one with Campbell and two women plus a young girl standing in front of them. They looked old photos, Campbell being much younger. The retired policeman noticed.

"That's my wife, Shona. Bless her," he said, looking glum. "We lost her five years ago now…" he thought hard, "no, six this coming October."

"I'm sorry," Duncan said. McLaren waved away the sentiment.

"It was a blessing by the end." He sat forward, resting his elbows on his knees. "Don't get sick when you're old, Duncan. It rarely ends well."

"Is that your daughter?" Duncan asked, indicating the picture with the young girl in it.

"No, that's my niece along with her mother, Shona's sister. I don't have any children of my own. Shona… well, children just weren't in His plan for us, I'm afraid."

Duncan nodded solemnly. "I'm sorry."

McLaren waved away the need for an apology and smiled warmly. "So, what can I do for you, DI McAdam?"

"I'm guessing you heard about the body we found—"

"Out Staffin way?" McLaren asked and Duncan nodded. "Aye, it's come up in conversation."

"And you know it was Bruce Dunmore?"

"I heard, aye."

"Well, I'm working up some background on his time on the island."

"I didn't even know he was back in these parts," McLaren

said, and that piqued Duncan's curiosity. The older man appeared to notice. "Until very recently, mind you." He frowned. "He got in touch with me a few weeks back." He was thoughtful, glancing up towards the ceiling. "It might have been a month ago actually… I'm not certain. All my days seem to merge into one now that I'm retired. Calendars mean very little."

"What did he get in touch with you for?"

"To catch up," McLaren said, sitting back again. "We hadn't seen one another for at least ten years, probably more. He said he'd come back to the island for good, losing interest in living in the big city. He was looking for a quieter life."

"Was he looking to retire?"

McLaren shrugged. "If he was, then that wasn't what he told me."

Duncan nodded. "When did you see him last?"

"A few weeks ago, like I said." His brow furrowed and he reached for a mobile phone on a small table beside his chair. Duncan spotted a glass of scotch next to it along with a set of reading glasses. McLaren put them on and began scrolling through his mobile. "I think… aye, here it is," he said, holding the phone aloft and flashing the screen towards Duncan. He was looking through old texts. "It was two weeks ago, the fourteenth. A Wednesday, I think it was."

"Where did you see him?"

"At his place," McLaren said. "I suggested meeting for lunch in Portree or he could come across to Dunvegan but he preferred to meet at his home."

"In Cuidrach?"

"Aye, he sold off the old family place years ago. Although he kept on the place at Cuidrach. I'd no idea at the time why he did, seeing as he hardly ever came back to the island."

"It has a way of doing that, the island, doesn't it?"

"There speaks the voice of experience," McLaren said with a dry smile. Duncan nodded. "I suppose you want to know what we talked about?"

"Aye, please," Duncan said. "You know the routine."

"When it's surrounding a suspicious death, I do, aye." Duncan was keen not to confirm anything, and so he said nothing under McLaren's watchful eye. He cleared his throat, shrugging ever so slightly. "He wanted to pick my brains, that's all."

"About what?"

"Police procedure, investigative techniques… that sort of thing."

"For what purpose?"

"He was writing a new thriller, and he wanted to set it around a police investigation."

"Surely, he already had contacts who could do that? It's not his first book."

"Aye, but he always wrote old spy thrillers set in the sixties and seventies." McLaren put his mobile down and picked up the crystal tumbler. He still had his reading glasses on, and he peered over the rim at Duncan. "I'm so sorry. How rude of me. Would you care for a wee dram?"

"No thank you," Duncan said. "I'm driving… and still working."

"Hah! How things have changed," McLaren said, sipping at his scotch. "Back in the day you'd be disciplined for not having a drink when offered."

Duncan guessed he was being hyperbolic but smiled graciously. "Times change."

"Aye, they do," McLaren agreed. "Sometimes for the

better," he said, tipping his glass towards Duncan in salute. "But not always."

"Agreed. What was it he wanted help with, for the book, I mean?"

"A relevant point we just had right here, Duncan," McLaren said. "Things change. Policing changes, a simple point of note that we now have a combined service, your employer, Police Scotland. Back in the sixties we were the Northern Constabulary, which was prior to the forming of the New Northern Constabulary in 1975 when we merged with Ross and Sutherland and the Inverness mob. Now it's all changed again… and not for the better. A poor decision in my book."

"Aye, you'll get no argument from me," Duncan said, "although it did make transferring home a bit easier."

"Every dog has his day!" McLaren said, draining his glass. He shifted to the front of his chair, wincing as he stood up, putting weight on his left leg. "Are you sure you'll no' have a dram? I'm on a single malt Talisker, just now."

"No, I'm fine thank you. So… he was after procedural detail from you?"

"Aye," McLaren said, glancing over his shoulder at Duncan as he reached the sideboard and took the stopper from a half-empty bottle, pouring himself a large measure. "He didn't want to be pulled up on getting the details wrong, names of the service, or force as it used to be, and how we used to go about things. Apparently, readers can get rather upset about that sort of thing."

"Was he basing the book on the island?" Duncan asked, unsure of whether this was something he needed to consider.

"I couldn't say," McLaren said, shuffling back to his chair

and sitting down. "Bruce kept the plot close to his chest, so to speak. I did ask, but he wasn't giving anything away."

Duncan nodded. "How did you get on with him?"

"Bruce? Pretty well, I'd say. We knew each other and had done for a very long time."

"Were you involved with him in his working life?"

"As a teacher?" McLaren asked.

"Or in his time running St Benedict's?" If the mention of the boys' home stirred any memory in Campbell McLaren's mind, he continued without hesitation.

"No, not specifically," he said. "Although," he arched his eyebrows in an exaggerated manner, "some of those boys were quite a handful and a number of the staff were young and inexperienced. Not much older than the boys in their charge, to be honest. On more than one occasion we had to visit the home, box a few ears." He swiftly held up a hand. "Metaphorically speaking."

"Was Dunmore a religious man?"

"Not particularly. Why do you ask?"

"St Benedict's had quite a reputation for being harsh when it came to distributing punishments."

"Ah… the piety of the church," McLaren said, and Duncan nodded. "I think Bruce was raised in that manner and he was certainly a wee free." He shrugged. "I'm not sure he carried that on when he left the island, mind you. The celebrity culture and a small, but not insignificant, fortune puts temptation in front of the best of us."

"Why did he leave the island?" Duncan asked. McLaren shot him a perplexed look. "I mean, I know he hit the big time with his writing, but you can write anywhere, can't you?"

"I suppose so, aye." He shook his head. "I've no idea. Seduced by the bright lights of the city… a desire for a more worldly life experience, perhaps? Writer sorts need that, don't they? Experience."

"It probably aids the creative process," Duncan said. "I was just wondering if he ever mentioned it to you."

"No, I can't say he did. But, although we knew one another, I'd never go so far as to say we were close."

"You got on well?"

"Aye."

"Did you ever fall out with him?" Duncan asked, thinking of Flora's description of hearing and seeing Campbell leaving the study on that one occasion. McLaren stared at Duncan with an unreadable expression. He wondered if he was going to answer the question.

"No, I wouldn't say that." He took a deep breath. "I recall a time when he wanted me to turn a blind eye to something I saw… but that was a long time ago."

"What was it?"

"I don't remember. One of his lads got himself into trouble and Bruce thought I could, and should, make an allowance for him. That was all."

"You disagreed?"

"Yes, I did."

"What was the outcome?"

McLaren thought hard. "I'm not sure I recall the details. I suspect he got a rap on the knuckles from the local sheriff and that was that."

"Do you remember the incident?"

He shook his head. "Sorry, I don't. Why do you ask?"

"I'm just wondering," Duncan said, paying close attention for any potential reaction, "whether it had anything to do with a case file we came across in the archives."

"What case?"

"That's just it," Duncan said. "When we got to the file it was empty."

"Empty?"

"Aye. All we have is the folder and a crime reference number. Nothing more."

McLaren cocked his head. "That's odd. What was it to do with Bruce?"

"St Benedict's," Duncan said. McLaren's eye narrowed and he concentrated, cupping his chin and striking a thoughtful pose.

"The only thing that comes to mind was when a couple of the lads – staying at the home – made a complaint against one of the staff."

"What was the nature of the complaint?"

"Two boys made some claims, allegations, about a member of staff." He shrugged. "I suppose you are here because I was down as creating the case file?"

"Aye, that's it."

"Well, again, things were different back then. It would have been…" he sucked air through his teeth, looking up at the ceiling, "around 1972, I think. There was only one CID officer assigned to the island, and I reported directly to the senior officer on Skye. That was a uniformed inspector, and that rank remained the highest on Skye right the way up until I retired."

"Times have changed," Duncan said. "You were the most senior officer on Skye?"

"I was, for a while, aye. I remember that particular time very clearly, because around then I was being made up to sergeant and in the process of handing over my caseload – not that it was much at the time, mind you – to my successor. I was going back into uniform for my promotion. The complaint was made and I created the case file, as was procedure, but it was someone else who carried out the actual investigation."

"And who was that?"

"Ooo… you're testing me now." McLaren thought on it for a few moments. "He was a young lad, handsome fellow, a detective constable who was coming across from the mainland. He was on the Kyle CID team, if my memory serves. McLintock, I think his name was, but he only lasted eighteen months and then he was off down to Glasgow. They were drawing a lot of ambitious people down there at that time following a wee crime wave that hit the city. The next generation of gangs were on the up in the late sixties, and they were considered worse than the legendary Razor gangs of the 1920s. It was all knife crime and turf wars… and it got very messy. You remember?"

Duncan laughed. "I wasn't even born then, but I read about it and had to study them for my exams."

"Exams!" McLaren chuckled. "They teach you detective work at school these days, don't they? In my day – and I swore whilst serving that I'd never use that phrase after I retired – we learned everything through experience."

"There's a place for both," Duncan countered. "Can you remember the outcome of the investigation?"

"St Benedict's? I think… but don't quote me… that the boys withdrew the allegations. They admitted to having made it all up."

"They were lying?"

"So it seemed, aye. No charges were brought anyway."

"And what were the details of the allegations, specifically?"

"Like I said, I didn't investigate it. I was over at Lochalsh for my training before coming back to the island to take up my new role. It was pretty much done by then."

"I don't suppose you remember the names of the accusers and the person they made the complaint about? Could it have been Bruce Dunmore?"

"No, it wasn't Bruce. I'm certain of that," he said, shaking his head. "Bruce was certainly working there at the time, but it wasn't him. As for the boys… I'm sorry, I didn't have much to do with them."

"Right," Duncan said, failing to mask his disappointment.

"I'm sorry lad. I wish I could help more." McLaren sipped at his scotch and seemed to be gauging Duncan for some reason. "Are you going to tell me what this is all about?"

Duncan smiled. "I would say it was just routine, but I don't want to insult you."

"I appreciate that, Duncan," McLaren said. "If you're digging into a man's past from fifty years ago, then it tells me something untoward has gone on over at Staffin."

"I couldn't possibly comment," Duncan said.

"I understand."

Duncan rose from his place on the sofa. Jocko lifted his head, but didn't follow suit, lying back down again and resting his head on his paws.

"Forgive me for not seeing you out," McLaren said. "My knee is playing up something chronic today. It's the damp, so I'm told."

"I'll see myself out," Duncan said.

"You look a lot like your father, you know?"

Duncan hesitated, and Campbell McLaren noticed a change in his expression. "I've been told that before."

"It was a shame what happened to him, your father, I mean."

"What happened?" Duncan asked, unsure of what he was referring to.

"Aye, the manner of his passing. That was very sad. I..." McLaren paused, glancing out through the picture window and staring at some point in the distance, "did what I could... to do right by your mother." He looked back at Duncan. "I hope it was the right thing to do."

Duncan held McLaren's gaze and nodded. "I'm sure she appreciated it."

"I do hope so," he said. "I stuck my neck out for her, but that's what we do on the island, isn't it? We take care of our own come what may."

"Aye, we do. Good night," Duncan said, making for the door into the hall.

"Safe drive home, Duncan," McLaren said. Something in his tone made Duncan prick up his ears, but he couldn't pinpoint what or why. He left without another word.

CHAPTER SIXTEEN

"GEORGE FRANCIS MCLINTOCK," Alistair said, lifting his cup to his lips as Duncan peered over his shoulder at the screen. Duncan was nursing his own cup of coffee in his hands. The fresh-faced individual depicted in the digital file open on Alistair's screen was in black and white, and the young man had wavy hair, cut close on the sides and parted from the left. "He was in the service from 1962," Alistair said, reading from the details below the picture. "A detective constable from 1967, and stayed in the polis until he retired having served his thirty years in 1992." Alistair went to sip from his cup and was both surprised and disappointed to find he'd finished it and set the empty cup down on the desk in front of him. It was pushing ten o'clock at night now, and the team were still working to establish the foundations of their investigation. The first forty-eight hours following any murder were deemed the most critical with regard to reaching a successful outcome.

"Where is he now?"

"Dead," Alistair said, sniffing. "He died in a car accident back in 2002."

"Damn," Duncan said. "There goes another lead."

"Ah, we're not done yet," Alistair said. He saw a reflection in his screen of Angus walking behind them. "Angus!" The DC stooped and looked over.

"Sarge?"

"Put the kettle on would you? I'm gasping for a cup of coffee here."

"Is there anything else to say about him?" Duncan asked, referring to McLintock.

"His clean-up percentage was pretty good," Alistair said. "He'd make it onto my team, certainly." He glanced over at Russell who was at his desk with a steaming brew and grazing his way through another packet of ready salted crisps. "He'd perform better than some of these reprobates anyway."

"Okay, thanks for looking it up, Alistair. If you need me, I'll be in my office until the end-of-day briefing."

"Right you are," Alistair said. Angus Ross approached him, stirring something in a cup. "You are an exceptional detective, Angus," he said, smiling broadly and gratefully accepting the mug. He glanced at Russell. "Unlike some others."

"Appreciate your support, Sarge," Russell said, totally unfazed, through a mouthful of crisps.

Duncan closed the door to his office and sat down at his desk. He logged himself into the police national computer, opened a search window and hesitated, his fingers hovering above the keyboard. He took a deep breath and typed the name into the box. The returned list of entries flashed up quickly. There were a few in the system under the name of Duncan McAdam. He paused, staring at the list. The most recent report was over twenty years ago. It documented the investigation into his father's death.

Duncan glanced through the window into the ops room but

everyone was busy and he thought it was unlikely that he would be disturbed. Exhaling, he double clicked on the report and it opened in a new window. He knew the circumstances surrounding his father's death. He'd been out on the town, drinking heavily which was not an unusual occurrence. In fact, it would have been unusual for him to have been at home and even more so if he'd been sober. Even though he was sure he knew the passage of events, he read through the report. He'd never sought the official findings of his death, never having the urge or feeling the need to.

Following a day of heavy drinking, passing through the many pubs in Portree, Big Duncan – as he was known, distinguishing him from wee Duncan, his son – had stumbled down to the harbour side having been refused entry to another establishment. On the island, Big Duncan McAdam was a well-known drunkard, and for him to be refused service highlighted just how intoxicated he'd been that day. The last sighting of him had been around ten-thirty that night, on the quayside of the old harbour. He'd propositioned a young lady who was returning to her nearby home. She'd dismissed him and he'd ambled away, leaving her annoyed but not threatened.

Duncan McAdam's body was hauled from Portree Harbour the following lunchtime after it'd been spotted by a fisherman returning to port. Duncan read the note on the report stating that the procurator fiscal – following discussions with local police – deemed that a Fatal Accident Inquiry was not in the public interest. The cause of his father's sudden death was clear. His blood alcohol concentration was recorded in the post-mortem at 0.35 percentage by volume which was almost the equivalent of a surgical anaesthesia. It was certainly enough to impair his physical state, cause nausea and leave him open to potentially fatal levels of blood poisoning. Any measure above 0.4 would very likely lead to respiratory failure, coma and probably death. The report stated he stumbled and likely fell into the harbour, leading to his death by drowning.

Duncan sat back in his seat, staring at the screen. The investigating officer who filed the report was none other than Campbell McLaren. He was an inspector by this point, and the most senior ranking officer on Skye.

"Why would you be investigating my father's death?" Duncan asked quietly. "That's a little beneath an inspector's level." McLaren had told him that he'd tried to do right by Duncan's mother, Big Dunc's wife. What did he mean by that? Closing his eyes, he felt tired, and pressed the heels of his palms into his eyes. Little lights danced before his vision in the darkness. A knock on the door snapped him out of it and he minimised the window on his screen before responding. "Come!"

Russell McLean entered, his notebook in his hand. "Sorry to disturb you, sir."

"Not at all, Russell. What is it?"

"The sarge has had me looking into Bruce Dunmore's affairs."

"Aye," Duncan said. "What do you have?"

"The usual," he said. "I'm into his bank accounts and I've been looking for trends, spending patterns or anything odd that comes or goes. Like I said, the usual stuff."

"And?"

"Regular payments leaving his account – substantial amounts too – each month, like clockwork."

"And where are they going?"

"To Iain Lambert," Russell said. "He owns—"

"Skye Lights," Duncan said. "I know. Alistair and I spoke to him already. He said he'd done some work up at Dunmore's house in Cuidrach and he was chasing him for payment."

"Well that's interesting, sir, because Dunmore's bank statements report that he's been paying him five grand a month, every month, for the last six months."

Duncan pursed his lips. "Thirty grand… that gets you a lot of window."

"And he still owes him for more?" Russell said, scoffing. "And if those windows of the Dunmore house are brand new, let alone worth thirty grand, then I'm a walking advert for healthy living."

Duncan smiled. "It sounds like Iain Lambert has been misleading us. I wonder if the threat of a defeating the ends of justice charge might see him tell us the truth. Anything else?"

"Aye, loads," Russell said. "I've got Dunmore's phone records too. They came through just now. The phone company must be working the back shift. Bruce Dunmore has had several conversations with Iain Lambert, lengthy ones at that. Well over an hour in some cases."

"When was the last one recorded?"

"Two days before he died, sir. On the Friday, last week."

"That strikes through the reason for Iain Lambert to be chasing him in the street for payment late on Saturday, if they'd been talking the day before. Who called whom?"

"Um…" Russell checked his notes. "Don't know. I'll go and check. There is something else though."

"Go on."

"Didn't the housekeeper, what's her name?"

"Flora McQueen."

"Aye, Flora... didn't she say that Dunmore kept himself to himself and didn't appear to socialise or speak to many people?"

"Yes, she did."

"Well, for a guy who likes to keep to himself, he hasn't 'alf been spending a lot of time on the phone to other folks on the island."

"Any particular names?" Duncan asked, intrigued.

"One number is unregistered, and so I don't know who owns it—"

"A burner?" Duncan asked, referring to a mobile that is not registered to any individual or business and is often used by people keen to evade the law, because it is untraceable. Russell nodded. "How many calls?"

"A dozen in total," Russell said, reading from his notes. "Seven of which came in the last four weeks."

"That's interesting. Do we have transcripts?"

"No, sorry. I've gone back to the service provider to see what they can find but I'm not optimistic. Data protection laws and all that," he said with a shrug. "There's another old boy on the island Dunmore has been talking to though. He lives out at Milovaig. Robert Hamilton. Do you know him?"

Duncan shook his head. "Should I?"

"No, no reason to. He hasn't got a file with us."

"An old friend of Dunmore's perhaps?"

"Maybe, but I had a chat with young Angus there," Russell said, inclining his head towards Angus who was seated behind his desk, a telephone clamped to his ear. "The sarge has him looking at An Corran and also he's been mooching about the history of St Benedict's as well. The thing is," Russell said, speaking faster, perhaps sensing Duncan's weariness, "we cross referenced the telephone numbers along with the names we have with the beach and the boys' home."

"Please tell me you have something," Duncan said. "Otherwise I might lose the will to live."

"Aye, I'm getting there. Hamilton also worked at St Benedict's at one time. Although the home had charitable status, it still needed to file accounts and to explain where the money they received came from and where it went, and all that sort of thing. Hamilton is listed as their caretaker."

Duncan shrugged. "Then he probably knew Dunmore and they were colleagues, if not old friends."

"Aye, that's… more than likely, and it might be nothing," Russell said, the wind going out of his sails momentarily. "But then there's one more number, an incoming call that Bruce Dunmore received at home. It lasted three minutes before the call ended."

"And?"

"The call originated from the Huxley estate."

Duncan's heart skipped. "Lord Huxley's?"

"Is there another?" Russell replied. Duncan realised he'd been holding his breath. He released it slowly.

"Do we know who on the estate called him?" Duncan asked. "They must employ dozens of people before you even count the family."

"Aye, a lot of people are employed on the estate," Russell said. "And I did check. The number that called was just one of the many landline numbers allocated to the estate. Obviously, they host weddings out there, tourist group parties, and then they sell the curated plants through the nursery, and they have the farm shop as well. They opened a wee kiddies' play area this past summer. It's great, you should go."

"I might be a bit big for that," Duncan said.

"Aye, right enough," Russell replied. "The thing is, Lord Huxley was a patron of St Benedict's as well, back in the day, like." He flicked through his notebook. "Angus found a reference to when the boys of St Benedict's would make a visit to the estate, camping there on the lawns each summer, doing a bit of hiking across the trails over the surrounding moorland."

Duncan rubbed his chin absently. The Huxleys were a real influence on the community of the island and Lord Huxley himself was well known for his philanthropic interests. In recent years he'd been leading a call for rewilding of the Highlands, a cause that put him at odds with many of the landed gentry of Scotland. That the Huxleys would support a children's home was very much in keeping with their ethos. It would be quite a leap to suggest there was anything untoward going on in anything that Russell had presented him with so far. However, in this day and age, nothing would surprise him or could be ruled out, bearing in mind the scandals that had been revealed from within both the Catholic and Anglican churches of the same period, let alone with the celebrity revelations of the period too. The links Bruce Dunmore had with his fellow islanders all appeared to be tied to his time at St Benedict's in one way or another.

"I'm not sure I like where this is heading," he muttered quietly.

"Sir?" Russell asked.

"Who have you told about this?"

"No one," he replied. "Other than you, and Angus obviously."

"This complicates things somewhat," Duncan said. "Keep it to yourself for now, and away from the information boards."

"Sir?"

Russell was confused by Duncan's reaction, which was

understandable. Although Duncan, personally, had no truck with the Huxley family being named in this investigation, he was well aware of the media frenzy that would follow if it slipped out that they were connected to any of this, even loosely. The last thing Duncan needed was to be spending precious time and resources, namely his own and his team's, on deflecting questions from the media and central command about the status of his investigation.

"We need to keep this on the QT, Russell. At least for now."

"Oh aye, I get you," Russell said, tapping the end of his nose. "Should I… keep checking?"

"Keep doing what you're doing," Duncan said. "If you find anything else, *anything,* then I want to hear it first. Understood?"

"Absolutely, sir."

"Good work. On your way out, can you send in Alistair for me, please." Russell turned and was halfway out of the door before Duncan called him back. "Give me Hamilton's address in Milovaig too, please."

Moments later, DS MacEachran entered his office. "What's got Russell so excited? I haven't seen him this happy since we restocked the honesty box with a multi-bag of branded crisps."

"Close the door, Alistair."

He did as requested and took a seat opposite him. "What's going on?"

"That's what I intend to find out."

Duncan relayed what Russell had told him, and also his concerns around this information becoming public knowledge. Alistair listened closely, clearly resisting the urge to interrupt. Once Duncan was finished, the DS sucked air through his teeth.

"This could get very messy," he said, "very quickly, if we're not careful."

"That was my thinking too."

"You know," Alistair said thoughtfully, "it would all go a lot smoother if we could find another angle to pursue, rather than St Benedict's."

Duncan was shocked. "I never had you pegged as someone to cover up—"

"I'm not! That's the furthest thing from my mind."

"Then I've missed your point."

"If we had a bone that we could throw to the public, and the media while we're at it," Alistair said. "That would give us the space to do our job."

"For example?"

Alistair frowned, one hand cupping his chin and the other drumming his fingers on his thigh. "I suppose we couldn't produce a royal pregnancy or something. That always distracts the newspapers."

"I think that's beyond our ability to arrange," Duncan said.

"How about we put it out there, on the quiet, that we think it's a suicide after all? That way, the press stay off our case and the killer might just relax a little bit."

"We can't officially announce that," Duncan said.

"And we don't have to." Alistair glanced into the ops room. "Have one of the lads go out for a couple of beers in the pub… and tell constables MacDonald – Ronnie and Fraser – that it's probably a suicide and their respective partners will have it across the island in no time at all."

"That would give us some breathing space," Duncan said, checking his watch. "Get everyone together for a quick debrief, and then we'll send everyone home for the night, pick up again first thing tomorrow."

"You look exhausted," Alistair said. "Something on your mind?"

Duncan shook his head. Alistair got up and went back into the ops room. Duncan maximised the window on his screen, cast a furtive glance over the report of his father's death and closed the browser window. He shut down his computer and made his way into the ops room where everyone was gathering to hear him speak.

CHAPTER SEVENTEEN

DUNCAN WOKE WITH A START. Rain was gently drumming against the skylight above the bed, and he could hear the wind pummelling the house with repetitive gusts coinciding with an increased intensity of the rainfall. His chest felt tight, and his head was pounding. Grace had cooked him dinner earlier but when he arrived home late she reheated it for him and, despite having not eaten all day, he'd only picked at it. They then sat on the sofa together watching a television series they've both been into recently, but he couldn't remember anything about the episode. He'd been lost in thought, completely preoccupied.

He looked to his left, watching the gentle rise and fall of Grace's chest as she slept. He eased himself out from under the duvet trying his best not to disturb her. It was cold once out from the sanctuary of the bedcovers. Despite his best efforts at insulating the old croft house he grew up in, it was still draughty when the wind was up. And the wind was up a lot on the Isle of Skye.

He picked up the shirt he'd worn during the day, having

casually thrown it across a chair in the corner of the room, beneath the eaves. He pulled on a clean pair of joggers that were waiting to be put away and made his way out of the bedroom and onto the landing. A floorboard squeaked under his weight, and he paused, the sound was amplified by the silence of night-time but thankfully masked by the weather. Grace stirred but didn't wake.

Heading downstairs, Duncan picked up a glass and filled it from the tap. His mouth was dry, the exertion of coming downstairs also made his throbbing head worse. His throat felt like it was lined with sandpaper and he found it hard to understand why he was so dehydrated. He'd been drinking enough throughout the day, but he'd been unsettled by his conversation with Campbell McLaren and he'd struggled to get to sleep. His shoulders were tense, painful even, and it all added up to explain why he felt so rough.

Duncan saw off the entire glass in one go and refilled it. Walking across the kitchen to the French doors, he peered out into the gloom. With the thick cloud cover he couldn't see the whitecaps of the waves or even the outline of the hills across from the house. The only thing he did see punctuating the darkness was the flash of the automated lighthouse on a rocky outcrop of an island off the coast. It flashed as it passed, winking out almost as soon as he saw it. He stared out towards the light, waiting for it to return, looking between the runs of water as they made their way down the glass of the doors in front of him.

He wasn't sure how many passes of the beacon's light he saw before he was startled by Grace's hands wrapping around his waist. He hadn't heard her come down the stairs, let alone walk up to him. She leaned her head against his shoulder, and he tilted his head to gently rest against hers.

"You couldn't sleep?" she asked.

"No, sorry. I didn't mean to wake you."

"You didn't," she said, tightening her grip. "Something on your mind?"

"Aye." He didn't offer anything further. It wasn't that he wanted to shut her out, far from it. He just hadn't been able to figure out what he was feeling, let alone finding a way to articulate it to her.

"Do you want to talk about it?"

"I do… but I don't know where to start."

He made to turn and she withdrew her arms, allowing him to face her. He slipped his hands around her waist now and drew her into his embrace.

"You could start at the beginning," she said. "That's usually a good place."

He nodded. "It's this case… it's taking me places that I'm not ready to go to."

"Sounds ominous."

"It is," he said, "or it might be, I don't know."

"I've not seen you like this with any other case you've had since we've been together."

"This is different." He took a breath, looking away from her.

"You don't have to talk about it if you don't want to."

He sighed. "It's not that. It's my father."

"Oh… I wasn't expecting that," she said, angling her head away from his and failing to mask her surprise.

"I wasn't expecting it either."

"He's related to… Bruce Dunmore's death?"

"No, not exactly. It's just… I don't know," he said, wincing apologetically. "Something happened, back when he passed and," he shook his head, "I don't know what it is. I'm in the dark and I have this feeling..."

"What feeling?" she asked, inclining her head. Duncan gritted his teeth, and she smiled at him. He could read her supportive smile even in the dim light, and he was certain she could see his reticence. "Go on, what feeling?"

"The feeling that I'm the only one in the dark about it."

"About what?"

He shook his head. "His death... his life," Duncan said, exhaling heavily.

"He fell into the harbour, didn't he?"

"Aye, when he was drunk." Duncan arched his eyebrows, his tone flat. "He was always drunk."

"I vaguely remember my mum telling me about it. Obviously, I was only little."

"I wasn't," Duncan said, "but I was away to Glasgow by then. Roslyn phoned me... and she said Mum wasn't doing well." He cleared his throat, a knot of emotion sticking there. "Roslyn wanted me to come home, to help but... er... I didn't." He pursed his lips, closing his eyes as he felt them tearing.

"Why didn't you come home?" Grace asked but there was no hint of accusation in the question, no hint of judgement. He shook his head.

"Because... because I was relieved."

"Relieved?"

"Aye, relieved... pleased even, that he was dead," he said, looking at her. He expected her to be shocked, to withdraw from him, incredulous that he could say something so callous about his own father's death. She didn't though. She reached up with one hand and gently rested her palm on the side of his face. He could see her eyes glistening as he opened up to her in a way he never had with anyone else. "I was pleased it was over. I would never have to face him again. I would never have to try to deal with all of his… crap… ever again. It was like a weight was lifted off me. I was… free. I guess that makes me a proper selfish bastard, eh?"

"Oh, Duncan," Grace said. "I'm so sorry." He could see she was crying, gentle tears that ran the length of her cheek. She wiped his cheek with her fingertips, first the left and then the right. He realised then that he was also crying. She smiled and leaned into him. They embraced in silence, and nothing more was said. After a while, Duncan had no clue how long, she withdrew from his embrace, took his hand and guided him out of the kitchen and back upstairs. She undressed him and they got back into bed. With his arms encircling her, they snuggled together under the duvet and he listened to her breathing, her hands holding his close to her chest.

Duncan didn't remember falling asleep but when he woke in the morning, the skies had cleared and shafts of brilliant sunshine lit up the bedroom. He felt truly rested, a sensation he couldn't remember feeling in quite some time. Grace wasn't beside him and he got up, following the smell of grilling bacon, fried egg and the sound of the coffee machine grinding. He found Grace in the kitchen, and she smiled as he walked in.

"Good morning, sleepy head."

"Morning," he said, going to her and placing his hand on her hip and leaning in to kiss her cheek. "Did you sleep okay?"

"I did," she said, pointing him towards the dining table which was set out for their breakfast. "I thought," she said, steering him towards the table and picking up a cup of coffee from the machine as she passed, "we could have breakfast together before you disappear off to the office."

"I'm not going in this morning," he said, sitting down.

Grace put his coffee in front of him and returned to the hob, taking the frying pan off the heat before transferring the eggs to a plate. "Alistair is picking me up." He checked the time and then buttered a piece of toast, taking a bite out of it. Grace set the coffee machine running for herself. She put the grilled bacon onto the plate beside the eggs before returning to the table, setting the plate down beside Duncan.

"Where are you headed?" she asked, retrieving her coffee and joining him.

"We have to see someone out at Milovaig."

"What do you have to go all the way out there for? Can't you just use the telephone?" She smiled. "It would be much easier."

"Sadly, in my line of work I have to see people face to face. It's way too easy to lie to me over the phone."

"It must be difficult," she said.

"What must be?"

"Having everyone lie to you every day."

He laughed. "Only the ones with something to hide will go to the effort of lying to me," Duncan countered.

"That would be over half the people on this island then," she said with a rueful smile. "Everyone has secrets."

"Even you?" He winked at her.

"Especially me," she said. Grace slapped the back of his hand as he went to pick up a strip of bacon. "That one's mine. I've had my eye on it."

"Fierce and loving at the same time," Duncan said, shifting his choice to the next strip. He hesitated, his hand above it. "Is it okay if I take this one or have you also planted a flag in that one too?"

"No, you can have that one."

"You're very kind," he said, putting it onto his plate. A car pulled up outside, and Duncan glanced at his watch again. "He's early."

"You should have known that," Grace said. "Alistair is always early."

Duncan hurriedly gathered two slices of bread to his plate, putting an egg and the bacon between them with a healthy dose of sauce, before getting up and taking it with him upstairs. A figure appeared at the back door followed by a knock.

"Come in, Alistair!"

The door opened and a draught of cold air blew across the kitchen. Grace beckoned Alistair inside and he closed the door behind him.

"Morning," he said.

"Hey Al. Is everything all right?"

Alistair's nose wrinkled, causing his moustache to twitch. "I smell bacon."

"Would you like a roll to take with you?" Grace asked.

"Well, on the better half's orders, I'm supposed to be eating healthy these days and I've already had my bowl of oats as well as my fresh fruit this morning."

"Never mind then—"

"But if you twist my arm, then I'll no' put up too much of a fight lass," Alistair said with his tongue firmly in his cheek. "What the wifey doesn't see, the old man gets away with."

"I'll make you one," Grace said, hopping up from her seat.

"Where's sleeping beauty then?"

"He's upstairs, getting ready." Alistair leaned against the counter while Grace prepared him a bacon roll. "Brown or white bread?"

"A dirty white roll, if you don't mind," Alistair said. "If I'm going to break the rules then I'll do it properly." Grace laughed. "How is your man this morning anyway?"

She glanced sideways at Alistair, finding him watching her intently. She wondered what he was thinking. "Fine," she said innocently. "Why do you ask?"

"Only, he seemed a little… distracted yesterday."

"Oh, he's fine. You know Duncan."

"Aye, that I do," Alistair said. She handed him his roll and he accepted it gratefully. "Have I got time to eat this—"

"No, you don't," Duncan said, bounding into the kitchen.

"In which case, I'll bid you good day, lass," Alistair said, saluting her with the roll in his hand. "Thank you for my second breakfast."

"Anytime, Alistair."

Duncan gave Grace a kiss on the cheek. "If you need to get about you can take my car today. I'll not be needing it."

"Thanks. I have a few errands to run. Let me know when you'll be home—"

"I will," he said, offering her a wink. Alistair was already outside, and Duncan made to follow, but Grace took him by the forearm. He looked into her face.

"Duncan, no one will ever judge you as harshly as you do yourself," she said. "Give yourself a break, okay?" He nodded, kissed her again and turned to leave. "I love you," she said as he reached the door. He looked back at her.

"I love you too."

The engine was already running by the time Duncan climbed into the cabin alongside Alistair. He was part way through eating the bacon roll Grace had made him. He spoke to Duncan through a mouthful of bread and bacon, gesturing with his head towards the house where they could see Grace sitting back at the dining table, mobile phone in hand, drinking her coffee. "She's a braw lass that one, Duncan," he said.

"I know."

"You should be smart," Alistair told him. "Pitch your tent while you still can."

"What do you mean *while I still can*?"

"Settle down with her before she comes to her senses and realises that marrying a policeman is awful for your social life and your spiritual soul." He shot Duncan a knowing look. "Before common sense prevails and she does a runner."

"How come you're still married then?" Duncan asked.

"My missus, bless her, never could run very fast," Alistair said with a half-smile, putting the pick-up into gear and pulling away. Grace waved as they passed the window and Duncan returned it.

"I hope she never sees sense," he whispered quietly.

CHAPTER EIGHTEEN

Lower Milovaig was a scattered mixed crofting and residential settlement nestling on the south shore of Loch Pooltiel on the Duirinish peninsula. There were very few points on the Isle of Skye's Atlantic coastline that were further west than the township. The bright sunshine belied the chill of the wind, and Duncan stared out towards Uist in the distance, over the salmon farming pods that were located in the loch, admiring the view. On the northern shore of the loch, the land banked steeply with almost sheer cliffs around the headland, facing the Western Isles.

Alistair picked his way around the coast, the narrow single-track road winding uphill. The groundworks of a new property had been laid, fresh stock fencing erected around the perimeter to keep the grazing sheep from wandering onto the site. Not that the animals were on the move this morning. Duncan saw several sheep, lying down on the open croft land, perhaps enjoying the sunshine. The road surface was uneven, pitted and broken up in places, but Alistair's pick-up managed better than most vehicles would and they were soon approaching the crest of the hill.

The scene opened up before them, white-painted and wooden-clad houses were dotted around the landscape. Plumes of smoke rose from some and Duncan could see those who worked the land were visible on their respective plots. Alistair slowed down as they looked for the home of Robert Hamilton. It didn't take them long to find it. The house was positioned in the lee of the hillside with a steep bank behind it. Unusually, much of the property was shielded from view by growth of Scotch broom, a large, deciduous shrub with long, whip like stems and an ornamental green foliage that flowered bright yellow petals in the spring. It was very similar to gorse but without the spines and to the uninitiated looked quite beautiful. However, unchecked, it grew like wildfire and was something of a nuisance if left uncontrolled. Hamilton appeared not too bothered about taming it.

The house was a traditional stone property, painted white as most were these days but the paint was blistering and peeling in many places. The salt of the coastal sea air wreaked havoc on exterior paintwork in these parts. Whereas most properties would have a traditional slate roof, this one was covered in corrugated steel panels, and these were warped and showing signs of discolouration and rusting. In front of the property, piles of materials had gathered over time, old offcuts of wood, rolls of stock fencing wire and general debris. There was even an old metal bathtub beneath some of the wood, piled within and around it.

Alistair exhaled heavily, studying the front of the property. "He's not very house proud, is he?"

"It takes all sorts," Duncan said, cracking the door handle and getting out. He was immediately struck by a gust of wind and he realised how exposed they were out here on the Atlantic coast. He drew his coat about him and Alistair fell into step as they walked to the front door, ducking beneath an overhang of the extensive broom. The shrub had grown across the front of the house, covering the two ground-floor windows to either side of the front door. Given another couple of years and they'd need a machete to cut their way through to the door. There was no bell and Duncan had to hammer a fist on the frame.

The glass panel of the door was mottled to shroud the interior but even if it had been clear, the inside was in darkness. Duncan knocked again, but they still didn't see any signs of movement. He stepped back, peering at the upper windows in the dormers. The curtains were drawn, but Duncan could see and smell the smoke coming from the chimney, the wind dispersing it but blowing it in their direction. Alistair bent down and pushed open the letterbox.

"Police!" he shouted and then knocked on the pane of glass again. This time a figure passed across the hallway, little more than a shadow, a change in the darkness but it grew in size as it came to the door. The person stopped short of the door and a gruff voice, muffled by the closed door, could be heard.

"Who is it?"

"The police!" Alistair said, frustrated. "Open the door, would you?" He then lowered his voice, muttering. "Or I'll kick it in."

The man came forward and they heard a key turn in the lock. The door moved slightly and stopped, the wood seemingly warped inside the frame because it stuck, and it took some effort to open it further. A short, balding man looked warily out at them through a gap of roughly five inches. He was bearded, but it was scraggy growth with wispy ends that were mottled and greying. He blinked at them, his eyes struggling with the brightness of the sun, peering out from the dark and gloomy interior.

"DI McAdam and DS MacEachran," Duncan said, brandishing his warrant card. "We're here to see Robert Hamilton. Is that you?"

"Aye, what of it?" he asked, his expression hard to read beneath the mass of unkempt facial hair.

"May we come inside?" Duncan asked, seeing the muscles in Alistair's face twitch at the suggestion. "We'll not stay long," he said, forcing a warm smile.

Hamilton muttered something incomprehensible, shook his head but relented, stepping back and hauling the door wider. It still wouldn't open fully, and Duncan had to turn side on to enter the house. Hamilton stood in his hallway, wearing a once-white vest with body hair sprouting from his chest over the neckline and from the arm holes. The vest was more grey now than white, with food as well as other unidentifiable stains down the front. He was dressed in jogging bottoms, far too large even for the ample girth of his frame, the waistline sitting below a pronounced belly.

It was hard for Duncan to judge whether their host was always this anxious and agitated or it was simply their presence in his home. He rubbed at his chin and mouth, his eyes flitting between Duncan and Alistair, suspiciously. He kept shifting his weight between his feet; feet sporting slippers whose heels had deteriorated to make them more like padded slip-on sandals, his toes visible on his right foot. Alistair attempted to close the door behind them and, having laboured for a few moments, gave up and left it cracked open. He looked around the dark interior wrinkling his nose.

"Shall we go through?" Duncan asked Hamilton whose

whiskers twitched and then he gave Duncan a curt nod, turning and leading the way into the house.

"What an incredible smell he's managed to create," Alistair said under his breath as they made to follow their host.

The front door offered a bit of daylight through the glass pane but once they made their way from the hall and into the first room to their right, a sitting room, they were almost in complete darkness. The curtains were drawn across the window and the broom growing across the exterior also helped to increase the gloom. It was so dark that they could only make out the silhouettes of furniture.

There was actually nowhere for them to sit down. Every seat, bar one, had been used to keep things on. As Duncan's eyes adjusted to the lack of light, he saw that Hamilton was a hoarder. There were stacks of paper, be they newspapers, magazines or unidentifiable publications, boxes – cardboard and plastic – piled somewhat precariously on top of one another from the floor and almost to the ceiling, including on the sofa. The air indoors was stale, smelling of cigarettes and alcohol along with, what Duncan guessed, was a mixture of rotting food and poor personal hygiene.

"Any chance we could put the lights on?' Duncan asked. Hamilton grumbled almost inaudibly and Alistair found a light switch but flicking it on did nothing. Duncan looked and saw there was no bulb in the fitting.

"I don't have lights," Hamilton said.

"You don't have electricity?" Duncan asked.

"I do," Hamilton said. "But I don't have lights. I like it dark."

"How do you do your hair of a morning?" Alistair asked drily, but Hamilton said nothing.

"Do you live here alone?" Duncan asked.

"Aye. I don't like visitors." He lowered his gaze to his lap, mumbling something.

"I beg your pardon?"

"Don't like 'em."

"We'll try to get out of your way as soon as we can, Mr Hamilton. I'd like to ask you about Bruce, if that's okay?"

"Bruce?" he said, staring at Duncan in the gloom. "Don't know any Bruce."

"Dunmore," Duncan said.

"Nope," he replied, shaking his head firmly. "Don't know him. Never have."

"That's interesting," Duncan said, and Hamilton lifted his gaze to Duncan, "because our records show that the two of you have been communicating via telephone recently." Hamilton grumbled, looking away and seeming to shrink into himself. "You say you live alone?"

"I do, aye," he said, snarling.

"And so there's no one else who could be using your telephone without your knowledge?" Their host was grumbling but if they were actual words, then they were incomprehensible. "Mr Hamilton—"

"So what if I did speak to him?" he snapped. "Not a crime…"

"What did you talk about?"

"Old times."

"Can you be more specific?"

"No. Why should I?" he said, glaring at Duncan. "Bloody people, sticking in their noses to where it doesnae belong." The last comment didn't appear to be directed at Duncan and he took it as a general comment.

"Is someone else bothering you, Mr Hamilton?"

He shook his head, smacking his lips, shifting nervously in

his chair. Duncan wondered if this man had mental health issues. He was, at the very least, rather odd by anyone's likely definition.

"You are aware, Mr Hamilton, that Bruce Dunmore's body was discovered on Monday morning?" Hamilton looked up with gritted teeth but he didn't speak.

"Dead," Alistair said flatly.

"Best place for him," Hamilton said.

"That's quite a statement," Duncan said. Hamilton looked away, his eyebrows knitting together.

"Best place," he repeated, muttering.

"What did Bruce want to speak to you about?" Duncan asked. The man shook his head, smacking his lips again. He was showing signs of agitation again, nervous tics in his face and body. "The telephone records show that you spoke several times, calls ranging anywhere from fifteen minutes to thirty minutes long. Can you tell us what you discussed."

"Nothing. The weather… things."

"I would struggle to speak like that with my closest friends for that length of time, Robert," Duncan said, adopting a more personal style. "Were you friends?"

"Not friends." He shook his head. "I don't have friends."

"You worked with him at St Benedict's, didn't you?"

The nervous movements Hamilton was making ceased immediately. It was so obvious that Duncan saw Alistair shoot him a knowing glance. He remained staring straight ahead, his forehead creased.

"You were the caretaker at the boys' home, were you not?"

"I fixed things, aye," he said. "I struggled to find work after I left school." He looked nervously between them. "I don't read too well, and I was always considered a bit of a Jonah out on the boats like. But I was good with my hands."

"Was that what Bruce was talking to you about, your time as a caretaker at the home?"

Hamilton was breathing heavily now, his intakes of breath becoming shorter and quicker with each passing moment.

"Robert, we can talk about this now or we can take you back with us to the police station in Portree—"

"But we'd rather not do that," Alistair added quickly. Hamilton didn't respond or look up, but Duncan shot his DS an inquisitive look. Alistair lowered his voice, although it didn't seem like Hamilton was listening. "If we take him back, do you think we could get a uniform come out here to pick him up? It's a long way back and… he is a bit… in my pick-up, you know?"

Duncan shook his head, and Alistair splayed his hands wide apologetically.

"Robert, it's important that you answer my questions—"

"It's not a crime to speak to someone," he said, shaking his head firmly. "Not a crime."

"What was the nature of your relationship with Bruce Dunmore?" Duncan asked.

"Not a crime," Hamilton mumbled beneath his breath. "Not a crime."

Duncan and Alistair exchanged a glance, Duncan cocking his head in a querying manner. Alistair shrugged. They had no cause to take this man back to Portree, and Duncan had no reason to believe they'd get any more out of him if they did.

"Okay, we'll leave it there for now," Duncan said, resigned to their position. "But we may need to speak to you again," Duncan said, "and next time, if you aren't more cooperative then we may need to have the conversation down at the police station." He looked at the man who was sitting very still, staring straight ahead, his lips moving and his eyes unblinking. He wasn't making a sound though. "Do you understand, Robert?"

Hamilton's eyes slowly lifted to meet Duncan's gaze, his expression defiant. "Evil doesn't come painted red and wearing horns, DI McAdam. He comes as everything you've ever wished for." His eyes appeared to gleam in the dim light. "You should remember that."

CHAPTER NINETEEN

"We'll see ourselves out, sir," Alistair said, looking at Duncan and arching his eyebrows. Duncan broke the lingering gaze between himself and Hamilton and nodded. The tone of the man, the words he spoke – the only coherent thing he'd uttered since their arrival – had thrown him. Hamilton didn't move from his chair as the two detectives went back into the hall. Duncan looked over his shoulder at Hamilton, his back straight, staring at the wall in front of him. Looking along the narrow hallway towards the back of the house now, Duncan saw it was completely in shadow. He nudged Alistair's arm and pointed along the hall. Alistair nodded, taking up a position in the doorway and keeping a watchful eye on Hamilton while Duncan took a moment to explore.

He made his way further into the property coming to the kitchen and looking inside. Flies were buzzing around the room, and he was confident he'd found the source of the strange smell of rot that seemed to permeate throughout the downstairs. He tried the light switch but, just as they'd found in the sitting room, the lights didn't work. He went inside, noting that the kitchen window had been covered by something fixed to the outside. It looked like a couple of offcuts of wood because he could see cracks of daylight permeating through the gaps in the boards.

He cast an eye around the kitchen. Dirty crockery was piled up in the sink, standing proud of the stagnant water it sat in. On the stove he found pans that had unidentifiable residue on the sides and base, mould growing in some places. None of the surfaces, utensils or plates appeared to have been cleaned in weeks. He opened the fridge and immediately regretted doing so. The smell made Duncan retch, and he had to put his forearm across his mouth and nose to block it.

He returned to where Alistair waited and the two of them made their way to the front door, both of them keen to get out into the fresh air. Once outside, Duncan drew a deep breath, filling his lungs. Alistair struggled but did manage to close the front door this time around. He came to stand alongside Duncan, both of them looking down across Loch Pooltiel and breathing in clean air.

"That man," Alistair said, frowning, "is as soppy as a box of frogs."

Duncan couldn't disagree. He had the urge to contact someone and suggest they reach out to Hamilton or, at the very least, keep an eye on him for his own safety. "What I don't understand, Alistair," Duncan said, looking back at the house, "is what on earth would Bruce Dunmore have in common with that man?"

"A fair question."

"I mean, how could they make conversation last anything close to fifteen minutes? It's not plausible."

Alistair frowned. "You think he's not real?"

"Do you?"

"If that's not genuine," Alistair said, pointing at the house, "then he deserves an award for his acting skills."

"He can't hold even the most basic of conversations," Duncan argued. "Why would Dunmore want to speak to him? What would be the point?"

"Excuse me?"

They both turned to see a man standing at the boundary fence, roughly twenty feet away, trying to get their attention. Duncan walked towards him. "Can I help you?" Duncan asked.

"Are you..." he looked at Duncan and then past him to Alistair who was slowly coming to join them, "with social services?"

"Why would you ask that?"

"You look... official. I thought, maybe, you were here for him," he said, nodding towards the house. Duncan took out his identification, showing it to him.

"We're police," he said.

"Oh... I see."

"Do you know Mr Hamilton?" Duncan asked.

The man scrunched up his face. "No, not really. He keeps himself to himself much of the time."

"We noticed," Alistair said.

"My name is Neil, Neil Sutherland. I live down the way, there," he said, pointing to a timber-clad house a short distance away.

"Has he always been like this?" Duncan asked, believing the neighbour would know what he was referring to.

"I moved here a few years back," he said thoughtfully. "Old Robert has never been what anyone would call fastidiously tidy, you know." He shrugged. "He's never been one to keep on top of his maintenance, but he was always a pretty affable man, you know. Until recently anyway."

"That changed?" Duncan asked, thinking he saw nothing of the sort while he was inside. Although, a lot of people could react strangely to being around the police, especially if they had something to hide.

"Oh aye, it has."

"In what way?"

"Well... he's become very withdrawn of late. He barely speaks to anyone now, and before... although he was never one to stop by for a cuppa, he would shoot the breeze when you walked by. Like I said, I don't know him well but there's certainly been a step change in his demeanour."

"Does he have any family or friends?"

"No family that I'm aware of," Sutherland said. "I've been told by others he has a wife and child somewhere, but they must be long gone because I've never seen them."

"Divorced?"

"I believe so, aye," he said, "but I don't know the ins and outs of it."

"What about friends, visitors to the house?"

He shook his head. "No, I've never seen... oh, wait, there was a man who came by once or twice recently."

"Who was that?" Duncan asked.

"No idea who it was. I didn't know him, but you notice people when they don't really belong somewhere, don't you? I was surprised."

"Surprised?"

"Aye... he was... a bit different to Robert."

"In what way?"

"Well, he had a bit of money. He drove a really nice car,' Sutherland said. "And he dressed well too. You can tell when someone is used to looking their best. He seemed very much at odds with Robert. I mean… you've seen Robert, right?"

"Aye," Duncan said.

"Well, what you saw of him today is pretty much what he's like every day."

"This man was…"

"A professional," Sutherland said. "I did wonder if he was a solicitor or something, you know? He carried himself with confidence. The type of confidence you see in people who move in certain circles."

"Wealthy circles?" Alistair asked.

"Aye, that's it." He shrugged. "I could be wrong."

"But you don't know who it was?"

"No, sorry."

"Can you describe him for me?"

Sutherland blew out his cheeks, his forehead creasing. "Now you're testing me. It was a couple of months back, and I was just passing when he arrived. I only saw him getting out of the car. He was probably late sixties, perhaps early seventies. He had grey hair, which isn't a shock, I suppose. Balding." He arched his eyebrows. "That's about all I remember. Is it important?"

Duncan ignored his question. "What about the car, do you remember it?"

"I saw the car here several times. I only saw the driver once, but you remember a nice car like that, and there's only one road in and out of here. Cars like that stand out in these parts. They're not exactly practical for living around here. It was a German brand… a Mercedes. I don't know which model, but a saloon type of thing."

Duncan glanced towards Alistair. The description of the car and the driver could be a match for Bruce Dunmore. It didn't help their understanding of why he and Robert Hamilton would be meeting, but it did confirm they should dig deeper.

"Thanks very much," Duncan said. "You've been very helpful."

"Is…" Sutherland said as Duncan turned to leave, stopping him, "everything all right?"

Duncan turned back. "Yes. Is there a reason you think it wouldn't be?"

The man looked nervous, all of a sudden. "I… it's just… Robert." He looked beyond them, to the house.

"What about him?"

"He's been a bit strange of late. I… we, - my wife and I, - have been worried about him."

"Do you know him well?"

"No. I can't say that we do. Like I said before, he was always open to chat, in passing, but… he kind of gives my wife the creeps."

"I get that," Alistair said. "Any particular reason for that?"

"Look… I don't want to cast any aspersions on the man—"

"I think we'd prefer it," Duncan said, "if you spoke plainly with us." He looked over his shoulder at the house, thinking of the interactions with the occupant. "We've had enough deflection for one day already."

"My wife, and me, to be honest, found it a bit odd… the way he interacted with… with our children." Sutherland seemed pensive, despite being given encouragement to speak openly.

"And when you say odd, you mean what?" Duncan asked.

Sutherland grimaced. "Nothing specific… it's just instinct, you know what I mean?"

"Instinct," Duncan repeated.

"Aye. Have you never trusted your gut?"

"I have," Duncan said.

"Look, I don't want to get anyone into trouble, but…"

"Do you have a specific allegation?"

"No, no I don't."

Duncan nodded. He took out one of his contact cards and passed it across the fence. Sutherland took it, scanned the front of it and smiled weakly. "If you have the need to call me," Duncan said, "with something specific, then I'll be there to listen."

Sutherland raised the card before him and nodded, then tucked the card into his pocket. Duncan turned and walked back to the pick-up with Alistair.

"What does your gut instinct tell you?" Alistair asked. Duncan glanced over his shoulder and saw Sutherland making his way down the slope towards his own house. "Because mine is saying we need to know more about St Benedict's."

"I've been thinking about what Booth told us."

"Dunmore's agent?" Alistair asked.

"Aye," Duncan said. "About how he was writing this new book, and that he was keeping the plot pretty close to his chest. He had this big announcement planned for the event at the Portree Hotel this coming weekend."

"And? What about it?"

They'd reached Alistair's pick-up, and it wasn't locked. They both got in and Duncan closed his door, resting his elbow against it, cupping his chin and striking a thoughtful pose.

"What if… he wasn't writing a new Cold War thriller after all?" Duncan said, looking across at Alistair. "Maybe it was something completely different."

Alistair started the engine. "Such as?"

"I don't know, I'm just thinking aloud," Duncan said. "A memoir… his autobiography or the story of his time on the island. Whatever it was, he didn't want anyone to know until this weekend and if I was a betting man, I'd wager he was looking to make a splash with it—"

"And he's spent a lot of time speaking to people he knew from when he was with them at St Benedict's."

"It's curious – don't you think? – that Robert Hamilton starts going very odd around the same time that Dunmore comes back to the island and possibly coming around here, chatting to him."

"The timing is… certainly interesting, that's for sure. Are you going back to this authenticity angle again?"

"Aye, I am. The question is, why would he pretend?"

"If he is pretending," Alistair countered.

"All roads lead to St Benedict's," Duncan said. "I wonder who else Bruce Dunmore has been speaking to of late."

"I'll have the team look into it," Alistair said, putting the vehicle into gear. As they moved off, Duncan thought he saw a flicker of movement at the window from within the house, through the brush, but he couldn't be sure.

CHAPTER TWENTY

THEY HAD BEEN DRIVING for fifteen minutes, back towards Portree, when Duncan's mobile rang. It was Angus Ross calling from the station.

"Hello, sir," Angus said. "I'm sorry to trouble you."

"It's no trouble Angus. What can I do for you?"

"You know I've been looking into St Benedict's, cross referencing names of people who may have crossed paths with Bruce Dunmore, past and present?"

"Aye, what have you got for me?"

"You spoke with Iain Lambert, didn't you?"

"He was seen talking to Dunmore after an event at the bookshop in town, aye. Was Iain one of the boys who stayed at St Benedict's?"

"No, I've not got his name anywhere in the records but I did come across Grant Lambert. He was down as working at the home around the same time as Dunmore was there."

"A relation?"

"Iain's father, aye," Angus said. "I found an old photograph printed in the local paper in March of 1977. There was some special event for the children out on one of the estates—"

"The Huxleys' estate I should imagine."

"That's right. Do you think it's relevant?"

Duncan glanced sideways at Alistair who saw the look and was clearly keen to know what Duncan was talking about. "It might be. Where is Grant now?"

"He passed away some years ago, sir. Iain was his only child. It's interesting because we've been working on these names, and Russell looked up Lambert's company information off the back of what we discovered in his personal accounts."

"You're referring to the payments Lambert received from Bruce Dunmore?" Duncan asked.

"That's right, yeah. We looked up the history of his business accounts filed with HMRC. His company has been in a precarious financial position."

"How bad is it?" Duncan asked.

"He has averted two compulsory strike-off notifications in the last two accounting years," Angus said, seeming to read from something in front of him. "He was late filing in both of those years as well. Looking at the balance sheets available through the Companies House portal, his business has reported significant losses in each of the past three years. He lost seventy grand three years ago, that doubled the following year and the latest accounts show he's down a further two hundred thousand pounds. At the same time as he's reported all of that, he's also taken director's loans from the business. Presumably, that's in lieu of being able to pay himself a salary or draw any dividend income from the non-existent profits. Looking at it though, these losses are completely unsustainable." Angus paused, allowing Duncan to take it all in. "What do you want me to do with it, sir? Anything?"

"No, leave it with me," Duncan told him. "Alistair and I can swing by and see Iain. Perhaps our knowing of his position might help to jog his memory."

"All right, sir." Duncan was about to hang up but Angus stopped him. "Oh, there's another one as well, sir."

"Another what, Angus?"

"A link. You know that group of wild swimmers, the ones who discovered Bruce Dunmore's body on the beach?"

"Aye."

"One of them… hold on a sec," Angus said, and Duncan heard him shuffling paper on his desk. "Here it is, Fraser McEwan. He was one of the party. Did you speak to him?"

"No, not personally. What's the link with him?"

"He was one of the boys who stayed at St Benedict's," Angus said. "He was there for four years according to the official records we've been going through."

"Did his stay there coincide with when Bruce Dunmore was there?"

"Ah… that I can't say just now, sir. I'll keep digging mind."

"Thanks, Angus. McEwan left us his details though, right?"

"Oh yeah. We have a statement from him. Not that there was much to it. I read through it just now and he stayed well clear of the body. He said he's quite squeamish about dead things. I can't say I blame him."

"Send me his details will you, please, Angus?"

"Will do, sir. I've also just had a message relayed up to us from the front desk. A lassie from the local newspaper has been trying to get hold of you… Katie, I think her name is. She didna say what it was about though."

"Okay. Did she leave me a phone number?"

"She did. I can forward it to you at the same time, if you like."

"Yes, please. Thanks, Angus."

Duncan hung up and put his mobile back into his pocket. Alistair shot him an inquisitive look. "Are we changing course?"

"Iain Lambert," Duncan said. "It looks like his father worked alongside Bruce Dunmore and Iain has been working under some severe financial constraints in the last few years."

"Which Dunmore has been alleviating with the cash he's been transferring to him," Alistair said.

"That would follow, aye," Duncan said. "The question is, why would he be willing to do that?"

"I'm looking forward to him explaining that to us," Alistair said, taking the next turning to alter course.

They arrived at Iain Lambert's business unit on the trading estate on the outskirts of Portree a quarter of an hour later. The company vehicles were parked outside, in the same places as they had been on their first visit, Duncan thought as he surveyed them whilst getting out of Alistair's pick-up. He walked closer to them, noting leaves and detritus had built up around the wipers' blades at both the front and the rear windows. The tyre of one vehicle was also flat. It looked like these vans hadn't moved in weeks or perhaps months. He pointed these details out to Alistair.

"Do you think he's lost a lot of contracts or something?" Alistair asked.

"Perhaps. Maybe he's had to lay people off—"

"Or he's on the verge of ceasing trading altogether."

They walked up to the entrance door and Duncan tried the handle. The door was locked. He leaned closer to the door, cupping his hands against the glass and peering through into the interior. His view into the main area of the unit was limited due to having to see across the entrance lobby. He couldn't see any lights on beyond the double doors. Duncan knocked on the glass, more out of hope than expectation. Alistair walked over to the window overlooking the car park and stared through the glass.

"Looks like nobody's home," he said quietly. The door to the adjoining unit opened and a man came out, pausing as he saw the two of them.

"Are yous looking for Iain?" he asked.

"We are," Duncan said. "Have you seen him about today?"

"No," he said, shaking his head. Duncan sensed reticence in his response. He took out his identification and brandished his warrant card.

"Police. Can I ask who you are?"

"I'm Dougie. Dougie McCall," he said, pointing to the industrial unit alongside Iain's. "I work here, doing bespoke joinery and the like."

"Have you ever done work with Iain?"

Dougie laughed drily and shook his head. "I used to, but..." he sucked air through his teeth. "He's not a man who pays his debts, if you know what I mean?"

"He's been having trouble recently?"

"Aye, you could say that," Dougie said. "It's a shame because he's always been a pretty decent bloke. We used to hang out, go for the odd beer and that. If we had a bit of complementary that we could push each other's way, then we would."

"But not recently?" Duncan asked.

"No," he said, smiling. "Not recently, and I can't see me working with him again." He looked around them, as if taking in the entire industrial estate. "And no one else will either. He's formed a bit of a reputation for himself has our Iain."

"For not paying his way?"

"Aye. That's about the size of it."

"When did you last see him?" Duncan asked.

"He was here this morning, actually," Dougie said. "Not that he stuck around long. He shut up shop around half nine. I saw him leave."

"That's an early finish," Alistair said. "Business must be good."

"Not from what I heard," Dougie countered.

"The jungle drums beating, are they?" Duncan asked.

"No, I mean this morning." Dougie waved a lazy hand towards Iain's unit. "It was all going off in there this morning. Shouting and bawling. They made a right racket."

"Who did? Iain was arguing with someone?"

"I don't know about arguing, like… but there was a lot of shouting going on."

"Between who?" Duncan pressed. Dougie grimaced and looked away, avoiding Duncan's gaze. "Do you know?"

"Look… it's not really any of my business," Dougie said. "And I don't want to get involved."

"Fair enough," Duncan said. "But it might be important, and if something happened here today, then I might need to know about it. This isn't the playground. This is adult stuff, do you understand what I'm saying to you?"

Dougie appeared torn but he sighed heavily and nodded. "All right. I get it."

"What happened this morning?"

Dougie took a deep breath. "I got here, usual time—"

"Which was?" Duncan asked.

"A little after eight o'clock. Iain's car was already outside." He pointed to an empty parking bay to Alistair's left. "That's where he parks. Same place, every day."

"Is he usually here when you arrive?"

He shrugged. "Sometimes. This morning though, he had company. There was another car parked next to Iain's."

"Did you see the driver?"

Dougie shook his head. "No, I didn't see but later on I figured he was in with Iain because of all the shouting and hollering."

"Iain?"

"Definitely Iain, but there were a couple of other voices too."

"Are you sure there was more than one?"

"Oh aye," he said, nodding towards the units. "These places aren't exactly built to keep the noise out. They're basically metal-clad sheds, you know."

"They were arguing?"

"I don't know about arguing, but they were going off at one another for about fifteen minutes." He seemed embarrassed. "I kinda listened in for a bit, while I was making a cup of tea when I got in. Not that I could make out what they were talking about before you ask, but I paid attention, that's all. Anyway, it went on for a bit and then everything went quiet."

"And?" Duncan asked, hoping there was more.

Dougie shrugged. I looked out of the front window and the other car had already left. Shortly after, Iain came out, locked up and he took off as well."

"But they didn't leave together?"

"No."

"You said you don't know what it was they were shouting about?"

"No. Presumably it was someone else who Iain owed money to. That was my guess anyway."

"A guess based on what?" Duncan asked.

"Experience," Dougie replied, smiling.

"Did you see the other people at all?"

"Nah, can't say I did."

"What about the car they were driving? You saw that."

"I did. It was a Bentley," Dougie said. "The SUV one they make, you know? It's quite distinctive."

"I don't suppose you got a look at the registration number?" Alistair asked.

"I'm sure I did, but I wasn't looking," Dougie said. "Sorry." He looked between the two detectives. "What's this all about anyway? Has Iain been up to no good or something?"

"No, nothing like that," Duncan said. "We just need to speak to him on another matter. That's all." Dougie shot Duncan a sceptical look. "Do you have any idea where we might find him?"

Dougie laughed. "I doubt he's on a job anywhere, so I'd try his house."

"Thanks."

"Or the pub," Dougie said, checking his watch. "He'll probably be there by now, if he can rustle up a bit of cash. No one is giving him any credit these days, not even the bar staff."

"Do you happen to know where his favourite haunt is?"

"Wherever he can get served," Dougie said. "He always liked to start off at the Merchant."

"Bosville Terrace," Alistair said. "Nice place that, decent variety of scotch behind the bar."

"Aye it is. If he's not there then you could look at the West Highland. But I've no idea whether he still drinks in these places. Most folks are as sick of him as I am."

"Why is that?" Duncan asked.

Dougie shrugged. "Don't get me wrong, Iain was always a

nice enough bloke but… of late, he's been a bit weird. Although, he's been a bit more agreeable these past few months. I thought – everyone thought – that he was going under. He let a lot of his guys go, those who hadn't already quit on him anyway. We were waiting on winding up petitions coming through, but that's all gone quiet recently."

"Things were that bad for him?"

"Aye. He had judgements against him in the Sheriff's court and all sorts, but all of that went quiet in the last month or so." Dougie smiled ruefully. "Maybe he sold his soul to the devil or something."

"Maybe," Duncan said. "Thanks for your help, Dougie. I appreciate it."

He left them and Alistair came to stand alongside Duncan, his hands thrust into the pockets of his long coat. "The plot thickens," he said as they both watched Dougie get into his works' van and drive away. He acknowledged them both with a brief wave as he drove past them.

"Well, we knew Iain had financial problems."

"Dunmore had been giving him money, which may have kept the wolves from the door," Duncan said.

"If someone was giving you money on a regular basis, would you put it through your failing business or keep it personally?" Alistair asked.

"If you put it in the business you lose it. If it was me, I'd live off it rather than draw a salary."

"Aye, that would make sense," Alistair said, nodding. He looked around at the locked-up unit and all of the stationary works' vans belonging to the business. "It doesn't look like Iain Lambert has a lot of work on."

"No." Duncan looked sideways at him. "I take it you have a point."

"If he's not working and his business is facing Sheriff's court judgements and the like, owes money… and he's barely trading… how did he stop the rot? I mean, we know Dunmore was throwing a few thousand at him regularly, but that's not going to make up the shortfall, is it?"

"Good question. Let's find him and ask."

CHAPTER TWENTY-ONE

DUNCAN THANKED the bartender of the West Highland, returning outside to where Alistair was on the telephone. He shook his head, answering Alistair's unasked question.

"Aye, have everyone in uniform," Alistair said, "who's passing a pub, a hotel, restaurant… even an off-licence stop in and see if Iain Lambert is, or has been, there." He sighed, rolling his eyes as Duncan smiled. "I know that covers a lot of places. I'm no' daft, am I? Can you just put the word out for me please? Aye… thanks very much." He hung up on the call, shook his head and put his mobile away in his pocket. "You'd think I was asking uniform to round up all the sheep on the island or something. There are wiser on the hill eating grass," he said, quoting one of his best lines.

"He can't have gone far," Duncan said. "It's only a matter of time."

"Where should we go next?" Alistair asked.

"Well…"

Duncan didn't get to finish his thought. The radio in Alistair's pocket crackled into life with someone communicating directly with him. He took it out and turned up the volume before depressing the talk button. "Go ahead for DS MacEachran ."

"Sarge, it's Ronnie MacDonald. I've just had word come through… are you in Portree looking for Iain Lambert?"

"Aye, Ronaldo," Alistair said, leaning against his pick-up. "Have you seen him today?"

"Not just ten minutes ago," PC Ronnie MacDonald said. "He was wandering along Quay Street, heading down to the wee dock, so he was."

"Are you sure it was him?"

"Aye, of course. He looked a little worse for wear. Listen, I'm no' far away. I could head back down—"

"Thanks, Ronaldo." Alistair glanced at Duncan. "We're in Portree ourselves. We'll go and have a look. An extra pair of eyes wouldn't hurt."

"I'll see you down there," Ronnie said.

Duncan and Alistair got into the cab of the pick-up to make the short drive across the town and down to the harbour. Quay Street was a narrow road that ran along the harbour's edge, the brightly painted facades of the terraced buildings – a mixture of residential property, hotels and businesses – were a real draw for tourist cameras. The pier at the end of the street harboured a fuel terminal for oil deliveries as well as a seafood business, landing the fresh catch from the trawlers that still operated in the local waters.

Alistair drove slowly, both he and Duncan searching for any sign of Iain Lambert. They reached the pier and Alistair pulled up. There was a short path off to the right but it was pedestrian access only. He parked the pick-up in a narrow bay alongside several vans belonging to the seafood operator and they got out.

"You cannae leave your truck there, mate," a man said, standing outside the small warehouse, dressed in his skins to keep him free of the fish. Alistair brandished his warrant card, and the man nodded. "Aye, all right. Nae bother."

"We'll not be long," Alistair told him. "Have you seen anyone walking by here in the last fifteen to twenty minutes?" Alistair wrinkled his nose. "He may have been slightly worse for the drink."

"Aye, there was a fella. He was leaning against the railings over there for a time." He pointed along the path to his left, their right. "He stumbled off up the way there, towards Apothecary's Tower."

"Cheers," Alistair said, offering him a grateful wink. He and Duncan set off towards the park just as Ronnie MacDonald drew up in his patrol car. He wound down his window, acknowledging them with a nod.

"Any sign?" he asked.

"Your man over there," Duncan said, inclining his head towards the warehouse, "says he saw someone who could be Lambert making his way up to the tower. Can you drive around to the other side just in case he is heading down the way—"

"Or tries to make a run for it when we approach him," Alistair said.

"Will do," Ronnie said, making to turn his car around and head back the way he came. Duncan and Alistair began the walk up the hill towards the high point where the tower was located.

Apothecary's Tower was located on The Lump, an area of

walking trails with panoramic views of Portree Harbour, the bay and out across Loch Portree. On a clear day you could even see the Old Man of Storr on the horizon to the north. The tower had once been used to advise ships of available medical services and also acted as a dispensary but was now a restored monument for visitors to climb to the top and take in the view.

"He'd better be up here after all this effort," Alistair said, breathing heavily as they climbed the path. The clear skies that had greeted Duncan when he awoke that morning were a distant memory. Clouds had rolled in throughout the morning and the threat of rain was in the air. The top of Apothecary's Tower came into view and Duncan gestured towards it, spotting a figure on the roof. The man was pacing around the roof, occasionally lifting a large bottle to his lips.

"I think that answers your question," he said. The crenelated rooftop offered sweeping views of Portree and the surrounding land. Accessed from a spiral staircase, Duncan and Alistair approached the entrance. They stopped at the base of the staircase. Singing – out of tune singing – carried to them from above.

"Do you want to do rock, paper, scissors?" Alistair asked. "To see who gets to talk him down from the roof."

Duncan shook his head, leading the way. "Why do you think it will be difficult?"

"I think you haven't had to deal with a drunk for a while," Alistair said with a wry smile.

Once out of the sanctuary of the tower and up onto the roof, Duncan felt the wind cutting into him along with the first spots of rain. Judging from the shroud of darkness coming towards them it wouldn't be long before the heavens opened. Iain Lambert was clutching a bottle of scotch between his forearm and his side, pacing back and forth. He didn't appear to have noticed their arrival and nor did he react now they were standing close to him. His focus was on the bay far below them.

"Iain?" Duncan said, raising his voice to ensure he would be heard over the wind. Lambert stopped his pacing and slowly turned to face them. He didn't seem particularly surprised to see them which Duncan thought odd, although it highlighted how much the man must have had to drink. His cheeks were glowing red, despite the bitter edge to the wind, and he wasn't wearing an overcoat to protect him from the elements. Duncan looked at the bottle. There was less than half of the contents left. "It's a bit early for that, isn't it?" Lambert glanced down at the bottle nestling in the fold of his elbow now.

"Can a man nae have a drink in peace anymore?"

"Of course," Duncan said. "We've just been looking all over town for you."

"Is that right?" Lambert asked, accompanied by a sneer. He spread his arms wide but was careful to grasp the neck of the bottle first. "Well, here I am. You found me. Now what?"

"I'd like to speak to you, if I may?" Duncan asked. "Perhaps we could go somewhere? Maybe I could buy you a cup of coffee or something."

"Nah," Lambert said. "I'm all good, but thanks for the offer." He held the bottle aloft, tipped it towards them by way of a salute and raised it to his lips. He took a mouthful, swallowing hard but that was the only reaction to necking neat scotch from the bottle.

"I want to speak to you about your father."

"I've got nothing to say about him," Iain almost spat back.

"Nothing at all. The man is dead and gone, and I'm done mourning him."

"Then how about your business? Can we discuss that?"

"It's going great guns," Lambert replied, sarcasm evident, swaying where he stood, holding the bottle of scotch aloft triumphantly. "Can't you tell? I'm the king of my own here, little castle of shite."

Alistair offered Duncan an almost imperceptible look. He was concerned. Duncan shared it. He felt his mobile vibrate in his pocket but he ignored it.

"What's going on, Iain?" Duncan asked. "If you carry on like this then there won't be much of a business left."

Lambert laughed, but it was a wicked sound, dismissive. "It doesnae matter anymore anyway," he said, lifting the bottle to his mouth again. He drank deeply, but his eyes remained fixed on Duncan. Lowering the bottle, he dragged the back of his free hand across his mouth. He maintained the eye contact with Duncan. "McAdam," he said almost quietly. "Duncan McAdam."

"Aye," Duncan said, finding Lambert's tone curious. "Can we talk?"

"What is there to say?" Lambert said, his speech slurred, but his demeanour shifted. It was as if a veil of despair had been drawn down across his face. He took a step forward but misjudged the ground, lost his footing on the damp stone and stumbled. Overcorrecting for his error, off balance now, he staggered backwards and fell against the crenelations. The masonry was barely waist high and in his present state, Lambert pitched backwards. It was only the quick reactions of Duncan and Alistair, surging forward to close the distance between them that prevented him from falling off the tower. In the melee, Lambert lost the grip on his bottle and it fell, tumbling through the air before smashing on the stone at the tower's base.

Between them, Duncan and Alistair hauled him back over the lip and the three of them sank down onto the roof, breathing hard.

"Shame," Lambert said. "That was a bloody decent scotch, you know."

"No it wasn't," Alistair countered. "And you've had enough as it is."

Lambert sniffed, slumped against the stone wall. His eyes tracked Duncan as he stood up. "I'm really sorry, Duncan. For everything."

Duncan brushed off his coat. "That's a bit melodramatic," he said. "How about we go somewhere quieter. Maybe we could have that chat?"

"Should have…" Lambert muttered, "should have done… more."

Lambert's eyes closed and when Alistair was also back on his feet, he stared down at the man, his chin disappearing into his neck, his head gently bobbing with the rise and fall of his chest. His breathing was shallow however, and Alistair nudged the sole of Lambert's left foot. He didn't flinch and then he started snoring.

"I don't think he's going to be very communicative until he sleeps that off."

Hearing raindrops strike the stonework around them, Duncan looked skyward. His mobile vibrated again and Duncan cursed. He ignored the call, keen to get back under cover as quickly as possible. "Come on, let's get him to his feet—"

"He'll not be walking anytime soon."

"Then we'll be carrying him between us, won't we?"

It was almost three quarters of an hour later when Duncan saw the door to a cell closing back at Portree station. Iain Lambert was still asleep. The only contribution he made on the journey down from The Lump was to mumble beneath his breath but, other than that, he remained out of it for the duration.

"You'll keep an eye on him, and let me know when he wakes up?" Duncan asked.

The custody sergeant glanced at him and sighed. "I could do without babysitting a drunk, to be honest with you, sir. But I'll call you as soon as he comes around. What is he being charged with?"

"He hasn't committed a crime," Duncan said.

"That we know about," Alistair added.

"Oh, one of those is it?"

"He's not detained, but we do have some questions for him," Duncan said.

"Leave it with me and I'll call you as soon as he's fit to be interviewed."

Duncan stepped up to the door and looked through the peephole. Iain Lambert was lying on the blue plastic-covered mattress of the cell, his chest rising and falling. They would have to wait a while before he'd sleep off the alcohol, especially if they wanted whatever he may have to tell them to be admissible in court.

They left the custody suite and went back up to the operations room, finding the team busy at work. Angus saw them enter and he came bounding across to see them.

"Sir," he said, addressing Duncan. "I've got more information on Iain Lambert's business affairs that might be of interest. And that local journo has been on to us again."

"Katie?" Duncan asked and Angus nodded.

"She's keen," Alistair said. "I wonder what she's after? A steer on the Dunmore case I suspect."

"No, she's not working that one," Duncan said. "But I've no idea what she wants. It will have to wait." He turned back to Angus. "What did you uncover about Iain Lambert?"

"Well, you know we went through his company accounts, and he's clearly been struggling these past few years. I phoned through to HMRC on the off chance that they might have some more information than we could draw from the portal at Companies House. It turns out that there's an official letter that hasn't been uploaded yet."

"Which says?" Duncan asked, intrigued.

"It's a simple notice of a change in persons of significant control. There is a new director nominated, and a new investor who has taken on fifty-five percent of the business."

Alistair was incredulous. "Who would buy into a business failing so spectacularly as that one, let alone take on the controlling stake?"

"The Huxleys. George specifically," Angus said, referencing the eldest son of Lord Huxley, "has become a named director whilst the estate business has taken on the shareholding." Duncan also found this an odd turn of events. "I did read in the papers a while back that the Huxley estate was looking to expand into other local businesses to spread their portfolio a bit wider."

Alistair scoffed. "They could just as easily have started a new business without taking on the exposure of all the bad debt. What is going on?"

"Perhaps we should speak to George Huxley about it?" Duncan said.

"People like us don't simply walk up to people like George Huxley and ask them about their finances," Alistair said. He took on a posh inflection. "It's just not proper, old boy."

Duncan raised an eyebrow. "Then how does one go about speaking to him?"

Alistair smiled, pretending to doff his cap. "One puts in a request for an audience."

Duncan laughed. "He's not the king, Alistair."

"He is as close as we get to one on the island."

"Make the call," Duncan said.

"One more thing, sir," Angus said. Duncan gestured to him to continue. "The forensic report on the break-in at Bruce Dunmore's home has come back. They only found two sets of identifiable fingerprints in the study. Those of Dunmore himself, along with those of his housekeeper, Flora McQueen."

"Did someone take her prints?" Alistair asked. Duncan shook his head.

"Not that I know of."

"No, hers were on file already," Angus said.

"Flora has a record?" Duncan asked.

"A shoplifting offence, back when she was a teenager," Angus said. "No fingerprints were found on the safe or inside it."

"None at all?"

"None," Angus said. "The technician suggested it was wiped clean, as we don't even have Dunmore's on it."

"Stands to reason," Duncan said. His mobile rang in his pocket, and he excused himself, walking through into his office and closing the door. It was Grace. "Hello—"

"Duncan, where have you been? I've been trying to get hold of you for the past hour."'

"I was…" he glanced back through the glass, "I was working. What's wrong?"

"It's your mum, Duncan. You have to come and see your mum!"

"Wait… are you with her?"

"Aye, I am. They couldn't get you on your mobile, or Ros, and so they called the croft. Duncan, she's calling for you. You need to come down here."

He heard the fear in her voice. "I'm on my way."

CHAPTER TWENTY-TWO

DUNCAN GOT out of the patrol car as close to the entrance to the facility as he could. He thanked the uniformed officer for dropping him off and hurried into the building. Crossing the lobby, he was met by a nurse descending the stairs who seemed grateful he was there. "Thank you for coming, Mr McAdam."

"Is she in her room?" he asked, as she changed direction and climbed the stairs alongside him. Duncan was moving briskly and she had trouble keeping up with him.

"Yes, we managed to get her back into her room, although it was under protest. It took three of us to do it."

Duncan stopped, shooting her a confused look. His mother was infirm and he found it difficult to understand that would need so many people to get her back into her room. "Three?"

"Yes," she said. "Your mother can be… wilful."

"Aye, she can be," he said, setting off again.

"I've never known her to be this upset, Mr McAdam. She was hysterical."

"What was it that triggered the episode?" he asked, knowing that in her current state it could have been anything.

"She seemed quite content in the communal room, watching television, and then all of a sudden she just blew up."

Reaching the landing of the floor his mum's room was on, he slowed his pace. He was breathing heavily and he was feeling anxious. The care home had never felt the need to call him like this before, although they were probably more inclined to contact his sister before they called him anyway. Making his way along the corridor he heard a sickening ailing sound coming from one of the rooms and without entering, he knew it was her.

Duncan paused for a moment at the door, took a deep breath and then entered. There were two members of staff standing to either side of his mum's bed, and she was lying on it, her head thrashing from left to right, clearly upset. The staff were trying to keep her in the bed and to calm her down. They were not physical with her, but it was clear to him that she felt trapped. Grace was standing beside the bed too, having not heard him enter, she had her back to him.

"He's hurt, you don't understand!" he heard his mum say. She looked between the staff either side of her bed, imploring them. "Please, you must help me find Duncan!"

"Mum, I'm here," Duncan said, forcing a smile. His mum focused on him, Grace turning at the sound of his voice. Duncan could see she'd been crying. "It's okay, Mum," he said, holding his hands out before him as she stared at him warily. "I'm here. I'm safe. Everything is okay." He slowly walked to the bed, his mum's eyes never leaving him. He perched on the edge of the bed, sitting beside her and he reached out, taking her hand in his, closing his palms around it. "I'm here."

His mum's eyes glazed over, tears spilling onto her cheeks and he edged closer, pulling her gently towards him. She put her head on his shoulder, and he embraced her gently. She didn't speak but she continued to weep.

"It's okay, Mum. I'm here."

"I was so worried about you, Duncan," she whispered to him. "They don't see. None of them see what has happened to you." He withdrew from the embrace but only enough to allow him to make eye contact with her. He smiled and she returned it with a weak one of her own. "They don't know," she said.

"It's okay, Mum. I know," he said, tightening his grip in a supportive manner on her arms. "And it's okay. I'm safe—"

"No," she said leaning away from him and shaking off his touch, her smile dissipating. "I'm not safe." She looked around the room at the three members of staff and then at Grace, although a hint of a smile formed when she looked at her. "I'm not safe, not here."

"You are," Duncan said. "We both are, Mum."

She shook her head, almost snarling as she pulled her hands away from him, shaking off his touch. "No, you're not. You just haven't realised yet."

"Mum—"

She snatched at his hands, grasping them so tightly that he was caught by surprise. She dug her fingernails into his skin, and Duncan felt sharp pain. "You must leave!" she hissed.

"Mum... I'm okay—"

"Leave now. Before it's too late," she said, through clenched teeth. "Take the children… and leave. They won't let me go." She lowered her voice to barely above a whisper. "I've tried… but they insist on keeping me here."

Duncan gently closed his eyes, ignoring the fact she was still clutching his hands and he could feel she'd broken the skin in several places. He didn't want to take his hands away though. She was having an episode, a moment where she thought everyone was against her. Everyone aside from him and, he suspected, Grace at any rate. He didn't know what to say. She couldn't leave. This was the best place for her. She was safe here, but it was galling for him that she felt threatened.

"I'm here, Mum." He shook his head. "I promise, no one is going to hurt you while I'm here." Her expression softened and she seemed relieved. It was fleeting though. It was like a shadow passing across her expression, disassociating her from the person he recognised.

"And who will keep you safe, Duncan?" she said before she drifted away from him again. Her shoulders sagged and she looked worn out after all of the exertion. "I want to sleep."

Duncan supported her head and upper body, awkwardly helping her to lie down. Grace drew a blanket over her and Duncan tucked it below her chin. His mum's eyes were still open as she rolled onto her side, staring at a blank wall. Moments later, she closed her eyes and it was like none of this had happened.

"I love you, Mum," Duncan said. She didn't reply, and he wondered if she was already asleep. The two staff members who had been either side of her retreated from the room, acknowledging Duncan as they left. The nurse who'd accompanied him remained. He looked at her and nodded. "I'll make sure she's settled and then I'll come and speak to you."

The nurse left and now it was only the three of them. Grace came and put a supportive hand on Duncan's shoulder.

"You are so good with her, you know?" she said. Duncan scoffed slightly. "No, you are. I mean it. Those nurses," Grace said, looking towards the door, "try their best and they're trained professionals, but you… you were here two minutes, and you'd calmed her down." She squeezed her hand on his shoulder. He was still watching his mum, checking her breathing which was shallow but steady. He was confident she was asleep. "I don't know how you do it."

"Neither do I," he said. "It's like – it's awful to say it – but it's like having a toddler, and you have to find a way to navigate their emotions because they can't regulate them themselves." He looked up at Grace. "She doesn't know how to express herself without going over the top when she's hurt, scared or in pain." He shook his head. "She doesn't know what to do and so her fear and confusion escapes in these outbursts."

He slowly got up from the bed, ensuring that the shift of his weight didn't jostle his mum and wake her. Grace slipped an arm around his waist and he pulled her to him. "I still think you're amazing," she said.

He smiled. "The really sad thing is that this is the best she's probably ever going to be. I don't think it's going to get any better, and it'll only get worse from here on in."

"Maybe not, you don't know," she said, but it didn't sound like she believed it herself, but it was a good attempt at offering him some hope.

"Let's hope so," he said.

The door opened and a flustered Roslyn hurried in, her eyes scanning the room in search of her mother, beginning at the window. She saw Duncan and then looked past him at their sleeping mother. She rushed to the bedside and tentatively reached out, but withdrawing her hand at the last moment so as not to wake her.

"Is she..."

"She's okay," Duncan said. "Don't worry."

"I-I... left my phone at the house," Ros said, glancing at

Duncan. "I'm sorry. I didn't get the messages until I got home from… I'm sorry."

Duncan wasn't sure who she was apologising to: him, Grace or their mother. She had no need to do so. Roslyn had carried the weight of their mother's care for years without his support. He was comfortable with sharing more of the load. Not that it wasn't lost on him that Grace had been the one to step up on this occasion.

"Don't worry," Duncan said. "I got here as soon as I could, and Grace came across as well. She was here well before me."

Roslyn looked at Grace, offering her a grateful smile. "Thanks, Grace. I'm sorry you had to be here."

"That's okay. I was happy to help," she said. "Although, I didn't really do anything." Ros came over to her and embraced her with a firm hug.

"You got here before either of us and you looked out for our mum. It matters," Ros said, with a firm grasp on Grace's upper arms.

"Okay," Grace said, smiling nervously.

"I mean it. Thank you."

"Agreed," Duncan said and when Ros let go of her, Duncan put his arm around Grace again. "Thank you," he said, kissing her cheek. Grace seemed embarrassed under the weight of the praise, but Duncan smiled at her and she eventually broke into a smile of her own.

"If you'll excuse me," Grace said. "I'll just nip to the ladies… I need to get out of this superhero costume."

Duncan grinned and Ros also smiled. Grace left the room and Duncan put an arm around his sister. They walked over to the window, looking out over the garden.

"She's getting worse, isn't she?" Roslyn said.

"Yes, I think so." He sighed. "She was worrying about me… or, I thought she was. She thought I was Dad again."

Roslyn smiled but she was glassy eyed. "You do look a lot like him you know."

"Are you trying to make me cry as well?" he asked. She gave him a playful thump in the arm with her closed fist.

"What sparked it all off?" Ros asked. "Do you know?"

Grace re-entered the room, looking between them apologetically. "Sorry, did I come in at a bad time?"

"No, you're all right, love," Ros said. "I was just asking Duncan what set mum off today?"

"She was in the communal room with everyone else," Grace said. "Then Lord Huxley came in, presumably with his little entourage that they pay extra for," Grace said, speaking conspiratorially from behind her hand, "and then it all went off apparently."

"Really?" Duncan asked. "The nurse I came up with didn't mention any of that."

"Oh aye," Grace said, "but that's one of the many benefits you get from dating me. Everyone who works here – under the age of forty anyway –drinks at the bar I work in. They tell bar staff things they'd never say in front of anyone else." She looked nervously between them. "But do me a favour and don't quote me okay?"

Duncan shook his head. "No problem. What is it about Huxley and his lot she hates so much?"

"Who knows?" Grace asked. "It could be anything, couldn't it?"

"What was she worried about?" Roslyn asked.

Duncan thought back to the moment he entered the room. "She said I should take the children – meaning you and me, presumably – and I should go somewhere safe."

"Somewhere safe?"

"Aye, she said I wasn't safe here." He frowned. "Well, not me… Dad, you know?"

"She said he wasn't safe."

"Aye, but it's all nonsense. You know what she's like when she goes off on one," Duncan said, lowering his voice for fear of being told off for saying such things about his mum in front of her like he had done before earning himself a roasting from his sister for the effort. Roslyn eased herself away from him. She moved closer to the window, her arms folded across her chest, staring out beyond the well-manicured gardens and across Loch Portree. Duncan moved to join her. Several boats were at anchor in the water, one was lit up, gently bobbing on the swell.

"I…. I see," Ros said.

"Ros?" he asked, sensing reticence in her tone. She glanced nervously at him.

"It's just nonsense," she said, forcing a smile. "Like you said, she does say this kind of thing. She doesn't know what she's saying half of the time." Roslyn sighed, dismissively shaking her head. "It's all too frequent these days, don't you think?"

Roslyn looked back out of the window, absently wringing her hands before her. Duncan glanced at Grace whose lips were pursed. It wasn't just him. Grace had picked up on it too, whatever *it* was. Duncan's mobile beeped and he stepped away from Ros, moving to stand beside Grace before taking it out of his pocket. His gaze shifted back to his sister, who seemed minded to be alone at the window. She seemed distracted, pained even, and even though he knew their mum's condition weighed heavily upon her, Duncan couldn't help but think there was something else behind her demeanour. He glanced at his mobile. It was a message from Alistair. He read it and then dialled his mobile.

"Alistair," he said. "No, I want to come with you to speak to Fraser McEwan."

"Is everything all right there?" Alistair asked.

Duncan looked at his sister again, and then glanced at their mum, still sleeping soundly in her bed. "Aye, everything's grand. Wait for me. I'll not be long."

"Right you are," Alistair said, hanging up.

Duncan put his mobile away, looking at Grace. "Any chance you can drop me back at the station?"

"Of course," she said. He nodded his thanks, then looked at his sister.

"Ros?"

She seemed not to hear him and then snapped out of it, turning to look at him. "Sorry, what was that you said?"

"I have to go back to work," he said.

"Okay," she replied. There was no judgement or accusation aimed at him for leaving.

"You'll be all right?" he asked. She nodded but said nothing. Duncan went over to her, placing his hand on the small of her back. "Are you sure?"

"Yes. I'm sure," she said quietly. She looked over at their mum and smiled at Duncan. "I'm sure, honestly. It's fine. I'll stay for a while just to make sure she's okay."

"Right," Duncan said. "If there's any change then—"

"I'll call you. I promise," she said when he shot her a questioning look. "I will."

He leaned in and kissed her cheek, then he crossed to their mother, and he did the same. She stirred but did not wake. Grace was waiting for him at the door and she waved to Ros before leaving. In the corridor, Duncan collided with a man who was walking along, eyes down, checking his mobile. He was so distracted that he didn't see either of them leave the room until it was too late. His mobile fell from his grasp as he bumped into Duncan, sending it clattering onto the polished surface of the floor.

"Damn it!" he said, stooping to gather it up.

"Sorry," Duncan said reflexively, but he didn't feel at fault.

"Watch where you're going, would you," the man said, glaring at Duncan and making to leave.

"Aye… I will if you will," Duncan said hotly. The man hesitated, stared at Duncan and then he glanced at Grace, nodding almost imperceptibly at her, before moving away. "What an arse," Duncan said.

"Soon to be Lord Arse of the Islands," Grace said, "if his father dies anytime soon."

Duncan looked at her, then at the back of the man now reaching the end of the corridor. He glanced back at them before entering the last room and disappearing from view. "Was that...?"

"George Huxley," Grace said. "Aye."

"You're not telling me he drinks at your bar too?"

She laughed. "Hell no. He'd not be seen dead in my place… but I read the papers, and the gossip magazines. He's quite the eligible bachelor around these parts."

Duncan stared at the space where George Huxley had been. For a second, he contemplated going down there and trying to strike up a conversation around his recent investment into Iain Lambert's business but quickly dismissed it. This wasn't the time, or the place and he knew he'd have to tread carefully around someone like Huxley. It would be better to speak to a sober Iain Lambert first. He put an arm around Grace's shoulder, steering her towards the stairs. He leaned into her. "Do I have to watch my back?"

"You should always be on your toes, Duncan. You never know who you might bump into."

"Then I'm pleased to have been here," Duncan said, playfully pulling her into his embrace as they reached the stairs, "so I could knock his mobile out of his hands, thereby distracting him so he doesn't realise the opportunity of his lifetime is in front of him and doesn't derail our beautiful relationship."

"You think I'm the opportunity of his lifetime?" Grace asked, smiling broadly, pushing her shoulder into Duncan's chest.

"Who was talking about you?" Duncan replied. "I meant me."

CHAPTER TWENTY-THREE

THEY REACHED the lobby at the foot of the stairs and Grace took Duncan's arm, stopping him. She looked around to make sure they wouldn't be overheard by anyone nearby. He cocked his head, sensing she was nervous about something.

"What is it?" he asked.

"Roslyn," Grace said, glancing to the stairs as if she could see up to the room where Ros was still with Duncan's mother. "What did you make of her reaction?"

"So it wasn't just me who noticed then?"

She shook her head. "It was… odd, don't you think?"

Duncan couldn't argue. "Aye, that's what I thought too. But… it's my family and so… you know?"

"You're all a bit odd?" Grace said and Duncan tilted his head to one side. "Although that is true, her reaction was a bit weird. I'm sorry. I'm not trying to be mean about your sister—"

"No, I get it," Duncan said. "The thing is, where Roslyn and our mum are concerned, they have this," he frowned, struggling to choose the right word, "symbiotic kind of a relationship. They know things about one another that… I just have never been a party to."

"Why is that?"

Duncan sighed heavily. "My fault, primarily." He shrugged. "I'm not exactly the most emotionally available of people."

Grace smiled, taking his hand in hers and patting it gently. "I'm so pleased you're reading that self-help book I got you for your birthday. You're really growing."

Duncan laughed. He was well aware she'd bought him that particular book purely as a wind-up, never expecting him to read it. "Well, I'm on a mission of self-improvement."

"It's amazing," she said, looping her arm through his and they set off again.

"What is?"

"The progress you've made through that book, despite it never leaving the shelf from where you left it having read the back cover."

"I've picked it up once or twice," Duncan countered. "The spine is really thick, and I can lean my mobile up against it when I'm streaming something."

"Aye, that's about right," she said, laughing.

"DI McAdam?" They both stopped, turning to see who was calling him. It was Katie, the journalist from the local paper. She got up from a seat on the far side of the lobby, struggling to slip the strap of her bag over her shoulder as she hurried over to them. "You're back again?"

"And you're still here?" Duncan asked. Grace glanced sideways at him. "This is Katie," he explained. "She works for the local paper."

"Sorry to trouble you, Detective Inspector," Katie said, coming to stand before him and adjusting her jacket which was now snagged on the strap of her bag. "Could I have a quick word?"

"Well, I was just off back to the station—"

"Please. It won't take a moment," she said hopefully. Grace patted Duncan's arm.

"I have to go and get the car anyway. I'll see you out front in five minutes?"

He nodded and Grace smiled at Katie, excusing herself and leaving them. Katie looked around, Duncan pointing to a couple of chairs to the right of the entrance, nestled beneath a large potted tree of some kind that he didn't recognise.

"Sure," she said cheerfully, and the two of them sat down.

"What can I do for you?" Duncan asked her.

"Well… I'm here to see Lord Huxley."

"Again?"

"Still," she said, wincing. "I had an appointment scheduled with him. Have you any idea how far in advance you have to book these things?"

"Someone mentioned it, aye," Duncan said, Alistair coming to mind. "He agreed to see you here?"

"Oh no, not here," Katie said, lowering her voice. There was no one within earshot. "I was supposed to see him late last week but then… they just cancelled on me. By email too, not even a phone call."

"That must be frustrating," Duncan said.

"Worse than that. I think I told you my editor sent me on this one—"

"You did, I think."

"He's unhappy that it looks like I've blown it. Luckily for me, this whole Bruce Dunmore thing has distracted him—"

"Less lucky for the man himself, though," Duncan said, taking a deep breath.

She grimaced. "That sounded bad, didn't it? It's not how I meant it."

"That's okay. What… er… would you like from me?"

"I don't know, not really," she said, but she seemed rather coy. She looked around again. "I was just wondering, if you'd heard anything?"

He leaned in towards her, lowering his voice to a conspiratorial whisper. She leaned closer expectantly. "About what?" She sat back and exhaled. Duncan smiled and then felt a guilty pang. "I'm sorry."

"That's okay," she said, despondent. "I'm not expecting you to give away any secrets." She slumped in her chair and exhaled. "You know, I always thought I'd love to be working as a journalist. When I was at school, I loved writing and keeping up with current affairs. As it turns out, it's just a lot of sitting around… even when you think you have a story to tell it can just evaporate before you like steam in the air. My editor doesn't want me looking into investigative things. I get all the fluff pieces. It's a bit dull."

Duncan felt for her. The timing struck him as being a little off though. "When did you say you agreed this interview?"

"It was supposed to happen last week, but we'd agreed it last month," she said. "I'd made multiple phone calls. They changed the dates on more than one occasion, too, and then they pulled the plug on it."

"And you're here to… what… try and ambush him in the corridor?"

She shook her head. "I've been trying to get close to one of the family, to see if we can do something else instead… a tour of the family home, a history of their business enterprise… something."

"To keep your editor off your back?"

"Something like that, yes. I'd like to have something to show for all this effort."

"Have you tried," Duncan said, glancing at his watch, "using the phone or sending an email?" He didn't mean to make her feel foolish but sitting around Lord Huxley's care home wasn't likely to yield positive results.

"Of course I have. They aren't responding to me," she said, exasperated. "This is my last shot at it. I don't understand, I really don't. It's like there's been some sort of an EMP or something. Total digital silence."

"An EM… what?"

"An EMP, an electro-magnetic pulse… and it's knocked out all their communication and electronic devices."

"Right," Duncan said, imagining the horror of such an event occurring.

"I'm starting to take it personally."

Duncan smiled warmly. "Stick at it. Perseverance can get you a long way."

"Thanks," she said. Duncan checked his watch again. He wanted to get going. "I'd been working on this for months and now… he's too ill and I can't even get a statement from him or his family. I'm a hair's breadth away from being hammered by my editor for this. They've played it so close to their chest. No one knew." She was talking to herself now, Duncan thought. "So… how could I know! I'm being blasted for this, and it really isn't my fault. You know what I mean?"

"I do, aye. Listen… I have to go." He stood up, taking the opportunity to leave before she started talking again. "I'm sorry I couldn't be of more help."

"DI McAdam?" she said, and he stopped, looking down on her. She stood up and rummaged through her bag before passing him a business card with her mobile number on it.

Duncan glanced at it in his hand. "If you happen to – I don't know – come across something that *maybe* I could run a story about, would you mind letting me know? Not that I expect you to break the law or anything. Just… well, I'm not great at building contacts and… you know?"

Duncan smiled. He had no intention of doing so but he accepted the card and tucked it away in his pocket. "No promises," he said, "but if something comes up then I'll think of you."

She blushed. "Thank you."

Duncan turned and headed outside. The threat of rain was in the air, he could feel it, but mercifully it was still dry. Grace was waiting for him, and he got into the passenger seat.

"What was all that about?"

"Just someone looking for a bit of help," Duncan said.

"And could you help her?"

"Nope," he replied, putting on his seatbelt. Grace pulled away. "It's a strange one though."

"What is?"

"Ah, it's probably nothing."

"When you get that feeling it never turns out to be nothing," Grace said. Duncan laughed.

"Aye, usually."

The remainder of the short drive up into the centre of Portree was made in silence. Duncan was preoccupied. The conversation with Katie was playing on his mind, but he couldn't decide why that was. It had nothing to do with him, and it wasn't as if he was concerned with her career prospects. She seemed a pleasant enough person, but there was something about what she'd said that was interesting to him.

Duncan knew from personal experience, witnessing the deterioration of his mother's health, that dementia seldom manifested out of the blue. It was a gradual process, quicker in some than in others but, nonetheless, it took place over a period of time. The Huxley family, or those who represented them, must have known about his condition. To agree to an interview, arranging it for a week prior to his admission to the home struck him as odd.

Grace pulled up at Somerled Square in front of the police station and he pushed thoughts of the Huxleys to one side. Who was he to pass judgement on how the family went about their business? Perhaps Lord Huxley had deteriorated in recent weeks, and they hadn't realised how bad it was. Perhaps the family were in denial about the nature of his decline. After all, you never really know how you'll react until you find yourself in a particular set of circumstances yourself.

He leaned over and kissed Grace on the cheek. "Thanks for the lift."

"Will you be home for dinner?" she asked.

"Probably," he said. "But I've no idea what time."

"Give me a phone when you're done, and I'll come and get you."

He nodded and got out. Poking his head back into the cabin, he smiled at her. "Thanks for looking out for my mum."

"I didn't really do anything, Dunc, but you're welcome."

"You were there," he said. "And I appreciate it." She smiled, then blew him a kiss. Duncan closed the door, and she pulled off. He waved to her and then made his way into the station.

CHAPTER TWENTY-FOUR

"WHAT DO we know about this guy?" Duncan asked Alistair who was driving them towards Brogaig, a small village a little way north of Staffin on the Trotternish peninsula. Alistair turned off the main coast road and onto a narrow single-track road, pitted and uneven, headed towards the water's edge. The houses dotted to the left and right were situated in an elevated position, all looking down towards Staffin Bay. In the failing light, Duncan could see the island off the coast opposite An Corran Beach where Bruce Dunmore's body was found.

"He's an interesting character," Alistair said. "He's never been in trouble with the law, but our uniformed colleagues have made his acquaintance on occasion."

"In what capacity?" Duncan asked, turning his gaze away from the sweeping panorama before them.

"He was sectioned back in 2002 after a suicide attempt," Alistair said. "His partner reported him for a physical assault the previous week and he was out on bail at the time. She withdrew her statement though. They had a frenetic, somewhat combustible relationship it seemed, and from what I read in the report, no one was really sure whether the complaint was genuine or six of one and half a dozen of the other. There was certainly no supporting evidence to the claim other than a few scratches and bruises."

"That should be enough," Duncan said.

"The injuries were on him, not her."

"Ah… right. Is there anything more recent?"

"There's another domestic violence incident on file, only this time it took place five years ago," Alistair said, pulling to the side of the road in a passing place to allow another car to pass coming from the other direction. The driver waved and Alistair acknowledged the gesture with one of his own. "It was Ronnie who dealt with it. I asked him and he remembered the call out. A neighbour called it in - a couple arguing – and Ronnie attended, speaking to them."

"Fraser and his wife?"

"Aye," Alistair said. "In Ronnie's opinion it was alcohol fuelled, and it all seemed calm enough when he got there. Both husband and wife denied there was any need for police involvement and Ronnie said he gave Fraser a stiff talking to and left it at that."

"Nothing since?"

"No, nothing on file."

"What did Ronnie make of him? Did he say?"

"He couldn't remember much about it, to be fair," Alistair said. "He described him as a wispy sort of fellow, anxious, with a ratty face."

Duncan shook his head. "Did he put that in his report?"

"Knowing Ronnie, I'd say so, aye."

Alistair slowed his pick-up, looking for the right house. He pointed towards it and they drove over a cattle grid at the entrance to Fraser McEwan's croft house. It was painted white, two dormer windows looking out across the water and the garden – such as it was – sloped away from the house. A plume of smoke drifted from the chimney before being dispersed by the breeze. A solitary light was on inside the house.

They approached the door and before they could knock, a dog began barking from inside. Duncan looked to the left to see a border terrier clamber up onto the window sill, staring out at them, its tail wagging furiously as it observed the newcomers. Duncan rang the bell.

A light came on in the porch above them, the front door unlocking a moment later. The door opened and Fraser McEwan peered out at them, his features illuminated by the light above Duncan's head. He could see that Ronnie MacDonald's description was befitting of the man before him. His hair was thinning, shot through with grey, and his thin, almost gaunt appearance made him look older than his sixty years. He had several days of stubble growth, and he scratched at his chin, causing a rasping sound, as he eyed them warily.

"I'm DI McAdam—"

"Aye," Fraser said, casting a wary eye over him. "I remember you from the other day." He craned his neck to look past Duncan at Alistair.

"This is Detective Sergeant MacEachran," Duncan said. McEwan stood in the doorway, nervously shifting his weight between his feet. "May we speak to you, Mr McEwan."

"Aye, come in," he said, but he did so begrudgingly. The terrier appeared at his feet and Fraser McEwan tried in vain to shoo him back inside and away from the visitors, but the dog bypassed him easily and set about smelling the arrivals. Alistair dropped to his haunches and the dog recoiled momentarily before making a judgement on Alistair's character and returning to accept a gentle petting. McEwan whistled and the dog turned and hastened back inside, seemingly happy to have made their acquaintance. "Make sure you close that behind you, it's hard enough staying warm as it is without the door being left open."

Alistair did as they were bid, ensuring the door was closed. McEwan had already returned to the living room, Duncan hurrying to catch up with him. An open fire flickered in the hearth and the smell of burning peat permeated the room. McEwan sat down in a tatty old leather chair beside the fire, gesturing for them to take any of the available seats. Duncan sat down on a sofa but Alistair remained standing. A folded newspaper lay on a small table beside their host, a pair of reading glasses lay on top of it, and a glass tumbler beside it on a coaster. The dog settled on the rug by his feet.

"Is it just you here tonight, Mr McEwan?" Duncan asked.

"It's only the two of us," McEwan said, looking down at the dog, who lifted his head, ears pricked. "The same as it is every night."

"There's no Mrs McEwan then?" Alistair asked.

"N-Not any more… no."

Alistair nodded. "The peace and quiet must be nice."

"What can I do for you, Detective McAdam?" he asked, ignoring Alistair's comment.

"I wanted to ask you about your time at St Benedict's."

McEwan's expression changed, his lips parted slightly as his eyes flitted between Duncan and Alistair. "My time… um…" he swallowed hard.

"At the boys' home, St Benedict's," Duncan repeated. "You

stayed there for… what, four years was it?" he asked, checking with a quick glance at Alistair who nodded.

"I thought you'd be asking about the dead man."

"We are, in a roundabout sort of way, Mr McEwan," Duncan said. "May I call you Fraser?" He wanted to be less formal, have McEwan relax in the conversation rather than be on his guard.

"Yes… of course." His forehead creased and he looked at his hands in his lap. "Aye, I did stay there for a time," McEwan said, gathering himself. "Was it four years? I-I'd forgotten. I remember it being less than that."

"How do you recall your time there?"

"At St Benedict's?" McEwan said, arching his eyebrows and lifting his head, his eyes searching the room but settling on nothing in particular. "It was okay, I guess. Some days were better than others but I had a roof over my head, so you can't grumble too much can you?"

"Why were you there?" Duncan asked.

He shrugged. "My mother got ill and my father was working. He found it hard, and so it kinda made sense for everyone if I stayed at St Benedict's. It was good for my parents."

"How about you?"

He shrugged again. "Okay, I guess."

"So you knew him, Bruce Dunmore, I mean?"

"Ah… yes, I knew him. He was… er… one of the staffers at the time, aye."

"You knew him well?"

"Not very, no. I was a wee lad at that time, and there were five or six of us there." He chuckled. "Tearaways, one and all. We gave the staff a bit of a hard time I can tell you."

"Have you had any contact with him since you left St Benedict's? When he returned to the islands perhaps?"

"No," he said, splaying his hands wide. "I haven't. I... er... didn't even know he was back. Not that I would have given it much thought anyway." He absently scratched at his chin, before cupping his hands in his lap again. "Why... why do you ask?"

Duncan smiled. "We're just trying to build a picture of his recent life here on the island as well as his past. Where he went, who he spent time with... what he was doing in and around Staffin that night."

"Which night?"

"The night he died, Fraser."

"Oh, right aye," McEwan said, nodding, his lips pursed. "I was under the impression his body had been left there, on the beach, I mean."

"It was," Duncan said, "but we don't know why. It turns out he was up this way the night before."

"Was he, aye?"

"Any idea why that might have been?" Alistair asked. McEwan's head snapped around and he looked up at him. "Maybe he was meeting someone. Perhaps you?"

"N-No, I didn't. Why would I?" He looked from Alistair to Duncan, his lips parting into a nervous smile. It was artificial. "Why would he be meeting me? I have nothing in common with him, eh. I reckon he'd barely remember me anyway. It was all a lifetime ago."

"Speaking of St Benedict's," Duncan said. "Do you recall an allegation being made to the police?"

"An allegation?" McEwan shook his head. "I don't think so, no."

"Two boys at St Benedict's contacted the police regarding their treatment at the home—"

"No, no, I wouldn't know anything about that," he said, shaking his head forcibly.

"You're sure?" Duncan asked. "Because the police came out to investigate… and later on the boys retracted their allegation. Is this ringing any bells with you?"

"No, no," McEwan said, still looking down at his hands, clasped together in his lap. "Nothing like that at all, no. I would remember."

"You'd think so, aye," Alistair said. "What about rumours?"

"Rumours? Rumours about what?"

"Past residents and their experiences," Duncan said. "There's always gossip. Everyone has a story to tell about their parents, a rogue teacher or someone who did bad things, right?" Duncan looked at Alistair. "Everyone knows someone."

"Aye," Alistair said. "We had a teacher at my school who we knew used to eye up the girls. He must have had a thing for girls in uniform, I reckon. We used to call him—"

"You get the idea," Duncan said, cutting Alistair off.

"No, not me," McEwan said, shaking his head. "Sorry, not me." He laughed nervously. "Nothing like that." He got up from his chair, gathered his glass, and crossed to a sideboard. Opening the door, he reached for a half-empty bottle of scotch. Almost as an afterthought, he turned to them. "Can I offer either of you a drink?"

"No thank you," Duncan said, "but don't mind us." McEwan took out the stopper and poured himself a large measure. Duncan noted his hand shook almost imperceptibly as he did so, but if he hadn't been paying attention then he may have missed it. McEwan returned to his seat, taking a sip from the glass as soon as he sat down.

"You're sure you don't recall any of these events?" Duncan asked.

McEwan looked thoughtful, then shook his head. "No, sorry. I wish I could help, I really do... but it was all such a long time ago."

"That's okay, Fraser," Duncan said. "We appreciate your time." He stood up and both he and Alistair turned to leave. The dog sat up, watching his owner as he also got up to see them out. "Oh, one thing, Fraser. Do you have a mobile number that we could contact you on?"

"Um…"

"Just in case," Duncan said.

"Of course," McEwan said. Duncan took out his own mobile and opened his contacts, looking expectantly at McEwan. He read out his number and Duncan typed it into his phone. He then rang the number to check it was accurate. McEwan's mobile sounded, coming from the kitchen. Duncan smiled. "Thanks very much."

They walked to the front door and were ushered out quickly. The door was closed on them as soon as they were clear and Fraser McEwan disappeared back inside.

Alistair stopped as they walked to his pick-up, and he looked back at the house. The dog was once again at the window, watching them.

"He's lying," Alistair said, jabbing his key fob in the air towards the house.

"Aye," Duncan said. "But what about, and why?" Duncan took out his mobile and phoned the ops room. It was Russell McLean who picked up. "Russell, I'm going to send you a mobile number. Cross reference it with the mobile records we got for Bruce Dunmore and see if they've been talking."

"Will do, sir." Duncan was about to hang up but Russell

stopped him. "Oh, sir… the custody sergeant has been on the phone."

"Has Iain Lambert sobered up?"

"They let him go, sir."

"They did what? When?"

"About three quarters of an hour ago, sir."

"Why?"

"The custody sergeant said it wasn't his call."

"Then whose call was it?"

"Didn't say, sir. Sorry."

Duncan balled a fist and wanted to punch the roof of the car. He caught himself in time, cursing silently to himself. "I want him found, Russell. I don't care how—"

"We've been told we can't do that, sir."

"Who the hell said that?"

"A memo came down from above not ten minutes ago," Russell said, "addressed to everyone in the investigative team. We're to *cease any and all harassment* of people or businesses linked to the Huxley estate, sir. Unless we receive prior approval from a senior officer."

Duncan felt his anger growing. Alistair was looking at him with an inquisitive expression.

"Aye, well," Duncan said through gritted teeth, "we'll see about that." He hung up and thrust his mobile into his pocket. Looking at Alistair, he shook his head. "Do you ever have the feeling that everyone else around you knows exactly what's going on?"

"Everyone except you?" Alistair asked. Duncan nodded. "Aye, of course I do. I have a wife and kids." He winked at Duncan, opening his door. "I'm the last one to know what's going on in my house." He hesitated before getting in, looking across at Duncan. "It's frustrating when someone keeps you in the dark, isn't it?"

Duncan met Alistair's gaze for a moment, reading something unsaid in his expression. "And what do you mean by that?" he asked. Alistair snorted with derision, shook his head and got in. Duncan did likewise. Whatever he'd meant by the comment, Alistair didn't elaborate further and they drove away from Fraser McEwan's house in silence.

CHAPTER TWENTY-FIVE

THEY LEFT BROGAIG BEHIND, Alistair turning left onto the main road towards Staffin. Duncan looked across at his detective sergeant. He could see he was ruminating on something.

"Come on, Alistair," Duncan said. "Whatever it is, spit it out."

"It's nothing."

"It's not like you to be shy and retiring," Duncan said. "If you have something to say, then say it."

Alistair drummed his fingers on the steering wheel, obviously contemplating what to say next. He glanced sideways at Duncan, inclining his head before dismissively shaking it. "Forget it. You'll tell me when you want to."

Duncan scoffed but before he could respond his mobile rang. He answered it without looking at the screen, his eyes still focused on Alistair. "McAdam," he said flatly.

"Sir, it's Angus. I've just heard a call go out over the radio regarding a distressed man up at Lealt Falls. Uniform are on their way—"

Duncan looked forward, checking where they were. "We're a little way north but headed that way," he said.

"The thing is… the man's description matches Iain Lambert," Angus said. "After we heard he'd left the station, I thought I'd try and find out who he was in contact with because I figured you'd want to know. I checked the CCTV cameras on the front of the station and Iain was met at the door, getting into a car as soon as he stepped out of the foyer."

"Who picked him up?"

"That I can't say. The car was facing away from the camera and never got to see the driver, but Lambert definitely got into it whoever was at the wheel."

"Did you get the registration number?"

"Aye. It's a car registered to the Huxley estate."

"Is it now?" Duncan said, tongue firmly in his cheek.

"Is it too much of a coincidence that it could be Iain Lambert?" Angus asked. "He didn't look overly stressed on the footage I watched when he was leaving the station. I checked with the staff of the custody suite and they said he was quiet, and probably still under the influence as well."

Duncan covered the microphone of his mobile with his hand. "Alistair, pull in at the Lealt Falls viewpoint, will you?" Alistair nodded and Duncan went back to Angus. "What else did you find out?"

"Only that once he'd had a nap, he asked to make a phone call. The custody sergeant approved it."

"Who did he call?"

"We don't know, sir, but shortly after making the call the custody sergeant was instructed to release him."

Duncan realised that was how it came to pass that the Huxleys were off limits. "Okay, good work, Angus. What is the estimated time of arrival for uniform at the falls?"

"On their way now, sir. Ten minutes, perhaps less."

"We'll be there before that."

Alistair picked up the radio he kept in the side pocket of his door. He depressed the call button. "DS MacEachran to control. Myself and DI McAdam attending at Lealt Falls."

"Confirmed," a disembodied voice crackled through the receiver. Alistair put the radio down, looking across at Duncan.

"This could get interesting," he said quietly.

They came upon the turn-off into the car park for the Lealt Falls viewpoint. The landmark was not only a spectacular local stretch of landscape but the route of the river over the falls cut a path through a gorge down to the coast. In days past it had been a busy stretch of shoreline when there were few roads and everything was transported around the island by sea. Scores of local workers were employed either in the salmon fishing industry or in processing diatomite, a white clay that was dug out of the ground around Loch Cuithir, some four miles inland. Now though, tourists flocked to the viewpoint to overlook the waterfall and to see the ruins of the buildings the workers used to frequent.

Alistair parked the pick-up and they got out. On a dry, summer day, the car park would be rammed with barely a space available throughout the day, but there were only a handful of vehicles present. Rain was falling again, the intermittent rainfall of a typical Highland day continued unabated. Beyond the viewpoint there were walking trails that wound their way down to the shoreline. At points they were narrow, unprotected by fencing, and could be treacherous in wet and windy conditions. The only person they could see was the operator of a mobile coffee cart which had become a semi-permanent pitch of late.

Duncan approached, taking out his warrant card and showing it to the man behind the counter. "Someone called in about a distressed man?" He pointed through the nearby gate to Duncan's right.

"I tried speaking to him, but I thought I was only making things worse, and so I thought I'd better come back here and wait for the police."

"My uniformed colleagues are on their way," Duncan said. "Did he say anything to you?"

The man shook his head. "He was completely unresponsive. There's a guy standing nearby, but he didn't have any joy with him either."

"What makes you think he's thinking of doing himself harm?"

"You'll see."

Duncan joined Alistair at the gate and together they made their way along the path. The viewpoint itself was a wooden platform structure, its supports anchored into the slope of the hillside allowing the platform to extend out into the gorge, offering an unparalleled view of the waterfall. Today, the platform was deserted. They made their way along the path, little more than a dirt track and barely a foot wide. The path tracked the line of the gorge which widened as it approached the sea and they could hear the waves breaking upon the rocky shore far below them.

Where the path curved briefly inland, away from the steep, rocky outcrop they came across a man dressed for the elements. He held a walking pole in one hand, his puffer coat fastened up to his chin and a hood pulled up over his head. He didn't hear their approach and Duncan startled him when he came alongside. He looked at Duncan and then Alistair, hope in his eyes.

"Are you here for him?"

Duncan nodded and looked down the slope to where the man had been staring when they approached. They could make out the top half of a figure below them, standing close to the edge. The route of the path cut inward at this point because the ground was showing signs of slipping into the gorge, and landslips grew increasingly likely following heavy rainfall. Signs were posted at close intervals warning of the danger of standing too close to the edge.

Duncan could see it was indeed Iain Lambert standing barely thirty yards away from them, facing away from them. "Have you tried speaking to him?" Duncan asked.

"I did… but he completely ignored me. I think he's going to jump."

Duncan nodded to Alistair and the two of them stepped away from the path and began to descend to where Lambert stood. The grass underfoot was damp and the surface uneven, so they had to be careful where they placed their feet. The going was tricky and one misstep could spell disaster. The hill-side sloped away from them before disappearing into the gorge. Duncan figured the drop was easily eighty to a hundred feet onto the gnarled basalt rocks below. The water flowing over the falls would not be deep enough to break anyone's fall. To go over the edge would result in almost certain death.

The rain was falling steadily but it wasn't hard, falling in a misty drizzle that seeped through everything after a period of exposure to it. Duncan ran his hand through his hair as he came to stand as close as he dared to Iain Lambert, roughly six feet from him.

"Fancy meeting you here," he said cheerfully, blinking the water from his eyes. Alistair had taken up a position on the other side of Lambert, away from Duncan, but he was no closer and Duncan hoped he wouldn't try to forcibly intervene. He had visions of seeing Lambert pitch over the lip, taking Alistair with him and Duncan had no desire to watch them plummet to their deaths. Iain Lambert seemed not to hear him, and Duncan was about to repeat himself but Lambert slowly turned his face towards him.

"You shouldnae have come, Duncan," he said, raising his voice to be heard over the roar of the water falling nearby, thundering down onto the rocks below them.

"Unfortunately," Duncan said, "it's my job." He took a step nearer to the edge and peered down into the gorge. The view made him nauseous, and he wished he hadn't looked. "We also didn't get to have that conversation we started earlier."

"There's no' a lot to say," Lambert stated evenly. Water was running across his face, his clothing was saturated, but he showed no signs of caring.

"How did you get all the way up here?" Duncan asked.

"Does it matter?"

"It does if you're planning on doing yourself in, aye," Duncan said. Lambert was staring straight ahead, into the gorge now. "It's quite a drop, you know? What if you change your mind on the way down."

"I'll no' be changing my mind, Duncan."

There was a finality in his tone. He didn't sound drunk. He sounded clear of mind.

"Listen," Duncan said. "I know things are tough with the business and all—"

"Who gives a stuff about the business?" Lambert said. "It's no' mine any more anyway. Not really. They're only keeping me around to keep control, to make sure I keep to my end of the bargain."

"What bargain?"

Lambert didn't respond. He simply stared down into the gorge. He was only a step away from the edge and Duncan looked nervously at the long grass underfoot. It could be solid beneath his feet or it could give way under his weight at any moment. Iain Lambert may not even make the choice for himself. Mother Nature could decide to intervene and choose for him.

"Iain, there are better days to come… this isn't the answer," Duncan said, daring to take a step closer. He noticed Alistair flinch in the background, inclining his head. A silent communication to Duncan, signifying he was unhappy with him getting closer and putting himself in harm's way. Duncan understood. He wasn't exactly happy about it either, but he needed to get through to Iain and calling to him from behind just wouldn't have the same impact. He was now in line of sight, and precariously close to the edge himself.

Iain Lambert's eyes shifted to meet Duncan's, but only briefly. "You shouldnae be here, Duncan. I told you."

"I know you did, but I have no choice."

"There's always a choice," Lambert replied. "And I made mine a long time ago, and there's no going back."

"What choice?" Duncan asked. Iain remained staring ahead. He took another half step forward, tantalisingly close to the edge. Duncan held up a hand. "Iain, what choice did you make? Tell me, please." Lambert shook his head, looking down at his feet. It took a moment before Duncan realised he was crying. "There's nothing you've done that's so bad it's worth your life, Iain. Believe me."

Lambert lifted his eyes to meet Duncan's gaze, slowly shaking his head. "I'm sorry, Duncan. I should have said something. I should have done something to stop him… but I couldn't stand up to him. I never did."

"You should have stood up to who?" Duncan asked. "I don't understand."

"Your father did, Duncan," Lambert said. "He had the courage that I never did. I saw him do what I couldn't."

Duncan was momentarily thrown by the mention of his father. "My father? What has he got to do with any of this?"

Lambert offered him a pained look. "I'm sorry. I should have helped him, but I was too scared to."

"Helped who… my father?" Duncan noticed Alistair taking the opportunity of Lambert's focus on him, to move into a position where he might be able to safely intervene. Duncan needed to keep him talking. "You knew my father?"

"Only by name," Lambert said. "He was in the care of St Benedict's. He was in the care of my father."

"How should you have helped him?" Duncan asked.

"I was… there," Lambert said. "I was there when it happened."

"When what happened?"

Alistair had manoeuvred himself into place now. He was almost within arm's reach of Lambert, approaching him from behind and downwind. Duncan was confident he wouldn't be seen and certainly not heard, provided he could keep Lambert engaged. He repeated his question, seeing Iain Lambert's lower lip trembling either through a reaction to the cold, fear or raw emotion.

"What did you see happen, Iain?" Duncan asked. "Tell me!"

Alistair was readying himself to take Lambert down, checking his surroundings to ensure he didn't get it wrong. If he did, then there was every chance of them both pitching over the lip and into the depths of the gorge below. As soon as Alistair made his move it would be on Duncan to close the ground between them as quickly as possible, and only then could he be sure they could secure all of their safety.

"I saw them arguing," Lambert said. "That night."

"My father was arguing with—"

"Mine," Lambert said. "I was walking home with him. We lived nearby back then."

"They argued? What about?"

Lambert shook his head. "I don't know, honestly I don't but Duncan… your father… he pushed my dad, and they struggled. I… watched, and I saw your father was drunk, h-he stumbled and fell to the ground." Lambert was staring at Duncan now, openly weeping. "He was bleeding from his head," he lifted a hand to the side of his own face, his expression displaying that he was living the memory through his eyes now, "a gash to the side of his head. He tried to get up but he slumped back down onto his knees, clutching the railing on the quayside." His focus returned to Duncan and he extended his hand towards him, held aloft as if he was apologising. "I'm so sorry, Duncan. I should have said something, but... I didn't."

"Where were you?"

"We were not far from home," Lambert said. "We stayed at a house on Quay Street back then. We were only a dozen yards from home."

At the mention of Quay Street, Duncan's mind leapt back to the procurator fiscal's report, and the decision that it was not in the public interest to investigate the discovery of his father's lifeless body after it was hauled from the waters of Portree Harbour.

"What did you see?" Duncan asked, barely above a whisper, but somehow, he already knew. He didn't need to hear it confirmed. Instinctively, he just knew. Lambert stared at him, and his expression was all he needed to see to know it was the truth.

"I'm so sorry, Duncan."

"What did you see?" Duncan asked, more aggressively than he intended. Lambert's bottom lip quivered and he threatened to break down. *"Tell me,* what did you see?" Duncan asked through clenched teeth.

"Please forgive me… I was just a kid back then—"

"What happened?" Duncan snarled. Lambert's shoulders sagged, and he shook his head. Ready to pounce now, Alistair hesitated. He must have sensed they were on the cusp of learning something significant. This may be the only chance they would get to hear Iain Lambert speak openly, to learn something that might unlock this entire case.

"My father—" he looked at Duncan, speaking through raw emotion, "—pushed him into the water." Duncan thought he must have heard wrong. That wasn't what happened at all. His father had been drunk and had fallen into the harbour. Lambert was wrong. He had to be. "I'm sorry, Duncan. I saw my father let yours drown… and he laughed as he watched."

"No, that's… that's not what happened," Duncan whispered.

"I'm so, so sorry," Lambert said, just as Alistair reached for him, but his fingers grasped only thin air. Iain Lambert didn't scream as he fell. He'd made his choice, and he didn't make a sound even when his body broke upon the rocks below.

CHAPTER TWENTY-SIX

"DUNCAN!"

He broke away from staring at the space where Iain Lambert had been standing only moments previously. Feeling the breeze on his face, Duncan stared straight ahead. How much time had passed, he couldn't say. Alistair was standing at the lip of the cliff face, trying to see down to the foot of the gorge, his mobile clamped to his ear.

"...scramble the Coastguard helicopter," Alistair said, shouting into his mobile to be heard over the wind. He continued speaking but Duncan was only picking up fragments of what he was saying. "Aye, one man has fallen into the gorge."

Duncan felt ill. He thought he was about to throw up and he backed away from his position, clutching his stomach with one hand and covering his mouth with the other. Doubled over, his chest constricted, and he realised he'd been holding his breath. He sank down onto his knees, ignoring the dampness of the grass and soil beneath him. Feeling a supportive hand on his shoulder, he didn't look up. He couldn't breathe, a stabbing pain repeatedly struck at his lungs.

"Try and calm down," he heard Alistair say. "You're in shock." That was easier said than done, but just as he felt he would pass out rather than draw in oxygen, he gasped, sucking cold air into his lungs. "That's better."

"I… it can't be true," Duncan whispered. Whether Alistair heard him or not, Duncan didn't know. The member of the public who'd been watching their conversation with Lambert made to approach but Alistair instructed him to keep his distance.

"Breathe slowly," Alistair told him, one hand still on Duncan's back between his shoulders. Movement to his left saw Duncan glance up, eyeing the arrival of their colleagues. PC Fraser MacDonald, and his namesake, Ronnie, hurried along the path towards them in their high-vis coats. Alistair stepped away from Duncan, intercepting the constables and issuing instructions. Duncan couldn't hear what was said but Fraser set off along the path, probably heading down to the shore. From there he could track back following the course of the river through the gorge to try and locate Iain Lambert's body. PC Ronnie MacDonald crossed to where the onlooker stood.

Alistair returned to Duncan's side. He was breathing regularly now, the pain dissipating, but he still drew breath in ragged gasps.

"How are you doing?" Alistair asked.

"I've had better days," Duncan said. Now that he'd recovered from the initial shock, the gravity of the situation he was in came to mind. Lambert's revelation changed everything, at least where Duncan was concerned anyway. He looked at Alistair, making to get up. Alistair offered him his hand and he accepted, his DS hauling him to his feet. "Did you hear?"

Alistair fixed him with a stern look. "If I heard, then someone else will need to be drafted in to complete this investigation," he said, glancing around them. No one was within earshot.

"And did you?" Duncan asked. "Did you hear?"

"Well that depends," Alistair said.

"On?"

"The extent of what you haven't told me. You've been keeping something back from me pretty much since the moment we entered Bruce Dunmore's study." He bit his bottom lip, inclining his head. "Forgive me for being self-centred and all, but I can't have this coming back to bite me. If you know what I'm saying?"

Duncan could see Ronnie taking notes from the onlooker, but there was only Alistair within earshot. Duncan couldn't allow himself to be removed from this case. There was already too much that had been missed, by accident or on purpose, he couldn't decide, but he needed to understand how his father died. The only way he could ensure that happened, bearing in mind the investigation had been screwed up the first time around, was to do it himself.

"On the shelf, in the study, was a photograph," Duncan said, keeping his voice low and a watchful eye on Ronnie, standing nearby.

"Aye, you were transfixed on it. That was when I realised you were keeping something to yourself. I assumed you had your reasons."

"I did. It was my father in the picture," Duncan said. "He was one of the boys in the photo with Bruce Dunmore."

"Your father was at St Benedict's?"

"Apparently," Duncan said. "Not that I was aware of it, mind you."

Alistair frowned. "All this makes this investigation more complicated."

"I know, but I need to see it through—"

Alistair scratched at his forehead, deep in thought. "I'm no' sure that's such a good idea."

"I need to know what's going on," Duncan said.

"It might just be…"

"What?" Duncan asked, but Alistair shrugged. "I need to know."

"If I were in your shoes, I'd want to carry on working the case as well, but—"

"I need this, Alistair. If I'm sidelined then this entire investigation goes back to square one," Duncan said. He pointed to where Iain Lambert had been standing. "And you can see what the result is. Who demanded his release and who authorised it?" Alistair shook his head. "Think about it, Al… there are people who don't want us asking questions about any of this."

"I don't know," Alistair said.

"Who do you think will be put in my place? Do you really think they'll send someone who wants to get to the bottom of it or will they ensure it all ends up down there, on the rocks alongside Iain?"

"It's not only that to consider though, is it?" Alistair said. "What happens to a case file when we put it before the procurator fiscal and they see you and your father's name listed… and you're the senior investigating officer." Alistair grimaced. "A defence advocate will have a field day with that information—"

"I get it!" Duncan said firmly, spying Ronnie MacDonald

lift his gaze to them. He lowered his voice. "We don't know that my father's death is actually related to any of this. Let me find out, and if it is… I'll recuse myself immediately."

Alistair exhaled through his teeth. He wasn't happy, but if he was nothing else, Alistair was loyal. Perhaps too loyal for his own good. He nodded.

"Give me your keys," Duncan said. Alistair didn't ask what he wanted the use of his pick-up for. He simply took the keys from his pocket and passed them to him. "Thanks."

Duncan turned and headed for the car park. Above the sound of the wind he heard a repetitive thumping noise signalling the approach of the coastguard's Sikorsky search and rescue helicopter, crossing the Minch from its base in Stornoway on the Isle of Lewis. Duncan didn't look back, climbing into the pick-up and starting the engine. There was someone he needed to speak to whom he hoped could help unravel this mess.

THE ISLAND WAS in the grip of nightfall by the time he'd driven for over an hour to reach his destination on the bank of Loch Vatten. Duncan passed an ambulance heading north towards Lealt, as he passed through Portree before cutting west and heading for Dunvegan. The house was in darkness when he pulled up on the driveway. The converted barn was closed up, as was the separate garage, but Duncan saw a car parked inside. Standing in the gloom, he surveyed the area. He couldn't be far away on foot.

Duncan decided to wait but was too restless to sit in the car; his curiosity got the better of him and he made his way around the property. Its perimeter fence along the boundary, and a cattle grid between the gate posts of the driveway's entrance were the only security attempts at securing the plot. Access around the exterior of the building was freely available. There were the CCTV cameras though, a level of security that most people in these parts didn't bother with.

The retired detective, Campbell McLaren, still took his personal security seriously. Duncan stopped at the picture window he'd looked out of on his last visit, only this time he cupped his hands against the glass and peered inside. There was nothing untoward to see. The interior was tidy, and very much as it had been the last time he was here.

Duncan thought about calling Alistair or turning his mobile phone on to see if he'd received an update. He decided against it. He'd turned his mobile off for a reason. He didn't want anything official that could document where he was or what he might be doing, just in case it could be used against him at a later date. This was an off-the-record visit; albeit possibly a waste of his time. He had no idea when or even if Campbell McLaren would return this evening. He sighed deeply, turning, startled by a figure coming out of the shadows.

"Geez!" he said, raising a hand to his chest. "You scared the daylights out of me."

Campbell McLaren stepped forward, an over-and-under shotgun broken across his shoulder. He was dressed for stalking in boots, a camouflage smock over a thick coat and a woollen hat which completed the ensemble. His West Highland terrier came forth, wagging his stump of a tail. Duncan knelt down and the creature came to inspect him.

"He remembers you," McLaren said, sniffing hard.

"Aye," Duncan said, ruffling the dog behind the ears. "Hello, Jocko, how are you doing, wee man?"

"Are you looking to make a habit of calling round at night or something?" McLaren asked as Duncan stood up.

"Aye, sorry," he said, "but it couldn't wait."

McLaren sniffed, training a beady eye on him. "I guess you'd better come inside then, eh?"

Duncan nodded, following the retired policeman to the back door which he unlocked, allowing the dog to enter first before beckoning Duncan to follow. He stripped off his outer gear, and if Duncan's unannounced arrival had unsettled him then he didn't show it. They went through the house and into the living room. McLaren crossed to the wood burner, donning a fireproof mitt, he opened the door and stoked the embers which were still aglow. He added a fresh log and increased the airflow, holding the door ajar slightly to aid the fire. Soon, small flames were licking the base of the log and McLaren closed the door, discarding the mitt and brushing his hands as he rose.

"So, what is it you're after me for this time, Duncan? I told you everything I knew about the allegations last time you were here."

"Oh aye, it's…" Duncan winced, "about something else."

"Oh," McLaren said, indicating for Duncan to take a seat. He preferred to stand but he did sit down opposite his host. McLaren splayed his hands wide. "You have piqued my curiosity, Duncan. What can I do for you?"

"The last time I was here," Duncan said, choosing his words carefully, "you referred to my father's passing."

"I did, aye."

"What did you mean when you said *you thought you'd done right* by my mother?"

McLaren took a deep breath, his chest rising and he inclined his head. He frowned before settling more in his chair beside the fire. "Can I take it..." he said, fixing his eye on Duncan, "that she never spoke to you about it, about what went on?"

"No, I can't say she ever did."

McLaren grimaced, nodding slowly and arching his eyebrows. "That's awkward."

"That's as it may be, but I can't exactly speak to her about it now," Duncan said. "I wanted to but she's not really present very much these days."

"I see," McLaren said, drawing breath and exhaling heavily. "Are you sure?"

"Am I sure about what?"

"That you want to pull on this particular thread," McLaren said, sitting back and, with one elbow on the arm of his chair, he cupped his chin with his hand. "Your mum probably chose not to tell you for a reason. Maybe it was a good one."

"And maybe that's my choice to make, and not hers."

McLaren nodded, glum. "I guess so. You're a grown man after all. You should know... that maybe some things are best left in the past."

"I need to know," Duncan said. McLaren met Duncan's gaze and they sat in silence for a moment.

"Fair enough, lad. It was just my attempt at imparting some wisdom, that's all."

"What happened to my father?" Duncan asked, sitting forward, his hands clasped together before him.

"Your father was quite a troubled soul, Duncan," McLaren said. "I was being kind before when I told you he was no worse than any of the other lads on the island of the time. He sighed. "He had demons inside him, and it was a struggle he had to keep them in check."

"Demons don't manifest themselves," Duncan countered.

"No… that's true," McLaren said. "The causes of such personal struggles can come at you through life, sometimes from the most unexpected of places. Hell, you may not even realise it until it's too late."

"My father?"

"Your father couldn't face what life threw at him, Duncan." He shook his head. "Sometimes… when people are at their lowest ebb, they make decisions that don't bear up under any form of logical scrutiny. Their decisions are irrational at best, and downright mad at their worst."

Irritated, Duncan held up a hand to interrupt him. "What are you saying to me?"

"I'm saying – as softly as I can – that your father chose to end his suffering."

"What?"

"He took his own life, Duncan," McLaren said quietly. "And, although I've made countless relatives and loved ones aware of such a reality countless times before now, this is really hard for me to say. I knew your father… and your mother, in particular, very well. Especially after what your father did, and it pains me to be the one to tell you."

Duncan shook his head, trying to piece this together. "Why would he do that?"

"Why does anyone do that, Duncan?" McLaren said, shaking his head. "When someone chooses to leave the rest of us behind, we're the ones who have to try and understand it. We have to make rational sense of what is an irrational act. There are no answers, not really."

"What you said… what you did for my mum—"

"Is what any decent person would have done, Duncan." He sat upright, sucking air through his teeth. "Your mum was worried."

"About?"

"She was a religious woman, Duncan. She was terrified about what it would mean for word to get around that Duncan – your father – had taken his own life."

"Like anyone would care," Duncan said. "He was a drunk, a violent drunk—"

"Who would be judged by a higher power," McLaren said. "A higher power than any of us could ever hope to achieve. And that was what your mother was concerned with."

Duncan scoffed, remembering his childhood where he and Roslyn were frogmarched to church each and every Sunday without fail, even if they were ill. "Surely, He will know my father's intentions—"

"Yes, without doubt, Duncan, but I could read between the lines. Your mother, bless her, wasn't thinking of the shame in the eyes of the congregation but she was thinking about you and your sister. Your father was a drunk, undoubtedly. A violent drunk. But your mother wanted you to live your life without any more stigma attached to it than you had already."

Duncan was about to protest but McLaren held up a hand. "I know that sounds daft now, but it was a different time even only a few decades ago. Society changes, morality changes… and people's views on this sort of thing change as well. Society is much more forgiving around mental health matters these days than they used to be. If those events happened now, then maybe the outcome would have been different. Your father may have had more help available to him."

Duncan's head was pounding. He was processing so much information in a short space of time. "How sure are you?"

"About what?"

"That it was a suicide?" Duncan asked. "How can you be so sure that something else didn't happen that night?"

"I investigated it, Duncan—"

"To what extent?" Duncan heard the note of accusation in his tone. McLaren picked up on it too.

"I did what I did for your mother's sake, and for you and your sister!"

"Aye, so you say," Duncan countered. "But did you come at it with a preconceived idea or did you actually do your job?"

"I don't think I like your tone, young man. I was looking out *for you*!"

"How do you know it was suicide?"

"Because I spoke to people who saw him that night. They knew how worse for the drink he was, how morose he was throughout the day. I spoke to those who spoke to him, saw how he was behaving… all day in his little drinking marathon." McLaren shook his head, affronted. "I know it's hard for you to accept, Duncan, but your old man was a proper head case. His mind was addled by the drink, and he chose a way out of his pain… without regard for your mother or his children. I'm sorry that it hurts, I really am, but that's the way it is."

"Did you even countenance another scenario?"

McLaren flinched. "Such as what? The only other outcome was exactly what was written on his file… he fell into the harbour accidentally—"

"And the blow to his head?"

"The wound to his head," McLaren said. "The post-mortem documented it, but it was most likely caused by him hitting the harbour wall having gone into the water."

"Or someone struck him and pushed him into the water," Duncan said.

McLaren scoffed. "I know it's hard to hear, Duncan… but

where in your right mind are you getting that idea from? I'm not a fool, you know. I did speak to people. We knocked on every door, and other than the lassie your father propositioned that night on the street, no one else saw or heard anything. Where are you getting this idea from?" McLaren got up and crossed the room to a drinks cabinet. He opened it and took out two crystal tumblers. Pouring a measure of neat scotch into both glasses, McLaren returned to his chair but passed one to Duncan on the way. Duncan held it in his hand, staring at the contents.

Duncan was reluctant to say what was on his mind. "How do you know? I mean *really know* what happened?"

Campbell McLaren thought hard, perched on the edge of his seat, meeting Duncan's gaze. His expression lightened. "Experience, Duncan. I was a policeman on this island for thirty-one years. That's a period of time you probably find hard to fathom, but when you've been in as long as I was, I think you'll understand. I've seen too many of these sorts of… incidents not to know." He held up an apologetic hand to Duncan. "Please, don't take offence. I mean no insult to you. You're an experienced detective in your own right but, believe me, when I say I just knew." He frowned, sitting back and offering Duncan an open-handed gesture. "You tell me what I should have done differently."

"I would never hide the truth," Duncan said with conviction. "No matter what the outcome might be."

"Is that right?" McLaren said, and Duncan's conversation with Alistair, a little over an hour previously, leapt into his mind and he winced. McLaren noticed. "You understand. I know you do. I can see it in your face. It's not something they teach you during your training, is it? Everything is black and white when you're prepping to take your exams. When it comes to real-world policing, sometimes you have to go with your instinct, and your conclusion can be…" he grinned "similar to a leap of faith."

"What if… something else happened that night?"

McLaren's grin faded, his forehead creasing deeply. "I saw no evidence—"

"But go with me for a moment, what if something else did happen and it didn't go down the way you think?"

"Can you give me a for instance?"

Duncan shook his head. "I can't, no."

"Your father couldn't face his demons, Duncan. He drank to numb the pain he felt, and in the end it all became far too much for him. It was all consuming." McLaren lifted his glass, tilting it towards Duncan. "Don't let your father's demons shape, and destroy, your life too. You have so much more to offer than he ever did." He lifted the glass to his lips and drank from it, but his eyes remained fixed on Duncan. Duncan lifted his own glass and without saying a word, emptied it in one swift motion. He set the glass down on the table before him, staring at Campbell McLaren with an unwavering gaze. "Is there something else on your mind, Duncan?"

"No," Duncan said quietly. "I believe I have everything I came here for."

CHAPTER TWENTY-SEVEN

DUNCAN DROVE Alistair's pick-up back to Portree, resisting the urge to turn his mobile phone on. The last thing he wanted was to have further complications presented to him. Entering the police station via the rear, he ducked into the custody suite and poked his head around the door into the sergeant's office. The custody sergeant was momentarily thrown by Duncan's appearance.

"Hello sir," he said. "I—"

"This afternoon," Duncan said, cutting him off. "Iain Lambert. Who did he call?"

"He didn't say, sir. When he woke up he started a banging and a hollering at the cell door. When I spoke to him, he demanded to be allowed to give someone a phone." He shrugged. "He wasn't under arrest, and so—"

"No, no that's fine," Duncan said. "I would have done the same, but who did he say he was going to call? Family? A girlfriend… solicitor?"

"Like I said, sir. He didn't say. I figured it would be a partner or something. Anyway, I allowed him to make a call –

obviously – and within ten to fifteen minutes, I was getting an instruction to release him." He winced under Duncan's scrutiny. "I suggested that I might give you a phone first, but I was told in no uncertain terms that he was to be released."

Duncan nodded. Glancing down at the sergeant's desk, the officer made an attempt to hide the plastic tub of pasta he'd been munching his way through whilst sitting at his desk. But Duncan wasn't looking at that. A thought occurred to him. "Which phone?"

"Say again?"

"Which phone did Lambert use to make his call?"

"Er…" the sergeant looked down at his desk, and then out into the custody suite. "Come to think of it, I let him use my phone."

Duncan pointed to the landline phone on his desk and the sergeant nodded. "Has anyone used it since?"

"No," he said, shaking his head. "I don't think so. Why?"

Duncan gestured towards the unit. "May I?"

The sergeant nodded. "Aye, knock yourself out."

Duncan picked up the receiver and pressed the redial button. The phone began ringing at the other end but no one picked up. Duncan allowed it to stay connected, waiting for an answering machine or voicemail system to kick in and, hopefully, play him a recorded message. A standard machine voice answered and Duncan chose not to leave a message. It was curious to him that the call was answered earlier that day and it led to a swift release from the station for Lambert, only now, a mere two to three hours later, the call went unanswered.

Before hanging up, Duncan checked the display on the base unit. He took out a pen and jotted down the destination telephone number on a note pad. It was a UK mobile number. Duncan tore the page from the pad and replaced the receiver.

"Thank you," he said to the sergeant.

"Was it him then?" Duncan stopped, halfway to the door, and looked back. "Was it him who fell from Lealt Falls? Lambert, I mean?"

"Aye," Duncan said. "It was."

He didn't say anything else, but resumed his walk from the custody suite, heading up into the CID ops room. The only member of the team present was Angus, who was surprised to see him walk in.

"Hello, sir," he said, getting up from behind his desk. Duncan waved him back into his seat and didn't break step as he went straight through into his office, closing the door behind him and pulling the blinds down. He went behind his desk and sat down, opening his drawer and taking out the file he'd checked out from the archive detailing his father's death. He took a deep breath and opened it, distributing the various documents around on his desk in front of him. There was a knock on the door.

"Not now!" he called. Undeterred, the knock sounded again. Duncan sighed, hastily pulling the documents in front of him together and putting them back into the folder. "Come," he said, sitting back in his chair. The door cracked open, and Angus peered in. Duncan beckoned him inside. Angus smiled and entered.

"Sorry to bother you, sir."

"That's okay, Angus. What can I do for you?"

"You've had a message left for you, sir. He's been trying to speak to you on your mobile—"

"I've had it switched off, Angus," Duncan said, forcing a smile. "I had a few things to do. Is Alistair chasing me?"

"Yes, he has called asking to know if you'd been in," Angus said. Duncan nodded. "But it's not him I'm referring to."

"Who then?"

"Connor Booth," Angus said. "Bruce Dunmore's literary agent. He's been into the lobby earlier, asking for you at the front desk. Obviously, they couldn't raise you… if your phone was off."

"What did he want?"

Angus shrugged. "I went down and spoke to him myself, but he only wanted to speak to you or the sarge. Neither of you were here, so…" Angus shrugged again. "He did say he was still staying at his hotel but he was planning to check out tomorrow and head back to the mainland."

Duncan arched his eyebrows and then checked the time. Drumming his fingers on the desk, he wondered what Booth had to say to him. Quite frankly, Duncan was surprised he was still in Portree. "Okay, Angus," Duncan said, accompanied with a brief smile. "Thanks." Angus looked at the folder sitting beneath Duncan's left hand, resting atop it. "Is there anything else?" Duncan asked.

"No, sir," Angus said with a sheepish smile. "I'll let you crack on."

He backed out of the office, closing the door behind him. Duncan quickly opened the file again and laid out the documents. He'd already read the report written by the procurator fiscal, but he did so again just in case he'd missed something. He hadn't. Turning to the post-mortem report, he hesitated as he began reading. The fact this detailed his father's examination made it seem very real to him.

They'd always had a troubled relationship, Duncan and his father, and Duncan had wished him dead on any number of occasions. Once or twice he thought he might actually be the one to end his father's life, when he visited the darkest places of his mind. After all, that was the main reason behind his drive to leave the island as a teenager. His father had passed away a few short years after Duncan had left Skye. Duncan had returned for the funeral.

Being back on the island for those few days hadn't changed his mind about leaving, even if his father was no longer there to butt heads with. Roslyn, and his mum, encouraged him to stay but he was already building a new life for himself in Glasgow and saw no personal benefit for him to return. He couldn't wait to leave again, if he was honest. He'd never stopped to consider what had happened to his father. An old drunk who fell into the harbour and drowned. No great loss. Not for him, his sister and certainly not for their mother either. He doubted anyone on the island shed a tear for Big Duncan McAdam. Not least his son and namesake.

Pushing the melancholy of his youth aside, Duncan pored over the post-mortem results. He'd read countless such reports over the years and this one read no differently. Just as he was about to put the post-mortem report down, something caught his attention. He looked at the toxicology section of the report. It was all handwritten, and there appeared to be something about the ink that stood out. Switching on his desk lamp, he held the paper beneath the light, angling it slightly to change his perception. It certainly looked like someone had either added to or overwritten the numbers.

Studying the numbers, Duncan considered he might be looking for something that simply wasn't there. The same mental gymnastics that the human brain does when it sees familiar shapes in cloud formations. He took a moment to rest his eyes and then he re-examined the document, but he was sure he wasn't imagining it. Several of the lines appeared to have been written in a different ink. Not that he was an expert on ink, but it was the difference between writing with a ball point or with a fountain pen. Under certain light, and if you knew what to look for, you could see a change.

The number on his father's recorded blood alcohol concentration level had been amended. Could that be an error? Possibly. A simple typographical error that the pathologist needed to correct before sending the report. It was possible. He skipped through the remainder of the report but nothing else stood out to him. He put the paperwork back into the folder and away in his drawer. This time though, he locked the drawer which was something he never did.

Picking up his mobile, he left his office. Angus lifted his head but Duncan didn't stop. He hurried out of CID and back downstairs. The Portree Hotel was only on the other side of Somerled Square, something Duncan was pleased about when he stepped outside to find it was raining. He drew his coat around him and ran across the square seeking the shelter of the hotel's lobby. He walked up to the check-in desk and the young lady behind it smiled as he approached.

"Good evening, sir."

Duncan smiled and, in the corner of his eye, he caught a glimpse of Connor Booth in the hotel bar receiving a drink from the barman. Duncan tapped his hand gently on the reception desk and gestured towards him. "I see him. No bother," he said. She nodded and Duncan went through into the hotel bar. There were a number of patrons sitting at tables or at the bar itself. Connor Booth saw Duncan and gestured to the barman.

"What are you drinking, Detective Inspector?" Booth asked. "Or are you *still on duty* and must decline?"

"A Talisker, please," Duncan said, inclining his head. "A double if you'll stretch to it."

"I certainly can," Booth said, nodding to the barman who

reached for a glass from the shelf above him. Booth turned to Duncan. "Has it been a trying day, Detective Inspector?"

"Aye, it has."

The barman set down a paper mat and the glass on top of it. Booth smiled. "Please put it on my room." He then gestured for Duncan to accompany him back to his seat at a small table by the window, overlooking the square. They sat down.

"I did wonder whether you would return my message," Booth said, raising his glass. "Cheers."

"Slàinte Mhath," Duncan said, lifting his own glass and drinking more than half the contents. Booth raised his eyebrows but didn't comment. He put his glass down. "You wanted to speak to me."

"I did," Booth said but he seemed reticent, studying Duncan's expression. "Although, you are giving off quite a negative energy and I'm a little apprehensive about—"

"Whatever it is," Duncan said, "you bought me a drink, so I'm more than happy to listen to you."

"Fair enough," Booth said. "I have a confession to make." He raised both his hands in the air. "A minor one. I'm not a… a…"

"A murderer?"

"Yes, far from it," Booth said.

Duncan raised his glass again, seeing off the remainder of his drink in one motion. He grimaced slightly, taking a deep breath as he put the empty glass down. "Then what is it you wish to confess to me?"

"Would you like another scotch?"

"No, thank you."

Booth cleared his throat and then sipped at his own drink, perhaps summoning up the courage to speak candidly. "I have to admit that my motivation for staying here on Skye – as well as my visit in its entirety – have not been completely above board."

"Go on."

"You see, Bruce has been very… guarded about his current work in progress. Unusually so."

"You said that wasn't unusual—"

"No… not exactly," Booth said. He wrinkled his nose. "Bruce has a team around him, of which I am the grease if you like. I keep the parts moving, communicating with one another but I don't actually—"

"Do very much for your fifteen percent?" Duncan asked.

"It's more like twenty," Booth said, smiling momentarily, "but let's not get stuck on the detail. Anyway, I'd been talking with people and no one had any word of or conversation with Bruce about his new work."

"And so – I'm busy so I'll paraphrase – you came out here to find out what he was working on?"

Booth nodded. "I did. Needless to say, Bruce didn't see fit to enlighten me. I was staying for the announcement this weekend, as you know, and I was just as eager as everyone else to learn what it was he was beavering away at."

"And you know now?"

He shook his head. "No, I don't. But, following Bruce's demise, I did try…" he bit his lower lip ever so gently, "to find out." Duncan pursed his lips. He owed Alistair ten pounds. "I met Bruce at his house last week, and also the lovely lady who looks after his housekeeping."

"Flora," Duncan said.

"Yes, that's right. Flora is her name." He coughed awkwardly, his eyes flitting around the bar. "Anyway, I looked up Flora and sought her out."

"For what purpose?"

Booth hesitated. "I... er... thought that because she was spending more time with Bruce than anyone else, that she might... um..."

"Know where he kept his manuscript?"

"I was trying to find out if he'd told her anything about it but," Booth said, smiling weakly and jabbing a finger towards Duncan, "she came to the same conclusion as you did." He shook his head. "I was just making enquiries and she thought the worst of me. Just as you did."

"It comes with being a policeman," Duncan said. "Cynicism."

"That's what she said too," Booth replied, with a nervous laugh.

"Excuse me?"

"Oh, Flora said that she'd grown up around policemen and so she had the same cynical mindset as they did." He inclined his head, arching his eyebrows. "And you've rather reinforced her point, actually."

Duncan felt that there was something tantalisingly significant said there, but he couldn't pin it down. For now, at least, he pushed the thought aside. "Why did you want to see me?"

"I wanted to see you because," Booth said, lowering his voice to a conspiratorial whisper, "I don't think Bruce was working on a new thriller. At least, not one any of us would be expecting and that was why he was so secretive about it."

Duncan couldn't believe he'd run through the rain, wasting precious time to hear something he'd already considered himself right at the beginning of all this. He humoured the agent though. "Have you any idea what that might be?"

"None whatsoever," Booth said, lifting his glass. "But I thought you'd like to hear my theory." Duncan sat forward.

"What is your theory?"

Connor Booth stared at him. "I've just told you."

Duncan forced an artificial smile. "Did Flora tell you that Bruce's house was broken into?"

"No!" he said. "She didn't mention that at all. When was this?" Duncan studied him, taking in his reaction.

"Within twenty-four hours of us finding his body up at an An Corran Beach," Duncan said. "The locked door to his study was forced and his safe opened, the contents cleaned out."

"Oh… who would do such a thing?"

Duncan inhaled slowly. "I did wonder whether you might have done it."

"Me? Are… are you serious?" Booth asked and Duncan nodded. The man was flabbergasted. "Why would I do such a thing?"

"Perhaps to lay your hands on the last ever work written by your cash cow, Bruce Dunmore."

"I…I would never go to such lengths," Booth protested. "I am his agent. We have a contract. Whatever he was writing I would have the ability to place with any publisher. I would have no need to stoop to such levels—"

"Relax, Mr Booth," Duncan said. "I dismissed the idea quite soon after it entered my head. You wouldn't have anything to gain. Unless, of course, there was something in that book that you wouldn't want to be published."

"Like what?"

Duncan shrugged. "For instance, if Bruce was writing something about his past, detailing something dark that he was involved in. That would change your… perception, would it not?"

"It would harm his brand, certainly," Booth said, his eyes narrowing. "Could Bruce have been working on such a project?"

"Who knows?" Duncan said. "But he was killed for a reason, and no one seems able – or willing – to provide me with an alternative motive." Booth frowned, considering what Duncan had said. It would damage future sales if Bruce Dunmore's reputation took a hit. Not that Duncan knew if it would, but he suspected that if the motive he was forming in his mind was the reality, then there could be numerous people who would wish to see that that book never made it to print. "Thank you for the drink, Mr Booth." He stood up, much to the man's surprise. "Have a safe trip back tomorrow."

He walked across the bar feeling Connor Booth's eyes upon his back. Booth wasn't a suspect, but regardless of how close they were to one another, Duncan sensed that Bruce would only have kept the details of a forthcoming book secret from him if he worried about the manuscript's acceptance.

Reaching for his mobile phone, he switched it on as he withdrew it from his pocket. Almost immediately he began to receive notifications. Once he was alone in the lobby, he scanned through them. They were messages from Alistair and Angus. An image of Flora McQueen came to mind, and he recalled how she was so keen to express the depth of her loyalty when it came to Bruce Dunmore and, historically, to his family. She'd been prepared to withhold crucial information from Duncan and his investigation under the guise – honest or otherwise – of misplaced loyalty. He dialled a contact's telephone number.

"Hello, sir," Angus said.

"Angus, can you access the forensic report from the break-in at Bruce Dunmore's house."

"Aye, it's right here," Angus said, shuffling something on his desk. "What is it you're looking for?"

"Can you confirm the fingerprints picked up on the sweep."

"Sure, that's easy. Bruce and his housekeeper, but that was all."

"And specifically on the safe?"

"None at all, sir. The technicians thought it was thoroughly wiped clean."

"But the safe wasn't forced, was it?"

"No sir. It was a key safe," Angus explained. "That is to say it has a double lock requiring two keys to open it. There is no manual combination or digital access code. It's old school."

"Thanks, Angus."

"Is there anything else I can—"

"No, that's all I needed."

Duncan ended the call. He wondered just how loyal Flora was and how far she might be willing to extend it when it came to the other people in her life.

CHAPTER TWENTY-EIGHT

DUNCAN STEPPED out onto Somerled Square, his mobile still in hand. A young couple passed by him, arm in arm, and he smiled as they walked by. Even in the relative shelter of the hotel's facade, he felt the wind had dropped and thankfully the rain had stopped. He wondered for how long, but a quick glance skyward revealed stars on show despite the light pollution of the town centre. He began the short walk back to where he'd parked Alistair's pick-up and called his detective sergeant.

"Alistair, what's the state of play with you?"

"Coastguard chopper airlifted our man and transferred him to Raigmore Hospital," Alistair said, referencing the largest hospital that served the Highlands and Islands, in Inverness. "He was still breathing when they got to him."

"What state was he in?"

"Unconscious, and in a bad way but breathing. I've sent Caitlyn up to Inverness. She'll probably be able to get an update by the time she arrives. Hang on a moment, will you?" Duncan heard a scraping sound as Alistair was on the move, and the sounds in the background diminished. His voice returned moments later. "And where are you?" he asked.

"I'm…" Duncan wasn't sure how to answer. It wasn't that he was necessarily looking to hide anything from Alistair, but he was keen not to involve him in anything that could harm his position. "I have something."

"Care to share it with me?"

"No," Duncan said, emphatically. "I think it's better if I run solo on this one."

"That will not look good."

"I agree… but I think it's best for you if I do." There was silence for a few moments and Duncan checked his mobile to see if the call was still connected. It was. "You understand, right?"

"Aye," Alistair said. There was no judgement in his tone. "You know what's best. I'm not going to try and talk you out of it."

"That's a good job," he said. "Although, I'm not sure of my next move. I'm feeling… like I'm stuck between a rock and a hard place. If I do nothing then everything slides away from us but…"

"If you act then it might blow up in your face?"

"Aye, that's about the long and the short of it."

"Without knowing what the hell you're going on about," Alistair said, drily, "I can't help you with that. However, thinking about it, one of the first things they taught me about combat in the Parachute Regiment might come in useful."

"I'm listening," Duncan said.

"If someone's shooting at you… shoot back." Duncan heard the words, allowing them to sink in. "Do you understand, sir?"

"Aye," Duncan said quietly. "I do." He hung up, clutching

his mobile in his hand he raised it to his lips. "I get it," he said softly to himself, unlocking the door to Alistair's pick-up and getting in.

Duncan took a different route to that which he'd driven on his previous two trips across Skye. This time he headed out of Portree and headed directly west via Glengrasco, arriving on the coast at the mouth of Loch Beag, near Bracadale. Turning north, he drove up the coast passing through Struan and Garrymore. The roads were quiet at this time of night and the storm front appeared to have cleared the island. The dark, foreboding storm clouds were on the eastern horizon over the mainland now. The moonlight reflecting off the still waters of Loch Caroy signalled to Duncan that he was approaching his destination.

In adulthood, Duncan had never been the type of person to stumble into any situation without first formulating some kind of a plan. Most of the time those plans went to hell the moment he attempted to enact them, but he always saw that as a reflection of his failure to prepare adequately. He role-played scenarios in his mind as he drove, trying to decide what he would do in response to any number of scenarios he might encounter.

However, when he slowed the pick-up and made the tight turn into the driveway and pulled up before the property, he felt genuinely out of his depth. Switching off the engine, he looked at the house. Several lights were on. One in the hallway beyond the porch and another partially illuminating one of the upstairs rooms. Duncan got out and approached the front door, hesitating momentarily before he knocked. There was no answer although he heard a bark in the distance.

A few moments later, the scampering of tiny paws on shingle carried to him and Duncan saw Jocko come around the side of the building, hurrying to investigate the newcomer. Duncan dropped to his haunches and the dog stopped barely three feet from him, wagged his stumpy tail, eyeing him warily before turning and running back the way he came. Duncan followed.

At the rear of the house, towards the loch-side boundary beside a dilapidated byre, Duncan saw two figures standing around a brazier a dozen feet or so from the water's edge. The flickering orange glow of the flames illuminated them. The firelight danced, casting shadows on the wall of the nearby stone building. Neither man looked his way and Duncan approached cautiously. His hands thrust into his pockets he came to within ten feet of them before Campbell McLaren acknowledged his arrival.

"Good evening, Duncan," he said, with a trace of a smile. "Your visits are almost becoming habitual." He held his hands out to the fire, warming his palms. The other man, Fraser McEwan, avoided making eye contact with Duncan, standing with his arms folded, his chin tucked into his chest. The night air was still but the open skies had seen a dramatic drop in temperature. McLaren looked Duncan up and down. "Are you okay? You look like you've seen a ghost."

"They keep presenting themselves to me," Duncan said, solemnly, "at every turn."

McLaren slowly nodded, turning back to face the fire. "Come and warm yourself by the fire, lad. On nights like this, it's the best way to remember you're still alive." He glanced sideways at him. "It will keep the evil spirits from laying claim to your soul."

"I think it's too late for some of us."

McLaren's smile broadened and Duncan approached, pleased to feel the warmth of the blaze.

"What brings you here, Duncan?"

"I think you know."

McLaren cocked his head, then absently scratched at his cheek just below his ear. "And yet you come alone."

"Don't toy with this—"

Campbell McLaren glared at Fraser who averted his eyes, shuffling his weight between his feet.

"You will have to forgive Fraser," McLaren said. "He doesn't have the steel nerves required for any of this." He shot his companion a derisory look. "You were always the weakest link, Fraser. It's only your sincere ineptitude that kept you from harming all of us." He smiled at Duncan. "Fraser, here, just needed a little urging, a gentle reminder as to what happens to those who speak up." He looked at Fraser. "Didn't you, young man?"

Duncan understood the significance of Bruce Dunmore's placement on An Corran Beach now. "That's why you left the body there, wasn't it? To be found by Fraser when he came out of the water."

"A little theatrical, I'll grant you," McLaren said, angling his head thoughtfully. "But the message made it through. Fortunately for me, Fraser's mental history harms his credibility and without Bruce and his wretched, misguided confession of a manuscript, there is nothing left that can actually harm us. Anything Fraser says would be destroyed in a court of law by even the dumbest of advocates."

"And Bruce?" Duncan asked. "Why did he choose to write the book in the first place, after all this time?"

"Ah… Bruce," McLaren said, pursing his lips. "Bruce took his fame and his fortune and did the one thing that none of us could really afford, if the truth be known."

"And that was?"

McLaren stooped to a log basket, nestling at his feet between himself and Fraser McEwan. He scooped up a clutch of papers and dropped them into the flames. The dryness of the paper caught fire with a flash of intense orange light which lasted a few moments before the flames subsided. McLaren sighed.

"He spent far too long with those liberal… arty sorts who inhabit his grandiose publishing house and attend his self-indulgent speaking engagements. Rather than allow sleeping dogs to lie, he decided to apply a salve to his conscience." McLaren looked into the brazier, nodding to Fraser beside him who dutifully picked up another clutch of paper - the last as far as Duncan could see - and added it to the flames. Duncan edged closer and stared into the brazier, watching the printed words catch fire, blacken and shrivel up before his eyes.

"You mean he had a conscience," Duncan said.

"Developed one, yes," McLaren replied. "If he had one before, then it was securely kept for many years under lock and key in that safe of his."

"The safe that your niece, Flora, opened for you."

McLaren glanced at him and smiled. "Very good, Detective Inspector McAdam." He shook his head and seemed impressed. "I wasn't too sure the first time I met you, Duncan. You came across to me as rather naive – capable, I would say – but nonetheless a little green for your position. I doubted that assumption following your last visit. Even then, I figured the emotion surrounding the events of your father's death would be likely to cloud your thinking somewhat." He drew a deep breath in through his nose. "I see I underestimated you." He rocked his head from side to side. "At least, a little."

"Only a little?" Duncan countered, feeling a knot tighten in his chest.

"Why yes," McLaren said. He looked towards Duncan but past him, craning his neck to see more of the front of his land beyond the house. "You came here alone, didn't you?"

"I'm not afraid of you," Duncan said. "And neither was my father—"

"Oh, he was, Duncan." McLaren looked at him with a blank expression, but the firelight reflected in his determined eyes. "Your father was terrified of us. And rightly so."

"Lambert," Duncan said flatly. McLaren arched his eyebrows. "Yes, I know what happened that night."

"No," McLaren said, raising a pointed finger towards him. "You only think you know, and that is not the same thing, is it? It took a lot of alcohol over many years for your father to confront one of us and, even then, it was on the spur of the moment—"

"You altered the blood alcohol level in my father's post-mortem report, didn't you? You made it look like he'd drunk an almost lethal level of alcohol that night. You changed the pathologist's report."

McLaren was pensive, his eyes narrowing as he studied Duncan. "I did underestimate you, didn't I?" He chuckled. "Well, well... Big Duncan's son has become quite a good policeman, hasn't he, Fraser?" McEwan said nothing. He looked decidedly uncomfortable and still hadn't dared to raise his eyes to meet Duncan's.

"You... all of you," Duncan said, "mistreated those boys – even you, Fraser!" Duncan said, accusing the man who was downcast beside his abuser. "You had a chance to speak up with Bruce—"

"Aye!" Fraser said, lifting his head with tears in his eyes. "And look where it led Bruce. I helped him when he asked me to. I did."

Campbell McLaren flicked out with his right hand and caught Fraser in the side of the face. He immediately stopped speaking and looked at the ground. The power of the abuser rarely fades, even over the course of years. Duncan knew this, and he could bear witness to it right now before him.

"Those boys were in your care—"

"That's just it, Duncan. No one cared," McLaren said, spreading his hands wide. "They were the damned children. Those that a belligerent society had no need of or use for."

"Children betrayed by the system that was set up to support them. Betrayed by the likes of you."

McLaren shook his head. "You are so representative of the service nowadays, Duncan, you really are. Idealists," he said. "No one wanted these children. *That's* why they were in St Benedict's in the first place!"

"But not for scum like you to treat them as you pleased!"

"It was a different time," McLaren argued.

"No, some things have always been wrong. Only too many people failed to speak up," Duncan said, "or they came to someone like you for help and were dismissed outright or I suspect they were scared away."

"And you think I had the power on this island back in the day?"

"You were the most senior officer—"

"By the end of my time, when I came upon retirement, certainly." McLaren turned on Duncan and he instinctively took a step back although McLaren maintained the distance between them and didn't look to advance on him. "But do you think that was always the case? You think I wielded that much clout in these parts." He laughed and it was a wicked sound. "You just take your little theory and write it up, laddie," he said dismissively waving a hand in the air, "and just see how far it gets you."

"I'll do exactly that."

"No, you won't." McLaren sighed. "Because you don't have a shred of evidence to back it up. You write about what you think you know and watch your career implode within a matter of days." He pointed a casual finger at the flames. "It's a shame, though. It was a beautifully crafted tale of sordid happenings among the elite and the powerful. It's a tabloid dream if you could find anyone willing to run the story." He inclined his head towards Duncan. "The sort of salacious storytelling that makes a fictional bestseller but would never be believed by anyone in their right mind. Sadly, for you, no one will ever get to read it."

"That's a paper copy. There will be digital back-ups," Duncan said, hoping that was true.

"What, on a laptop for example?"

"Aye," Duncan said. McLaren fixed him with a stern look.

"By any chance, have you come across a laptop yet?" Duncan closed his eyes briefly and McLaren smiled. "I thought not. As for other copies, the back-ups you speak of. These ones, you mean?" McLaren asked, holding a memory stick up to Duncan before tossing it into the brazier. "My niece is an impeccable housekeeper. There is nothing that Bruce Dunmore did that went unnoticed. He confided in her too, you know. She was his rock in the storm of his life this past year. Bruce soldiered on following the death of his beloved Annie, but he never found anyone else to support him quite like she did. Flora filled that void recently. Had Annie not passed first, then Bruce would likely have forever kept his counsel, I'm almost certain."

"Why would she side with someone like you over a

Dunmore, who by her own admission saved her and her mother when they were at their lowest?"

"I may be a despicable human being, in yours and many other people's eyes, but there's a lesson in there. Blood is thicker than water, Duncan." He looked him up and down. "It's a pity you hadn't learned that yourself. Perhaps your father would still be alive."

Duncan felt a surge of adrenalin, drew himself up and stepped forward only for a movement in the shadows off to his right to stop his advance.

"You took the case file with you when you retired, didn't you? Everything surrounding the allegations at St Benedict's."

"Long before I retired, Duncan. Hard-copy storage areas are prone to inefficiency, loss and damage. Things… get lost *all the time*."

"I checked up on your record too," Duncan said. "You went to Lochalsh for your sergeant training the year after when you told me. You were the one tasked with investigating those allegations."

McLaren sucked air through his teeth and arched his eyebrows. "My memory must be deserting me. It happens when you get older." He looked at Duncan. "How is your lovely mother, by the way? I do hope you're not upsetting her with all these stories you're fabricating."

Anger flared in him and Duncan moved forward only for movement seen in the corner of his eye to make him hesitate. Out of the shadows, a man lumbered forward. McLaren turned to see who it was and Duncan saw a flicker of surprise matching his own as they recognised Robert Hamilton, coming into the reflected glow of the firelight. He stopped short of the three of them, perhaps six feet away. Fraser sidestepped to his left, although he stopped dead when Hamilton turned his gaze upon him. All three of them, Duncan, Campbell and Fraser were transfixed by Hamilton's arrival. He stood facing them, a double-barrelled shotgun pointing at Duncan.

Campbell McLaren, despite being momentarily shocked by the arrival, gathered himself swiftly. He smiled. "There's no need for you to be here, Robert. I have everything in hand," he said, glancing at the fire.

Duncan had his hands up before him, adopting an unthreatening pose. "Robert, please lower the shotgun."

"You heard the man," McLaren said. "There's no need for you to overdramatise this situation." He glanced at Duncan as Hamilton lowered the barrel of his weapon. "He has nothing. All he's achieving here is understanding his own impotence." His expression clouded. "What are you doing here anyway?"

"I'm here to atone for my sins, just as I promised Bruce," Hamilton said quietly, and Duncan realised his intention mere seconds before the barrel came up, only now it was trained upon Campbell McLaren.

"No!" Duncan yelled, but his demand was lost in the roar of the shotgun's discharge and something splashed against his face. McLaren was punched from his feet and flung back into the brazier, knocking it over and his body rolled onto the spilled hot coals and flaming wood, flames immediately licking around his torso. Duncan moved towards him only for Hamilton to turn the shotgun on him.

"Please, don't," Duncan said, holding his hands in the air.

"Let him burn," Hamilton said. "His soul will need to get used to the flames where he's going."

Duncan looked down at the stricken form of Campbell McLaren. He was groaning and the flames were already taking hold on his clothing. He didn't appear to notice. A shotgun blast to the chest at point-blank range. He would be lucky to survive even without the fire. Fearing he'd caught some of the shot himself, Duncan raised a hand to his face and, withdrawing it, he saw blood on his fingertips. After a cursory examination, he concluded it wasn't his. Fraser McEwan was on the floor, curled up in the foetal position, his hands over his head. He was sobbing.

Duncan was confident the retired inspector was already dead, but Hamilton still had a loaded shotgun pointing at him. He looked at the former caretaker of St Benedict's.

"Bruce came to you too then?" Duncan asked.

"He came to all of us," Hamilton said quietly, staring at Campbell who was no longer moaning. Duncan thought he was dead. "He told us what he wanted to do. That it was time for all of us to make our peace while we still could."

"Before what?"

"Before we passed on," Hamilton said. "We were unspeakably cruel to those boys. They grew up damaged, and suffering. Like they hadn't suffered enough before they came into our care."

"Iain Lambert?" Duncan asked.

"Watched his father commit murder, to keep their secret." He looked down at Fraser. "Those who were wronged… and still feel the pain."

"Who was in charge of it all?" Duncan asked. Hamilton looked at him, disconsolate. "Who?"

He shook his head. "There are some who will only face judgement in the next life, Detective Inspector McAdam."

"That's not how it has to be," Duncan said, stepping forward only for the barrel to elevate slightly higher by way of a warning. "Help me," he said. "Help me like you promised to help Bruce."

"I've got as far as I can, Duncan," Hamilton said. "And it's time for me to face my judgement." He spun the shotgun in his hands, pointing it towards himself, his right arm at maximum extension and before Duncan could speak, he pulled the trigger. Duncan watched in horror as the majority of the man's head disintegrated in less than a second.

Robert Hamilton's body instantly went limp and crumpled to the ground. Duncan's ears were ringing due to how close he'd been standing to the fatal shot and, as his hearing slowly returned, the sound of water gently lapping against the loch's shoreline and the occasional spit or crackle from the burning embers came to ear. That, and Fraser McEwan quietly sobbing on the ground nearby.

CHAPTER TWENTY-NINE

THIRTY-SIX HOURS LATER

DUNCAN OPENED the door for Roslyn and she got out of her car. She smiled warmly at Grace, adjusting her coat, a fine navy-blue three-quarter length coat with a bronze lapel pin that Duncan didn't recognise. It seemed strange to see his sister dressed in anything other than the clothes she wore to work on the croft.

"Is Ronnie not joining us?" Duncan asked and Ros rolled her eyes. "I'll take that as a no, then."

"He said this is for family," Roslyn said. Duncan nodded. He understood. His brother-in-law didn't care much for their side of the family most of the time, and even less when it came to spending time with Duncan. Why should this time be any different?

"Nae bother," he said, smiling weakly to try and reassure her that it didn't really matter. Grace looped her arm through

Roslyn's and gave her a supportive squeeze. She appreciated it and the two women smiled at one another.

"Come on then," Grace said, drawing a deep breath. "Let's go inside and get your mum."

Duncan nodded but saw Alistair's pick-up approaching on the access road to the care home. He looked at Grace. "You two head on up and I'll be with you in a minute." Grace steered Roslyn away and Duncan's sister shot a glance towards Alistair but did as she was bidden and set off into the building still on Grace's arm. Duncan walked over to meet Alistair as he pulled up.

"What are yer saying, Alistair?"

"All is well," he replied, cracking open his door and stepping down from the cabin. "Don't worry." He looked towards the entrance, seeing Grace and Roslyn disappear inside. He nodded to Duncan. "How are things yourself?"

Duncan cocked his head. "I've had better days to be fair."

"Have you cracked the seal on a fresh bottle of scotch yet?"

Duncan smiled. "No, and I won't. That might be my father's way of dealing with things, but I'm sure as hell going to make sure it isn't mine."

"I'm pleased to hear it," Alistair said.

"Don't worry. We're working through it."

"Roslyn?" Alistair asked, looking at the empty lobby where he'd seen them only moments before.

"I think," Duncan said, frowning, "that Mum had shared a few bits and pieces about Dad's life with her over the years." He shrugged. "Snippets… and nothing substantial but to learn of what he probably went through whilst living at St Benedict's…" he grimaced. "It's pretty hard to take. For all of us."

"She's a tough one," Alistair said. "The McAdams are hardy folk, right enough. You'll get through it."

"What have you gleaned from Fraser McEwan?" Duncan asked, keen to learn the latest in the case that he'd recused himself from. Learning of their worst suspicion, that of a lengthy period of abuse that took place over several years involving Duncan's father meant he could no longer be a part of the investigation.

"Nothing," Alistair said. "He's still reluctant to talk… and he's a witness not a perpetrator." He took a deep breath. "We're having to treat him with kid gloves and it's a slow process—"

"That's the way it has to be," Duncan said. "He kept his silence for all of his adult life until Bruce came calling… and seeing what befell him must have sent him into shock, and then some."

"Do you think he will open up?"

"I don't know," Duncan said. "Maybe if others come forward then he'll draw strength from them. Maybe Iain Lambert will—"

"He won't be able to," Alistair said, wincing. "That's why I drove down here because I didn't want to tell you over the phone." Duncan inclined his head, fearing the news but he'd already guessed it before Alistair confirmed it. "He died in the early hours of this morning."

"Damn," Duncan said. Iain Lambert had been airlifted to Raigmore Hospital in Inverness and had been stabilised by inducing him into a medical coma. He'd not regained consciousness though and his condition had remained critical. "What happens now?"

"The procurator fiscal is…"

Alistair didn't finish the statement. Duncan understood. The suspects they believed to be involved in the abuse were all dead. Bruce Dunmore, Robert Hamilton and Inspector Campbell McLaren were deceased, and the only witness to their crimes - as far as they were aware - was Fraser McEwan. With his mental health history, Campbell McLaren had been right, in that there was little chance that the fiscal would carry out an investigation on the strength of Fraser McEwan's word alone.

"We could appeal for people to come forward," Duncan said. "The world is a changed place now. People will listen."

"You think so?" Alistair asked, raising an eyebrow.

"You don't?"

Alistair snorted. "I'm already being asked to wind down the investigation."

"What? How can that be? Five people are dead because of this—"

"One being your father," Alistair said. "I know." He shook his head. "But it would seem that no one wants this story told. Not that you heard this from me, obviously. I still want to keep my pension too."

"Why? I don't get it. They're all dead. The boys' home closed down decades ago. Whose reputation are we looking to protect?"

Alistair tilted his head. "Now that is a very good question. And it's one that I don't see us getting the chance to find an answer to. If you know what I mean?"

"What about interviewing his Lordship?"

"Huxley?" Alistair asked. "His Grace is unable to accept the invitation to interview due to poor health. Should that change in the future, which it won't by the way, then perhaps the situation could be revisited. If he speaks to us he would have to explain why the family invested in Lambert's failing business. You and I both know it was to pay him off to keep him quiet. No," Alistair said, shaking his head. "The Huxleys will not be speaking to us."

"Is that right?" Duncan asked. Alistair nodded solemnly.

Duncan felt a stab of pain in his head, and not for the first time since he'd learned of what his father must have gone through as a teenager. The stress surrounding the magnitude of his father's secret history – secret to Duncan, at least – had made sleep almost impossible. Whether the pain was fatigue, stress or something else, Duncan didn't know. He was still processing all of it. The anger his father carried, the violence that seemed to manifest out of nowhere to be unleashed on himself and his sister, and their mum, all of it came from the pain he held inside and had never been given the chance to get rid of. He did what many people who went through the same experiences did, they found a way to numb themselves to what they couldn't process, what they couldn't understand.

"I'm sorry, Duncan," Alistair said. "I don't know what you must be feeling, just now. I really don't."

Duncan nodded. If the truth be told, he felt drained. An emptiness of spirit that he'd not known since he'd decided to settle back here on the island. He felt eyes upon him and he looked up, seeing Grace standing at the window of his mum's bedroom, looking down at him. She smiled and offered him a little wave and he returned her smile.

"Thanks for coming down, Alistair," Duncan said, turning and making his way into the building. "Keep me posted, aye?"

"Will do."

Duncan entered the care home, heading for the staircase. A ping sounded and the elevator door opened. A familiar face stepped out, George Huxley, accompanied by an elegant woman. Duncan hesitated at the foot of the stairs, catching George's eye.

"Mr Huxley?" Duncan said. The man stopped, casting an eye over Duncan.

"Yes," he said, seemingly trying to gauge whether or not he knew Duncan. "Can I help you?"

"Duncan McAdam," he said, closing the distance behind them. There was a flicker of something in George's expression, be it familiarity, recognition or something else, Duncan couldn't say.

"Detective Inspector," George said, smiling. It was an artificial smile. Duncan had seen thousands of them over the years. "I'm pleased to make your acquaintance. Are you here to see me, because I told your office—"

"No, I'm not here in an official capacity."

"Of course," George said. He glanced at his companion. "Darling, you take the keys, and I'll meet you outside in a moment or two." He passed the lady his keys and she took them, making to leave without acknowledging Duncan at all. He didn't mind, he only had eyes for George anyway. George Huxley, eldest child of Lord Huxley, guided Duncan aside from the main thoroughfare of the entrance lobby, lowering his voice. "What can I do for you, Detective Inspector."

"Your father is well known for his philanthropy, is he not?"

"Among many other things, yes. That is true."

"He spent a lot of time around St Benedict's too, didn't he?"

"My father was, and still is, heavily invested in many good causes—"

"And yet he won't speak about them on the record with the police!" Duncan said, staring hard at him. George appeared uncomfortable under the scrutiny.

"I don't care for your tone," George said, "or your insinuation."

"I didn't insinuate anything though, did I?" Duncan countered.

George Huxley held Duncan's gaze, and something unsaid passed between them. This man knew. Duncan was sure of it.

"I think it best, primarily for your sake, if we end this conversation here, don't you?"

"You know what he did," Duncan said, grasping George's upper arm tightly as he made to leave. He tried to shrug Duncan off, but it only saw him increase the strength of his hold tighter still. "Don't you?" he hissed.

George Huxley was unfazed. He stared at Duncan's hand and when he made no further attempt to walk away, Duncan released him. George straightened his arm, almost as if he was stretching out the muscles, but his eyes never left Duncan's. "I think you're making accusations far above your pay grade, Inspector Plod," George said, sneering. "My father is a well-respected member of the House of Lords, a retired politician and a man known for his charity work. *You* on the other hand, are a journeyman detective… looking to make a name for himself by rubbishing the reputation of a great man unable to defend himself because of his declining mental acuity." George smiled, and it was wicked. "How dare you seek to destroy my father's character."

"I'm doing no such thing."

"Is that so?" George replied. "Well, that's how it will be framed in the print media of every national publication I have access to. Do you have any idea how many of the owners, and editors, of these publications I either went to school with or know socially? And that's before we get to the media barons controlling the television networks and their in-house producers." He grinned at Duncan now, knowing he had the upper hand. "You're punching above your weight, Detective Inspector… or will it be PC McAdam by the time I'm through with you?" He stared at Duncan, who was standing between him and the route to the main doors behind him, indicating for him to step aside. Duncan held the eye contact for a moment longer before he turned sideways on to George, who brushed past him without another word.

Duncan seethed, watching him stride out into the morning sunshine, seemingly without a care in the world. He was correct though, and Duncan knew he was in a position of weakness. He suspected, and that was all he had. Without first-hand testimony from Fraser McEwan, and probably corroborative evidence from others, then there was little to no chance they would be able to approach Lord Huxley. Was his dementia real or was it a ploy to avoid a criminal inquiry into historical crimes?

There was no way a person suffering from severe dementia would ever face a trial in the UK. After all, if you are unable to give evidence or understand what it is you are accused of, then there is no chance of a fair trial. In this scenario, the case would never make it into a courtroom. George Huxley was well aware of this fact, and to pursue the matter would look like a witch hunt.

"Duncan?"

He turned to see Grace walking towards him. Roslyn was behind her pushing their mum in a wheelchair. She was well dressed for the elements with a thick tartan blanket draped over her lower half, tucked in at the sides of her chair. Grace slipped her arm around Duncan's waist, and she smiled at him, concern in her eyes as she read his expression.

"Are you okay?" she asked.

"Aye, I'm grand," he said, putting his arm around her and drawing her into him, forcing a smile.

"Shall we go?" Roslyn asked and Duncan nodded.

THERE WAS a stiff breeze blowing in off the water of Kilmaluag Bay as they stood in the graveyard of the ruined St Molaug's Church. Duncan stood shoulder to shoulder with his sister, their mother still in her wheelchair in front of Roslyn. Grace stood to Duncan's left, her arms tucked into her sides, bracing against the cold. Duncan hadn't planned a speech or anything like that. Neither had Roslyn, and somehow it didn't seem appropriate. They stood in solemn silence, each with their own thoughts.

Their mum stirred in her chair, twisting to look up at Duncan. Roslyn leaned down, placing her hands gently on her shoulders.

"It's okay, Mum," she said, choking on the emotion, her voice threatening to crack.

"He wasn't a bad man, Duncan," she said. "Your father. He didn't mean the things he did to you. Not to any of us. I always knew that."

This was the most lucid he'd seen his mother in months. Duncan's vision blurred and he blinked away the tears. Grace came closer to him, having respectfully kept her distance to allow their family moment. He took her hand in his and she squeezed it supportively.

"I know, Mum," Duncan said. He smiled at her and she returned his with a weak smile of her own. "I know that now."

Duncan disengaged from Grace, stepping forward and laying flowers before the headstone, and reading his father's name above the blessing engraved below it, *His journey has just begun.* An image of Callum came to mind, the son Duncan fathered with his teenage partner Becky. The boy was approaching the age Duncan had been when he'd decided to leave Skye, and his abusive father, behind for the bright lights and optimism of Glasgow. Duncan had wanted no part of his father's life, avoiding him until he returned following his untimely death, a death he now knew was a murder. If he knew then what he knew now, would he have made the same life choices? These thoughts could tear a man apart, but Duncan was less concerned with those. All he could think of now was how much he wanted to have a relationship with his son, with the teenager who didn't know who his father was. He'd taken the decision not to upset the boy's life, respecting Becky and her family's unity, as well as Callum's wellbeing. It would be selfish to upset all of their lives purely to satisfy his own needs. Setting that aside though, Duncan had a son and he wanted to be there for him, to guide him, to support him when he needed it. The sense of loss, of missing out on a relationship with his own father struck him as poignant. If he believed in a higher power, of any sort, then he could take these events as a sign. Or was he seeing exactly what he wanted to see and nothing more?

"God speed, Dad," he said, placing his hand gently on the top of the headstone. "I forgive you."

HAVING WALKED BACK to the car, parked at the viewpoint overlooking the bay, Duncan unlocked it and touched Roslyn's forearm to get her attention.

"Are you two," he said, gesturing to Grace as well, "okay to get Mum into the car? I just need a minute."

"Sure," Roslyn said. Her eye make-up had smudged slightly, but it didn't matter. Duncan thanked her and stepped away. Grace quickly went to him, touching his elbow.

"What are you up to, Duncan McAdam?"

"Me?" He shrugged. "Nothing. Why?"

She eyed him suspiciously, but backed away as he innocently took out his mobile phone and turned away from her once he was confident she was going back to the car to assist Ros. Duncan reached into his pocket and took the card out, reading the mobile number quietly to himself as he tapped it into his mobile. He pressed call and then looked back at the car. Grace and Roslyn were already supporting his mum and getting her into the rear passenger seat.

"Hello?"

Duncan focused on the call. "You said I should call if I have something for you."

"Definitely," Katie said, failing to keep the excitement out of her tone. "Do… you have something for me?"

"I do, but you should know that your editor will never run it in a million years."

"You make this sound like it's quite a scoop," she said, undeterred.

"You said you went into journalism to report the truth, to make a difference?"

"I meant it," she said. "Why wouldn't he want to run the story?"

Duncan paused, looking out across the bay.

"Because he'll be scared… or threatened with all manner of lawsuits, I suspect."

"If my editor is too scared to run with it, then I'll put it on my blog."

"If you publish it yourself online then you should know, they will come for you."

"Let them."

"I mean it, Katie. These are very wealthy people and they

wield a lot of power." Duncan doubted himself. Maybe he should not have called her. He looked over at the car. His mum and sister were sitting in the rear seats whilst Grace was leaning against the car, watching him.

"Mr McAdam… I live in the spare bedroom of my parents' house, and I earn minimum wage. What have I got to lose?"

He laughed. "You should know that they will try to destroy you, your reputation, your credibility… and you need to go into this with your eyes open. There'll be plenty of people who will want all of this to go away, and you along with it."

"What's the story?" she asked enthusiastically.

FREE BOOK GIVEAWAY

Visit the author's website at **www.jmdalgliesh.com** and sign up to the VIP Club and be the first to receive news and previews of forthcoming works.

Here you can download a FREE eBook novella exclusive to club members;

Life & Death - A Hidden Norfolk novella

Never miss a new release.

No spam, ever, guaranteed. You can unsubscribe at any time.

Enjoy this book? You could make a real difference.

Because reviews are critical to the success of an author's career, if you have enjoyed this novel, please do me a massive favour by entering one onto Amazon.

Type the following link into your internet search bar to go to the Amazon page and leave a review;

http://mybook.to/JMD-skye5

If you prefer not to follow the link please visit the sales page where you purchased the title in order to leave a review.

Reviews increase visibility. Your help in leaving one would make a massive difference to this author and I would be very grateful.

D.I. Duncan McAdam returns in 2025

Sticks and stones may break bones…
But your name is going to kill you…

ALSO BY THE AUTHOR

In the Misty Isle Series

A Long Time Dead

The Dead Man of Storr

The Talisker Dead

The Cuillin Dead

A Dead Man on Staffin Beach

In the Hidden Norfolk Series

One Lost Soul

Bury Your Past

Bury Your Past

Kill Our Sins

Tell No Tales

Hear No Evil

The Dead Call

Kill Them Cold

A Dark Sin

To Die For

Fool Me Twice

The Raven Song

Angel of Death

Dead To Me

Blood Runs Cold

Watch and Prey

When Death Calls

Life and Death**

FREE EBOOK - VISIT* ***jmdalgliesh.com

ALSO BY THE AUTHOR

In the Dark Yorkshire Series

Divided House
Blacklight
The Dogs in the Street
Blood Money
Fear the Past
The Sixth Precept

Psychological Thrillers

Homewrecker
Family Doctor

AUDIOBOOKS

In the Misty Isle Series

Read by Angus King

A Long Time Dead

The Dead Man of Storr

The Talisker Dead

The Cuillin Dead

A Dead Man on Staffin Beach

In the Hidden Norfolk Series

Read by Greg Patmore

One Lost Soul

Bury Your Past

Kill Our Sins

Tell No Tales

Hear No Evil

The Dead Call

Kill Them Cold

A Dark Sin

To Die For

Fool Me Twice

The Raven Song

Angel of Death

Dead To Me

Blood Runs Cold

Watch and Prey

Hidden Norfolk Books 1-3

AUDIOBOOKS

In the Dark Yorkshire Series

Read by Greg Patmore

Divided House

Blacklight

The Dogs in the Street

Blood Money

Fear the Past

The Sixth Precept

Dark Yorkshire Books 1-3

Dark Yorkshire Books 4-6

Psychological Thrillers

Homewrecker

Read by Tamsin Kennard & Alison Campbell

Family Doctor

Read by Eilidh Beaton